I CH

YOU

I CHOOSE YOU

GAYLE CURTIS

THOMAS & MERCER

Text copyright © 2020 by Gayle Curtis
All rights reserved.

No part of this book may be reproduced, or stored in a retrieval system, or transmitted in any form or by any means, electronic, mechanical, photocopying, recording, or otherwise, without express written permission of the publisher.

Published by Thomas & Mercer, Seattle

www.apub.com

Amazon, the Amazon logo, and Thomas & Mercer are trademarks of Amazon.com, Inc., or its affiliates.

ISBN-13: 9781542008181
ISBN-10: 1542008182

Cover design by Heike Schüssler

Printed in the United States of America

For my lovely parents, and Neil Diamond, whose music in the summer of 1976 I suspect had something to do with my appearance the following year.

And for my constants from the very beginning, Christopher, Paul, Susan, Catherine and Marty.

PROLOGUE

Holding a gun to a child's head isn't something I will ever forget. The small boy was just as startled to find me in his home as I was at discovering he was there. Shortly after the gun had fired, I heard a quiet, gentle sob and discovered him on the stairs. Fear had rendered him frozen and there was a dark stain seeping into his blue pyjamas, his anxiety taking control. We stared at one another for quite some time, his eyes eventually wandering slowly down to the gun in my hand. I had no idea how long he'd been sitting there, what he'd witnessed, what images would stay with him. Would he be able to understand any of it, in his innocence?

His position on the staircase gave him full view of the kitchen. I turned to look at what he'd seen. The man I assumed to be his father was sitting at the table, a bullet through the side of his head, an obituary that would be taken for a suicide note tucked under his left hand, the debris from the exit wound sprayed across the cupboards. I had been sitting opposite, observing the silence, the shift that death always leaves behind, a brief pause in time, when the sound of the young child had pierced the atmosphere.

I often wonder how I could have explained everything in a better way. I guess at such a young age, it was incomprehensible to him, way out of his reach, or so I assumed.

I can still remember the touch of his soft hair on my fingers as I guided him up the stairs, the muzzle of the gun pressed into his back with my other hand. He was silent the entire time, startled into a shocked kind of muteness – not one word came out of his mouth as he allowed me to guide him to his bedroom at the top of the stairs. The glow of his bedside lamp shone on the hall floor.

Having told the young boy to get back into bed and not move, I spent the next hour or so downstairs thinking.

It was over, the game had come to an end. I'd known it would one day. If nothing else, the similarities of each case would soon lead to suspicion.

Disappointment flooded me. I'd always anticipated my last participant would be a survivor, but John was none of the things he'd blustered about when I'd first met him. After we'd become friends, we spent many an evening discussing philosophy and the meaning of our existence. John said he knew the importance of life, how vital it was to evolve and embrace change, but when I asked him to show me, he failed to deliver. My game, even though we had talked about it before, shocked him, and I could see he hadn't been expecting it. This is nothing new – most of my participants are startled by it.

'Shoot yourself or be shot. Are you going to do it, or will I?' I said, placing one revolver on the table in front of me, and keeping the other in my hand. 'What's your answer going to be?'

'What?' John attempted to stand up, tipping his chair and almost losing his balance.

'Sit down, John. Otherwise I won't give you the opportunity to save yourself.' He sat down, they always do. 'You have sixty seconds to answer me. Plenty of time to think about it.'

'You're fucking crazy. I'm not playing this game.' John laughed and took a large swig of his whiskey.

'The clock is ticking, John.' I'd already started the timer on the watch I carried with me. 'What's it going to be?'

'I think that whiskey has gone to your head.'

I pointed the gun at him.

John put his hands up, as if I were a police officer about to arrest him. Most of them do this. It's a strange movement, but all sense of reason is lost when you're fearing for your life.

'You can't be serious!'

'Deadly.'

Let's just freeze this frame right here. It astounds me that, when you give people a proposition regarding their survival, they don't use the sixty seconds they have left wisely. They don't listen. Instead, they allow their emotions to override their ability to problem-solve. Such was the situation with John. So, it was a disappointing end to everything, but life is about change, and everything must evolve, eventually.

When I returned upstairs, the young boy was gone. His instinct to survive had kicked in and he'd fled. I searched the property, including the grounds, and eventually found him hiding in one of the barns behind a silo. I can sense a presence, and children, especially when they are fearful, don't have the ability to stay completely still. I could hear his heart beating like a skittish hare's, and when I caught him, he screamed like a young rabbit.

I led him back towards the house. The boy had seen me. He was a witness. I had no choice.

CHAPTER ONE
NOW

The pavement hit Elise on her right hip, elbow and shoulder, and the wall smacked her head, reminding her how much she hated herself, along with the rest of the world. Pins prickled the inside back of her nose, warm blood moved like a snake from her nostrils and into her mouth.

'Hey!' someone shouted at Mark Paton, the man who'd hit her in the face with the heel of his hand.

Having been snatched so sharply from Elise's arms, Louis was now in the full throes of a scream.

A few people shouted for someone to call an ambulance, the police, was anyone a doctor?

Mark ignored the crowd gathering and walked back into the shop where Elise had removed Louis from his pram. He emerged a moment later with the pushchair, angrily manoeuvring it one-handed, like it was an awkward supermarket trolley.

Louis was still screaming; the sound gave Elise goosebumps across her arms and neck. She tried to stand up but was firmly held down by a well-meaning bystander.

'You're a crazy bitch!' Mark shouted at Elise, violently shrugging off the man trying to restrain him. 'Get some fucking help and leave us alone.'

Elise pulled herself up to a sitting position. Leaning against the wall of the shop, she watched Mark shove his way through the people who had gathered at a distance. No one stopped him, and all she could manage to whisper was 'He has my son,' but no one could understand what she was saying – her lips were puffy and numb.

Jane and Mark Paton. Mark and Jane Paton. Paton as in 'Capon'. That's how she'd remembered it when she'd first learned their names. They were both consultants at the hospital where Elise worked as a coordinator for the delivery suite – Jane was a surgeon and Mark specialised in paediatrics. They lived two streets away from where Elise and her husband Nathaniel used to live. They had her son, the child she'd given birth to twenty months ago.

Elise had visited them weeks ago, not long after she'd spotted them with Louis – their choice of name, not hers – in the Maryon Wilson Park, where she would often walk. Elise felt she was on a bad footing from the get-go because they recognised her from the papers. Everyone knew Elise and Nathaniel Munroe. Any sympathy the public had for them had died long ago, when people learned all about their private lives and started to become suspicious. Now people frowned or smirked because they had reliable facts they'd retrieved from the tabloids that contradicted anything that Elise and Nathaniel might say publicly.

'Try and stand up, love.' Someone gently tugged at her arm. Another person told them to leave her and covered her up with a jacket, handing her a tissue for her bloody nose. That was when she realised the cold air she'd been feeling was because her skirt had risen over her thighs and stomach in the fall, leaving her exposed to everyone.

Elise threw the jacket from her legs as she heard someone say, 'That's Ida Munroe's mother.' She manoeuvred herself on to all fours and, pressing her right hand on to the wall of the shop, managed to stand up, staggering backwards slightly as she swiped at the hands that were trying to steady her. The helpers wanting to help, just so they could tell a good story at work or down the pub. She'd done it herself hundreds of times – told a good story. Elise knew how to tell a cracking good yarn.

She tried to walk, the opportunity to rescue her son fast slipping away now that Mark was out of sight. 'Stop that man!' she shouted, and then screamed, the force of her voice making her double over, and she staggered again. People were backing away now, and she heard someone say, 'Don't get involved.' All except one woman, who claimed to be a medical professional and tried to sit her on the bench a little way down the road.

'Fuck off.' Elise pushed the woman away, her words long and drawn out.

'I'll wait with you until the ambulance arrives.'

'I said, fuck off.' Elise tried to focus on the woman's face, but she was beginning to see double, visions sliding into her peripheral, reminding her of the kaleidoscopes she used to play with when she was a child.

'I've seen you before, haven't I?'

'Everyone's seen me before . . . Just piss off and leave me alone.' Elise crouched down and steadied herself by placing her hands on the pavement.

'At the hospital. You used to work there?'

Elise stared up at the woman, momentarily stunned that someone should recognise her in a different capacity.

'I'm one of the nurses on A & E. You used to be on the maternity unit. I know you, you're Elise Munroe.'

'That's right. What of it?'

'Nothing of it. We used to chat when we saw each other in the canteen. I'm Trish.'

Elise tried to focus on the small woman with the soft face. She was familiar. She wasn't familiar. She couldn't be sure.

'Listen to me, Trish. I don't remember who you are. I'm sure I did know you before I got into this state, but there you go. Do yourself a favour and go home.'

'Let's go and sit down and have a proper chat.' The woman gently pulled Elise to her feet and guided her towards the bench, where they waited for the emergency services. The crowds had dispersed, apart from the odd person glued to the spot, forgetting they weren't at home watching the soaps but an actual human being in the street. A couple of them raised their iPhones and took pictures of her.

Elise turned to look at Trish, squinting to see if she recognised her at all. There was a faint glimmer from another life that didn't belong to her anymore, when she hadn't been dosed up on prescription drugs.

'I'm sorry about your daughter,' Trish said.

'I need to go home.' Elise pushed herself up from the bench, throwing the tissue someone had given her to the ground.

'The ambulance will be here in a minute. I can hear the sirens. Let them check you over.'

'The police will nick me.'

'Look, I'll tell them I know you, you've had a bad day, you're going through a nasty divorce and you're a bit worse for wear. It'll be fine.'

'I'm not getting divorced.' Elise laughed. 'What gave you that idea?'

'Oh . . . I just thought – the man?' Trish gestured to where Mark had walked away.

'Those bastards have my son. They stole him from the hospital and he's mine, he belongs to me.' Elise stabbed at her bony chest and sat back down next to Trish. 'And I'll tell you something else, I'm going to get him back. Whatever it takes, I'll have him back. Even if it means killing Mark and Jane fucking Paton. That is a given.'

The two women stared at one another for a few moments, until Trish stood up, said she had to get home and walked away.

Unfazed, Elise pushed herself to her feet, pointed her finger as she always did when she was trying to get her bearings, and headed in the direction of their new home. The place where Nathaniel thought they'd be able to start again, away from the house they had shared with Ida, their daughter. Who, on her sixteenth birthday, had found herself in a situation so awful it resulted in a terrible turn of events.

Elise and Nathaniel hadn't been around the day Ida needed them. They were absent when they should have been saving her. Ever since, Elise had spent a lot of time thinking about the sequence of what happened that day, and how, if she'd altered things, even slightly, she might have been able to step in front of the fate that lay before her daughter. She hated fate, with all its surprises, and death with its unrelenting determination – they were fuckers. If she hadn't been so eager to return to work after the birth of their third child, and had taken the full amount of maternity leave she was entitled to, she would have been at home. There'd have been no late shifts and they'd have had dinner on time, as a family. Wouldn't they, she often thought to herself. Ida would still be alive, and no one would know who they were. They would be anonymous.

CHAPTER TWO
NOW

Begging was an undignified practice that Nathaniel had become all too familiar with over the last twelve months. He pressed the bell to the Patons' house and a long ring ensued, making sure they heard. Nathaniel was hoping Jane would answer the door, she was the easier one out of the two – calmer, more considered in her responses. Mark was hot-headed and tended to speak freely without thinking first.

Mark answered and immediately shut the door once he realised who was standing there. Nathaniel caught the door with his hand and foot before it closed fully.

'Please, listen to what I have to say. Just give me five minutes.'

'You've got to be joking, right? Get your foot out of the door or I'll call the police.'

Nathaniel pressed against the door harder. 'Look, just give me five minutes and then I'll leave you alone, I promise.'

'Let him in, Mark.' Jane appeared in the hallway. She was much taller than her husband, elegant and model-like, with fair hair and kind features. Against Mark's stocky figure and dark roughness, they looked odd together as a couple.

'Thank you. I promise not to take up too much of your time.'

'You won't, trust me.' Mark walked purposefully into the sitting room, a place Nathaniel had been before, when he'd asked them not to pursue their complaint about Elise stalking them. After quite a lot of persuasion they'd agreed to withdraw it on the condition Elise left them alone. Shamelessly, Mark had used Ida as an excuse, and had eventually guilt-tripped them into understanding that Elise was suffering mentally and needed help. Nathaniel had naively believed Elise had learnt something from the degrading and very public arrest, and would promptly accept some help and move forward with her life. Now, here he was again with the trickier issue of overcoming attempted child abduction, and he had nothing left to tell them about Elise, having used every possible excuse already.

'Say what you need to and please leave.' Mark sat down in one of the armchairs on the far side of the room. Nathaniel waited for Jane to choose a seat and then perched on the edge of the sofa, so he could address them both.

'I don't want to make this any worse than it is. I don't want to excuse what Elise has done. I simply want to apologise. If you decide to press charges against her, I'll understand. I know what she's done, how terrible it is . . . Let me finish.' Nathaniel stopped Mark from interrupting him. 'I can assure you I'll get Elise all the help and support she needs and she won't bother you again.'

'Your wife won't be bothering us anymore because we've applied for a restraining order.'

Nathaniel nodded, surprised they hadn't decided to do this before.

Jane leant forward. 'Have you taken advice from anyone? Has she been diagnosed with any kind of mental health issues? Post-natal depression or anything like that?'

'Everything changed after Ida, obviously. I'm not using it as an excuse – something changed between her and our son Buddy too. He's the same age as your little boy . . . Sorry, of course you know that.' Nathaniel had forgotten about the letters Elise had written to the Patons telling them she had their son and they had hers, and all the visits, the harassment.

'But why our son? I don't understand.' Jane leant back in her seat and crossed her legs.

'Elise thinks you were in the same delivery suite as her. She thinks she remembers you.'

Jane focused on the glass coffee table and Nathaniel could see she was trying to recall the people who had been there twenty months ago.

'I don't know why any of this is relevant.' Mark folded his arms.

'Mark,' Jane said, 'why don't you go and make us all some coffee while I have a chat with Nathaniel?' She turned to Nathaniel. 'Would you like some coffee?'

'Not for me thanks, I'm really not stopping.'

To Nathaniel's surprise, Mark stood up and silently went into the kitchen without any argument.

'I'm sorry, Nathaniel, I don't remember your wife. But then, I had a difficult birth. Has she been to see anyone to be assessed since we last spoke? I'm wondering, with everything that's happened, if she's suffering from post-partum stress?'

'It could be, but she has been assessed . . . it's slightly more complicated than that.' Nathaniel wasn't sure if he should reveal the last piece of information about his wife, which he'd so carefully managed to conceal from everyone, even the media, with some help from a few close colleagues. These days, people thought she was a bit of a drunk. They pitied her, felt sorry for her. But that wasn't the problem at all, not really. Elise had battled with prescription drugs, in Nathaniel's opinion, for a few years, all magnified since Ida's attack.

'Okay,' Jane said, 'I don't want to pry into your private business, but I do know people who might be able to help – colleagues in the medical profession.'

'That's really kind of you but we have a great therapist and doctor. We're just going through a particularly bad patch.' Nathaniel stood up and walked into the hall. Jane followed. He could see Mark through the open kitchen doorway, out in the garden smoking a cigarette, which again surprised him. He imagined them both being so controlled and tense, measured in everything they encountered, that smoking seemed an odd habit for either of them to have. Both medical professionals, and Mark and Jane seemed so clean-cut and stiff.

'I understand about addiction,' Jane said. She glanced behind her, and Nathaniel didn't know if she was nodding to Mark or checking he couldn't overhear. 'Get her into a rehabilitation centre. It'll make all the difference, trust me.'

'It's not alcohol – I know everyone thinks she's a drunk.'

'I know.' Jane squeezed his arm, and then he realised – of course they knew. How easy it was to find these things out when you worked in the medical profession. Elise had been a well-respected coordinator for the delivery suite. She'd been monitored a few years ago for codeine dependency – not an uncommon problem. She'd relapsed when their lives turned upside down and her GP had prescribed zopiclone, a sleeping tablet.

'I'm so sorry about everything, and Elise is too. Since the children . . . you know, it's been difficult, and I probably haven't been supporting her as much as I should. Buried my head in work.'

'It must be really difficult for you all.' Jane unhooked her bag from the bannister and pulled out a business card. 'Here's my number. Give me a call if you want any contacts. I know people who could help.'

Nathaniel took the card. 'I know you need to take this injunction out. I get it and, actually, I think it's the right thing for Elise . . . she needs to realise how serious this is. What she's done.'

'We have to, Nathaniel. We have our family to think about.'

'I know I'm not in any position to be asking for favours, but would you be able to put a good word in, tell the police we've spoken?'

'It's out of our control, unfortunately. The Crown Prosecution Service will decide if it's in the public interest to prosecute. You know that.'

Nathaniel nodded. 'I understand. Thanks for your time, anyway.'

'You still haven't answered my question about why your wife believes our son is hers.'

He sighed heavily. 'Elise says that when Buddy was born, he had an unusual birthmark on his right calf. The morning after he'd been born, and she'd managed to get some sleep, she said he didn't smell like hers, he seemed like a stranger – "an unfamiliar animal" were her actual words – and she felt something was wrong. That's when she noticed he didn't have the birthmark on his leg anymore. It's common. I spoke to one of the midwives about it and she said women can often be so over-whelmed and tired, they find it difficult to bond. For a while she totally believed he'd been swapped in the hospital until I managed to persuade her she was mistaken, but then it became an issue again a few weeks after Ida . . . I guess she felt like she was losing control – she'd lost one child and it cast more doubt on Buddy. She saw you at the hospital one day and recognised you from the maternity ward – said you'd spoken to one another quite a bit.'

'I'm sorry, I just don't remember. Thanks for calling round, Nathaniel. We appreciate your apology.' Jane opened the front door for him and he could tell by the change in her demeanour, the altered look in her eyes, that their son, Louis, had a birthmark on his right calf.

CHAPTER THREE
THEN

When Elise finally made it to the top of the stairs, with Buddy, her two-month-old son, asleep in his car seat hanging from one arm and her work bag under the other, she was alarmed to see the apartment door open. Her initial thought was that Nathaniel was home early from work, or perhaps it was Ida or Miles, their other children, already back from school. But then she remembered, they were going straight to their grandfather's because it was Ida's birthday and they were all going out for dinner.

Elise placed Buddy gently on to the floor and peered around the door frame. There was something wrong with the entire picture before her eyes, she could feel it. She pulled the door towards her and checked the Yale, which appeared to be intact until she touched it and the metal block moved away from the frame, the screws jutting out of their holes. Just as she decided the door had been forced and warned herself not to overreact, as she was so often accused of doing, Elise's phone began to ring, startling her and causing Buddy to stir from his warm slumber. It was Nathaniel calling.

'Where are you?' she whispered into the phone.

'I'm at work. I wondered if you wanted me to pick anything up on my way home. I'm leaving soon.'

'I thought you were in the apartment,' Elise said quietly, desperate not to wake Buddy or alert a possible intruder.

'No, I'm still at work. What's wrong?'

'Our front door is open. I'm not sure what to do.'

Nathaniel was silent for a moment. 'I bet it was Ida, she was the last one out this morning. I'm always telling her to give the door a good slam. Is there no one at home?'

'I haven't been inside to check. Ida and Miles are going straight to Dad's after school. It's her birthday, remember?'

'Of course, we're going out. I'm sure she just forgot to close it.'

'The Yale lock is loose, it's been forced.'

'Oh? Give me half an hour and I'll see if I can get away.'

'Don't worry, I'll call Dad,' Elise snapped. Maybe she was being ridiculous, but it didn't seem irrational not to want to enter a situation where she could possibly be faced with a burglar.

'Don't do that – it's fine, I'll come home. Just wait until I get there.'

Elise almost dropped the phone when she heard the door opposite open, then Tolek, their neighbour, peered out, startling her again.

'You made me jump.' Elise raised her hand to her chest, her voice made louder as it bounced off the walls in the small hallway.

'Everything okay?'

'No. I've just come home and found our front door open. There's no one home. I don't think there is, anyway.'

'I did notice and thought it was odd, but I didn't want to interfere in case you'd deliberately left it open for the caretaker or someone.'

'No, we wouldn't do that.'

'What's going on?' Nathaniel was still on the line, but Elise had moved the phone away from her ear.

'Tolek is here now.' And she hung up the phone, feeling easier now that there was someone more pragmatic to deal with everything.

Elise called the police while Tolek crept inside the apartment to see if anyone was there. While she waited for him to come out, she rang

Ray, her father, and asked him if he wouldn't mind coming over once he'd finished with his patients.

'Are Ida and Miles there yet?' she asked. 'It looks like we've had a break-in and the children aren't home.'

'A break-in? The children aren't here yet but I'll let you know as soon as they arrive. Are you okay?'

'Yes, kind of. I found the front door open, and the lock is broken.'

'As soon as they get here, I'll come over. Try not to worry, Elise, there's probably a perfectly good explanation. You're just being a bit irrational. I'm with a patient, I must go.'

Elise was glad he'd hung up; she didn't want to hear the psychiatric observations he always felt it necessary to impart. She probably was being irrational, but it wasn't the first time they'd been burgled.

One particular intrusion had occurred when they'd decided to have a brief spell living in the countryside, when the noise of the city had all been too much for her. That burglar had made their way in through the back of the house, smashing through two sets of uPVC doors. It hadn't been until the evening, when she was putting the children to bed, that she noticed the mess and the vandalism in Nathaniel's office. *Being so remote, you're more of a target*, the police had said. *Your husband being a journalist increases your chances*, they had added. Elise hadn't thought 'chances' was the right word to use, given the circumstances. Chances conjured up thoughts of being lucky and favoured. It seemed to her that, wherever they lived, they were targets for intruders.

'I'm not sure if anyone has been in.' Tolek appeared in the hallway again. 'Come, I'll make you some tea while you wait.'

Elise smiled, picked up Buddy in his car seat and followed Tolek into his apartment, so starkly different to theirs with its white walls and wooden floors. It was clean, sharp, and yet it always felt warm. He had moved into the apartment nine years ago and had lived there far longer than Elise and her family. Ida had been intrigued by him when they'd moved in four years ago; she was just twelve years old at the time and would ask him all sorts of questions about his home country of Poland. After he helped her with a school project, they became great friends. Elise hadn't approved at first and was suspicious of a man in his thirties who spent far too much time alone. He owned a deli on the next street and over time they got to know him, realising he missed his own children, having become estranged from his wife and family.

While she waited for Tolek to make some tea, she called Ida's phone, but there was no answer.

'Someone might have been in there, might not, I cannot tell.' Tolek shrugged.

'It's okay, I'll have a look when the police get here.' They weren't the tidiest of families and Elise knew anyone would find it hard to see if anything was amiss.

Nathaniel arrived at the same time as the police and showed them around the apartment while Elise waited in Tolek's sitting room.

Nathaniel appeared. 'Have you managed to get hold of Ida?'

'I tried to call her a little while ago but there was no answer. Dad said he'd come over as soon as they got back from school. What's wrong?'

Before the words left Nathaniel's mouth, Elise could feel the goosepimples rising, hurting her as though someone were peeling back her skin.

'Ida's room has been completely ransacked. Nowhere else has been touched.'

'Let me see.' Elise pushed past Nathaniel, who was blocking the doorway, and bumped straight into Ray, who had just come up the stairs.

'Hey, what's going on?' her dad said.

'I'm not sure. Nathaniel says Ida's room has been ransacked.'

'Let's not jump to conclusions, this is a teenager we're talking about.'

'Ida's tidier than we are.' Elise shoved her way past all the people who seemed to be accumulating in the hallway and went straight into the apartment, followed closely by two police officers.

'Have you spoken to your daughter today, Mrs Munroe?' one of the PCs enquired.

'Not since this morning,' Elise muttered as she began to take in the carnage before her. 'It's her birthday, we're all having dinner out and we're meeting at my father's.'

'Lucky girl to be born on February the twenty-ninth,' the other PC commented. She was a short, thickset woman whose male colleague was so tall they looked comical.

Elise had been expecting a few drawers pulled open, the duvet strewn on the floor, possibly an overturned lamp, but the scene before her was far more dramatic. The drawers had indeed been pulled open but were lying on the floor, the contents scattered everywhere. Ida's mattress appeared to have been thrown across to the other side of the room and was leaning awkwardly against the wall, reminding her of the drunks she saw in shop doorways on her way to work. The posters, all political statements, had been ripped from the walls, the remnants hanging there, like scraps on old billboards. Elise entered the room and noticed the wooden slats to Ida's bed had been smashed, as though someone had jumped across them, and the mirror above her dressing table was cracked right down the centre. It was definitely not how Ida kept her room, which was always neat and perfect.

There were two things that hadn't been touched. One was a large pinboard Ida was using for a family history project she was doing. It seemed to glow from the wall, in all its complicated and magnificent glory; Ida had gone beyond the space inside the frame and spread the project out like the sprouting branches of a tree. The second item was a box that was set on its side, containing a scene, not dissimilar to a set in a theatre, like a snapshot from a stage play.

19

'Ida's laptop is missing,' Elise said absent-mindedly, as she examined the strange scene on the dressing table. The female police officer followed her gaze.

'That's interesting. What is it?'

'I haven't seen it before.' Elise peered inside the box, which looked like it had been turned into a room from a doll's house. 'What I mean is, she's made these before, at my dad's, but I haven't seen this one until now.'

'Is it some kind of school project?' asked the male officer. Both of them were now interested in the miniature scene before them. It was a kitchen, complete with stove, fridge and units. In the middle of the room, a doll was sitting on a chair at a table, two tiny handguns in front of her, one placed under her hand. On closer inspection, you could see a messy blood wound on the side of her head. 'That's a bit macabre.'

'Did you have an argument with your daughter this morning?' the female officer asked.

'Just the usual teenage strop we have to endure on a daily basis,' Elise said, as Buddy's crying pierced the atmosphere. She pushed anxiously past the two officers and walked into the hall, where she found Nathaniel releasing Buddy from his car seat.

'Don't keep picking him up, you'll make him needy,' Elise snapped at Nathaniel. 'Where's Dad?'

'He's gone back to his to get Ida and Miles. He doesn't want them walking here to the apartment.'

'Has he seen them?' Elise was beginning to panic.

'Yes, stop worrying. Miles went back to school for basketball practice. He says Ida was in a terrible mood because she'd quarrelled with Alistair.'

'I told Miles he wasn't allowed to stay behind tonight. Why didn't Ida remind him?'

Nathaniel shrugged.

'Is Alistair a school friend?' the female police officer enquired.

'Yes,' Elise snapped. 'What are you going to do about all this?'

The police officers were now examining the extent of the damage to the front door.

'As long as you're sure you've been burgled,' the woman said, 'we'll call Scenes of Crime out to look. We'll need a statement from you, and then I'd suggest you carry on with your evening as planned.'

Neither Elise nor Nathaniel could believe what they were hearing.

'I should say we've been burgled, wouldn't you?' Nathaniel shouted above the sound of his crying son.

The two police officers looked at one another.

'We'll also need a statement from your daughter. It could just be an innocent misunderstanding.'

'A misunderstanding?!' said Nathaniel. 'It's her birthday, she was in fairly good spirits this morning when I left. She might be moody at times, but she certainly wouldn't do anything like this.'

'I'll call Dad and tell him we'll be over as soon as we've collected Buddy's things.' Elise ignored the two officers and turned to Nathaniel. 'We'll stay there tonight.'

'Can we have your father's name and address please?' the male officer asked. For the first time since they'd arrived, one of them had begun to take everything more seriously.

Elise sighed heavily as she tried to appease Buddy, who was whimpering in Nathaniel's arms. 'He needs a bottle.'

'I'll go and feed him.' Nathaniel picked up the nappy bag and walked across the hall to Tolek's apartment.

'It's Dr Ray Coe, Walnut Villa, Canterbury Avenue—'

'Dr Ray Coe?' the officer interrupted.

'Yes. That's my father.'

'I've read some of his books.' He looked up and studied her face, searching for the resemblance. 'Very interesting man.'

'Everyone says that, when what they mean to say is he's a nutcase.'

The officer's face coloured. 'Some of his theories are . . . well, a bit, well, unusual.'

'It's okay. You don't have to be polite, I know a lot of people think he's an arsehole. You shouldn't believe everything you read in the papers. Being in the police, I should imagine you know that.'

The officer nodded, and Elise could see he was eager for them to leave so he could tell his unaware colleague about the social experiment Ray became infamous for. In 1986, he'd organised a *Big Brother*-style television game on a remote island – the first of its kind. One of the participants was removed and the others led to believe that she'd been murdered, prompting research into trust and paranoia. Unfortunately, one of the other participants actually died from positional asphyxia and Ray was investigated and charged with manslaughter, but he was found not guilty in court. Several of the contestants were so traumatised by the whole experience, they sued him.

Later, making their way out of the apartment block and across the forecourt to their car, having finally managed to settle Buddy, both Elise and Nathaniel paused as they heard an all-too-familiar sound coming from the flower bed by the main entrance. It stopped, and then a few seconds later, it started again.

Nathaniel wandered over to the location of the sound; rain was beginning to pelt down. In the dark, he could see a lit-up screen, across it the name 'Alistair' distorted by droplets of water.

Ida's phone, vibrating amidst the shrubs.

CHAPTER FOUR

That was the game. Shoot yourself or be shot. What would you do? There was a way out, a solution – isn't there always?

Sometime during the late seventies, when I was commuting to work on the train, I met Sidney Mitford, the man who gave me the idea for the suicide game. We often had strange but interesting conversations, but this one made a mark on who I was to become.

'If you had to choose whether to shoot yourself or be shot, what would you do? What would your answer be?' Sidney leant forward and stared at me, his elbows resting on the table between us.

'I don't quite understand what you're asking.'

'Someone has handed you a gun and the question is, will you shoot yourself or would you rather your assailant did the deed?'

It was a few moments before I gave him my answer. Sidney was a barrister and he normally travelled with his clerk Frank, but on this particular day he was alone. In fact, there was no one else in the single carriage, unusual for a Monday morning.

Sidney would often throw random questions across the table, designed to surprise and shake whoever was listening from their mundane thinking.

My response was that I would opt to shoot myself, but then turn the gun on my assailant.

'That's not how the game works,' Sidney said.

'I didn't realise we were discussing a game. Is this one of your cases?' I enquired in a slightly mocking tone.

'I wouldn't tell you if it was.' Sidney leant back, resting his hands on his lap.

'I don't understand.'

'Answer my question. Shoot yourself or be shot – you have sixty seconds to answer and it's not possible to turn the gun on your assailant.'

'I think I would choose to be shot. Possibly. Who wants to shoot themselves? I would say that, to the very last second, I would be hopeful they might change their mind, or I would be rescued. If I had already shot myself, I would be giving in. Fight or flight, I guess.'

Sidney pondered on what I'd said and almost looked disappointed. I returned to my newspaper, unable to stop thinking about his question. Eventually, he spoke again.

'That says a lot about who you are. How much you value your life. Is that the kind of person you want to be?'

'Which person?'

'The one who opts to be submissive. Where is the fight or flight in that? Did you think there might be a solution to your survival if you thought about it?'

'But surely, with only sixty seconds to decide, how can I work out the solution?'

He didn't answer me, just raised his eyebrows.

It was the last time I saw Sidney on that train journey – or ever, for that matter. Two weeks later, when I saw Frank again, he told me Sidney had shot himself. Frank didn't mention anything about the game, but it hung in the air between us as we rocked to the vibration of the train.

'Does anyone know why?'

It was a while before Frank answered. 'He left two letters to his wife. One was a statement of the facts of his life – an itinerary, if you like, of the significant events. It was quite sad in places but in the main, happy.'

'And the second?' I leant forward, eager to know what was in the other letter – and so, it seemed, did the couple sitting next to me. Both were pretending to be absorbed in their reading materials.

'It was an obituary, of sorts. It was how Sidney wanted to be remembered, but also what he would have liked to do with his life had he taken a different path – his thoughts and aspirations.'

We sat in silence for a few moments as I thought about what he had said. The couple next to me had forgotten about being impolite and were openly eavesdropping, having lowered their newspapers.

'Can I ask where Sidney did it? Who found him?'

Frank shook his head at the sadness of it all and glanced at the couple, who quickly looked away.

'Sidney lived in a beautiful old house with a lake in the grounds,' he said. 'Just on the edge of the water was a large summer house he'd had built years ago. It was a Saturday, mid-afternoon, and, according to his wife, he poured himself a brandy and walked down to the lake – not an unusual thing for him to do on a weekend. Some moments later she heard a gunshot and Sidney's dog was barking and scraping at the door to be let out. He would never go down to the lake house without the dog. She knew exactly what she was going to find. Terrible business.'

'But I still don't understand why.' I was pushing a sensitive subject, but for some reason I needed an answer. I didn't want to leave the train never knowing.

'Sidney had been diagnosed with Alzheimer's. All those dreams and aspirations would never unfold, and he'd written them down, so he would always have a record of who he used to be, so he wouldn't forget, and neither would the people around him. They were things he could have done but never quite got around to. He used to be exasperated at how people arrogantly assumed they had all the time in the world, when in fact he was just the same as them. I think that's what he was trying to say, in the hope his loved ones would conduct their lives in a better way.'

'So it wasn't necessarily a suicide note?'

'Sidney's wife believes he wrote those letters some weeks before and just happened to read them again before he died. He left them for his family, so they could remember the person he was and not the one he would have become.'

We all sat back in our seats and there was silence for the rest of the journey.

That story stayed with me. Sidney didn't want to lead a life that, in his eyes, was diluted or poorly conducted, so he bravely ended it. This got me thinking about all the healthy people who waste their lives. What made them like that – and, given a choice, would they change their lives if they knew they might only have months left?

That's when the game started, when I began introducing people to death.

There are only a few people who have survived the game; Magda King – as she is known now, under her married name – is one participant I remember well. She played the game in 1986, when I knew her as Magda Bradshaw. We stay in touch, partly because I'm fascinated by her but also because she isn't dissimilar to me. She unexpectedly surprised me, and we share a lifelong secret like we're on a perfectly balanced see-saw – one will not disclose the other, so we remain suspended in mid-air, in perfect balance.

CHAPTER FIVE
THEN

The floodlight on the front of Ray's imposing Victorian villa lit up the driveway as he pulled on to the gravel. Behind the electric lantern, the house stood in complete darkness, not one window was projecting a warm glow, which Ray thought peculiar, seeing as when he'd left, Ida had turned on almost every one of them. She'd been antsy earlier, wanting food, wanting to know what was going on, it was her birthday, why didn't anyone ever tell her anything? Ray had told her to wait there so she could let Miles in when he got back and, being a defiant teenager, he guessed she and Alistair had gone to the van in the park for chips, purposefully turning all the lights out because it was another thing he nagged her about.

As he pushed the key into the front door and switched on the hall light, Ray picked up the phone and called Ida's mobile. No answer, so he dialled Elise. He put his hand on the bannister and peered up the dark staircase as he waited for her to answer.

'Dad?' she said when she picked up. 'We're still at the apartment. Please tell me Ida is there at the house.'

'It's pitch black here, not a soul. I've tried calling her phone but she's not answering. I'm going over to the chip van in the park, which is probably where I'll find the little scamps. It's like the bloody *Mary Celeste* here.'

'Dad . . .'

'Or maybe she's gone to meet Miles at school – basketball practice finishes soon. I think she's in a huff because it's her birthday and no one is here yet.'

'Dad . . .'

'I'll try her again, search the park and ring you back.'

'We've found Ida's phone. Out the front of ours, on the forecourt.'

Ray fell silent for a few seconds, not quite understanding what Elise was implying. 'Well then, she'll be in the building somewhere, gone to one of the neighbours I should expect.'

'We'd have seen her, Dad. She'd have come up to the apartment. I need you to check around and call me straight back. Isn't Sonny there yet?'

'No, he's still at work, said he'd meet us at the restaurant if he was going to be late. I'll call him. Try not to worry, I saw her before I popped over to yours, she was with Alistair and they were both absolutely fine. Call Alistair, he'll have his phone. Ring me if you hear anything.' Ray hung up and dialled his son Sonny's number. There was no answer, so he left a message on his voicemail for him to call. Sonny lived with him and worked as a barrister in the city. It was rare he ever came home early, or even on time.

The house was deathly silent, and Ray began walking through, switching lights on and peering briefly into rooms, calling for Ida as he went. It was a waste of time. Why would she have been sitting there in the dark? He made his way to the back door and out into the garden. Ida and Miles liked to work on projects in the old summer house and, as eerie as it was on a dark winter's evening, it would be just the sort of place she might be, especially as she'd been in a strange mood that day. He would often find her in there when she was feeling tetchy or had something on her mind, scarf wrapped around her face, thick woolly mittens curled around a mug of hot chocolate. But Ray could see from halfway down the garden there were no lights illuminating the summer house. He walked straight to the back gate, reassured that it was unlocked and open, which gave him the thought that Ida and Miles were out in the park that ran along the back of Ray's property. The children insisted on using it as a shortcut, but Ray liked to keep the gate locked, especially with some of the psychiatric patients who visited his house.

Ray took wide strides across the usually green but now quite muddy park, the rain causing him to squint. He stopped so he could visually sweep the area, illuminated by the streetlights, but there was no chip van. And then he remembered it was Monday. The chip van was never there on a Monday.

Ray went back into his garden, peering through the windows of the summer house on the way, just to make sure Ida wasn't in there. But making sure she was absent was quickly turning into needing to find her, as the places she could be began to diminish like sand in an hourglass, his heart rate starting to rise. Elise and Nathaniel had been burgled and Ida's phone had been found, her bedroom vandalised.

Then, as he went inside and walked through the kitchen on his way to check upstairs, he saw Ida lying on the floor in the orangery. He paused, wondering why he hadn't noticed her before. He rushed to where she was lying on her side, her back to him. Ray knelt on the stone floor and carefully gripped her shoulder, pulling Ida on to her back. Blood had seeped from her head, mouth and nose, but he couldn't tell if she was alive or not. Ray gently lifted her small frame towards him, handling her like a newborn. A rasping gasp came from her mouth as he folded her into his arms. She was alive. She was still alive. He knew he needed to call an ambulance, but he was frozen to the spot. Ida stared at him, her lids drooping over her big brown eyes, fading and barely conscious.

Ray grabbed a cushion from one of the chairs and put it under Ida's head, carefully placing her in the recovery position, taking his coat off and laying it over her before he went into the kitchen to use his mobile. Somehow, he made the call for an ambulance, stuttering over whether they needed the police as well. He hesitated when the operator asked for his address, which he simply couldn't remember for a few seconds, his mind filled entirely with visions of his granddaughter. He opened the front door as instructed and rushed back into the orangery, rested the phone on the table, and knelt down on the floor in front of Ida so he could hold her hand. He could hear the operator talking, asking him questions, but he didn't answer. Ray stared at Ida, she at him, as he felt the life ease its way from her grip on his fingers, the light gradually fading from her eyes like she could see a dark spectre standing next to them, overshadowing the scene.

Ray was barely aware of the click of a door, although later he would remember hearing it close, or open, he couldn't be sure.

Hearing the sirens in the distance, Ray left Ida's side and ran out the front to guide the ambulance to the correct address. To his dismay, it drove past and had to turn around. As soon as Ray was confident they'd seen him in the entrance to the driveway, he ran back inside to be with Ida.

The paramedics eventually found Ray in the orangery, where they all stared at the bloodstained floor, his black winter coat lying in a crumpled heap as though Ida had never been there.

CHAPTER SIX
THEN

The scene Nathaniel returned to was very different to the one he'd left. Ray's drive was now filled with two Scenes of Crime vans, three police cars and two ambulances. After the discovery of Ida's phone, they'd received a call from Ray telling them to come straight over, there'd been an incident, and when they'd arrived, the police had ushered them straight into the drawing room, which was the first room on the left by the front door. Nathaniel had explained they needed to collect their son from school, and he'd been permitted to go with a police escort. He hadn't wanted Miles to be dropped off by friends' parents, who would see everything and want to know what was happening. It also gave him a chance to talk to Miles on the way back, although he wasn't sure Miles was listening as he kept interrupting him to tell him about what had happened during basketball practice, in between exclaiming how cool it was to travel in a police car.

'What's going on, Dad?' Miles was more excited than alarmed by all the vehicles with flashing lights, and hadn't linked what Nathaniel had told him about his sister to the scene before him.

'I don't know at the moment, lovey, let's go and find your mum.'

What alarmed Nathaniel more when he arrived back at Ray's were the people in white overalls he could see at the end of the hall. One of them looked up and then quietly spoke to their colleague. The enormity of the situation tightened his throat and chest.

Nathaniel found Elise sat on the sofa, ashen-faced, her blonde hair dishevelled. She stood up when he walked in. Nathaniel went to embrace her, but she put her hands out to stop him.

'Don't.'

'What's happening? Where's Ida?'

'I don't know. Dad said he found her on the floor, he went outside to guide the paramedics in and when he got back, she'd disappeared. They searched the house and garden but couldn't find her anywhere. He says she was in a state.'

'In what way?'

'Badly injured . . . she was unconscious when he found her.'

Nathaniel nodded, shock rendering him momentarily speechless.

'We have to wait in here until someone comes to speak to us.' Elise reached out for Miles's hand and pulled him towards her; Buddy was sitting in the crook of her other arm. 'Have you explained what's going on?'

Nathaniel looked at Miles and nodded. 'I'm not sure how much of it has been understood, though.'

'I think we all feel like that.'

'Where's Ray?' he asked.

'I'm not sure. The police wanted to ask him a few questions at the station. Why would anyone do this to her?' Elise pulled a tissue from her sleeve and wiped her nose.

'I don't know. Let's just wait and see what the police say. Have they said anything at all?'

'No. They won't tell me what happened to Ida or Dad. I heard someone say Sonny was there as well, but I haven't seen him.'

'You've been in here the whole time?' Nathaniel asked, pacing the room, hands shoved into his pockets, trying to control himself and not be hysterical. He wondered if Elise was aware of the Scenes of Crime vans – what it all meant.

'I know as much as you.'

'I saw Uncle Sonny in the park earlier, but he ignored me,' Miles blurted as he wandered over to the television in the corner and picked up the control.

'We're probably going to have to book into a hotel tonight. We won't be allowed to stay at ours or Ray's.' Nathaniel was trying to ease the news for Elise, preparing her for what they were about to be told. Being a journalist, he'd seen these kinds of situations before. They weren't expecting Ida to survive, and once it turned into a murder enquiry, everything would change very quickly.

Elise stared up at Nathaniel and then turned to Miles, who'd found some satisfactory trash to watch on TV. 'What did you just say, love?'

'I shouted to Uncle Sonny on my way back to school, but he just looked at me and carried on walking.'

'You couldn't have seen Uncle Sonny. He was at work earlier.'

Miles frowned. 'No, he wasn't. Me and Ida saw him after school.'

'Hang on a minute. Why did you come back here? I thought you stayed for basketball practice after lessons, after I told you not to,' Elise said, letting him know he shouldn't have gone against her instructions.

Miles looked up, trying to think through the day's events, gauge if he was in a lot of trouble or not. 'I wasn't going to basketball practice and then I changed my mind because Ida met up with Alistair on the way home and I was bored, so Granddad said I could go back to school if I wanted.'

'And Granddad walked you back?' Nathaniel was always telling Ray he didn't want the children walking anywhere on their own, especially through the park.

'No, by myself. Granddad had a strange man here. He said he couldn't leave him.'

'A strange man?' Nathaniel looked at Elise, who was gently rocking Buddy.

'He came out of Granddad's office and said he was me, myself and I. He had an eye patch, like a pirate.'

'Okay. One of Dad's patients,' Elise whispered to Nathaniel.

'I thought you told him not to have patients here when the children are over?'

Elise sighed, as she always did when he questioned her father's actions, but he didn't care, especially when it came to his children. 'Come on,' she said. 'He can't help it if there's a bit of a crossover. And that's all it would have been, he promised me.'

'Bloody hell, Elise, you don't know what sort of nutcases he has on his books. And Miles isn't old enough to walk through the park by himself.'

'If they were that bad, they'd be locked up.'

'Look at the situation we're in now.' Nathaniel raised his hands.

Elise ignored him. 'Try Alistair again, will you? See if he knows anything.'

'I called already, he's not answering.'

Elise turned her attention back to Miles, who was now absorbed in the TV programme.

'So, Ida stayed at Granddad's with Alistair when you walked back to school?'

'I think so.' Miles shrugged. 'Granddad and Ida were arguing about something just before I left.'

'What were they arguing about, love?'

'Where's Ida?' Miles appeared to suddenly realise his sister wasn't there.

'She's with the doctors because she's poorly, they're trying to make her better.' Nathaniel dialled Alistair's number but there was still no answer.

'Are we staying at Granddad's tonight?' Miles switched the channel.

'Shush a minute, your dad's talking on the phone.'

Nathaniel left a message on Alistair's voicemail, telling him to call them urgently.

'Still no answer?'

Nathaniel shook his head. He was beginning to wonder if both kids had got themselves into trouble.

His thoughts were interrupted by the sudden arrival of a couple of detectives.

'Where's my daughter?' Elise demanded of them. 'What's happened to my dad?'

The detectives introduced themselves as DI David Davis and DC Alex Chilvers, the latter a woman, despite her name.

'Mrs Munroe,' DC Chilvers said, 'we don't know where your daughter is at the moment, but our officers are out searching for her and we're doing everything we can. We just need to ask you a few questions.'

Nathaniel and Elise looked at one another.

'What do you mean, you don't know where our daughter is?' Nathaniel asked.

'We believe your daughter was attacked sometime this afternoon. Dr Coe and Sonny Travers found her, but since then she's disappeared.' DC Chilvers allowed the words to settle.

Nathaniel and Elise stared at the officers, trying to take in everything they were saying.

Elise said, 'We were only told she'd been attacked . . .'

'I'm sorry no one has been in to explain everything to you, Mrs Munroe. As you can imagine, the first few hours in any investigation are crucial. Our priority is finding your daughter.'

'So she ran off? Her injuries couldn't have been that bad then?' Elise stood up and propped Buddy up on some cushions. 'I need to find her. I can't sit around here doing nothing.'

'Mrs Munroe, you need to stay calm and we'll explain everything to you, as soon as we have the facts. It doesn't help anyone if we speculate. Sit down, please.'

Elise reached for Nathaniel's hand and they both sat down.

'Firstly, I need to ask who lives here with your father. All of you?' DC Chilvers opened her pocketbook.

Elise and Nathaniel exchanged puzzled looks.

'No. Just my brother-in-law Sonny,' said Nathaniel, quickly becoming irritated. 'We live a few streets away from here. Our apartment was burgled earlier today.'

'Did you report it?'

'That's not quite right, Nathaniel,' said Elise. 'Our flat was broken into and Ida's room was trashed. We think her laptop was stolen.'

DC Chilvers looked up from her note-taking. 'You reported it?'

'Yes, for fuck's sake,' Nathaniel snapped. 'We reported it before all this happened. Before we knew someone had attacked our daughter. Do any of you talk to one another?'

'Nathaniel, little ears,' Elise hissed, nodding towards Miles, who was standing in front of the television, transfixed by his programme.

'Mr Munroe, you'll appreciate that when we're sent out to different jobs, it takes a while for information to be collated and compared. We're relying on all of you to tell us as much as you can remember. Can you confirm who lives in your father-in-law's house and who lives in your apartment with you?' DI Davis addressed them both.

'When are we having dinner?' Miles wandered over to Elise and leant against her legs.

'Just go and sit quietly for a few minutes and we'll sort something out.' Elise stroked the back of Miles's head and turned her attention to the police officers. 'My father lives in the house with my brother, Sonny. Sonny John Travers. Nathaniel and I live in our apartment with our children, Ida, Miles and Buddy.'

'And how old is your brother?' DC Chilvers continued to note everything down in her pocketbook.

'Thirty-six, thirty-seven, I'm not sure.' Elise was beginning to feel uncomfortable. She didn't like people prying into their private lives.

'You don't know how old your brother is?' DC Chilvers stopped writing. 'Is he a half-sibling?'

'No. Why do you ask?'

'He has a different name to your father.'

'My mother had him adopted just after he was born. Sonny employed an agency to find us. About three years ago, I think.' Elise lifted Buddy on to her lap; he was beginning to fidget. 'He's a barrister.'

'Yes, I know Mr Travers. I've met him in a professional capacity.' DC Chilvers showed no emotion, neither a smile nor an offer to elaborate any further. She just carried on writing. 'And your mother's name?'

'Ingrid Coe. She's deceased.' Elise glanced across at Miles, wondering how much he could hear, but he seemed totally absorbed in *Deal or No Deal*.

'Recent?'

'No, she died when I was eleven. Suicide. Well, we think it was.'

DC Chilvers frowned. 'You think it was?'

'Have you heard of the Suicide Watcher cases?' Nathaniel reached his arms out to Elise, so she could hand Buddy over.

'Yes.'

'Both our mothers were victims.'

'That's not quite right, Nathaniel.' It was a subject they had always disagreed on. Elise had attended a support group, set up for anyone dealing with the aftermath of suicide, and that's how they'd met. It had been founded by a woman called Donna Levisham, but she'd moved away, and it was eventually taken over by Magda King, Alistair's mother. The group had quickly become known as a place for the Suicide Watcher's alleged victims.

It irritated Nathaniel when she contradicted him.

'It doesn't matter,' DC Chilvers said. 'It's not important at this stage. We just really need to know who is presently in Ida's life. People she spends time with on a regular basis. We also need to know if there's anyone you might be worried about. Anyone who might have upset Ida recently?'

'I can't think of anyone. Is my father hurt?'

'No.' DC Chilvers frowned. 'Mr Travers found your daughter and may have chased her assailant from the property. As far as we know, neither he nor your father was involved in the attack.'

'Sonny found Ida?' Nathaniel stood up. 'You need to tell us exactly what's going on. We didn't know that.'

'Where are my father and brother?' Elise got up from the sofa.

'They're at the station answering some questions. The most important thing is that you tell us everything you can remember. Is there anyone you can think of who might have been bullying Ida?'

'No, I just told you.' Elise gripped her face and began to cry. 'Why aren't you out looking for her?'

'We have officers out there right now. At this stage, we don't know what's happened to her. Your father says he found her lying on the floor with what he thinks was a head injury. He called an ambulance, and sometime between your father going outside to get the paramedics and coming back into the room, your daughter disappeared.'

'But you just said Sonny found her. Which is it?' Nathaniel was becoming more irate.

'It appears that Mr Travers found your daughter first, but believes he saw an intruder in the garden, so he pursued them.'

'Why didn't Sonny call an ambulance?' Nathaniel frowned, trying to make sense of what was being said to him.

DC Chilvers paused and observed them both. 'Mr Travers believed your daughter was dead when he found her.'

'Does he know who it was? In the garden, I mean?' Nathaniel leant against the wall, wanting to fall through it like he was in a dream.

'Unfortunately, we don't know any more.' DC Chilvers stood up, excused herself and left the room. They could hear her talking to someone outside the door.

'I'm sorry no one has been in to explain things to you in more detail.' DI David Davis took over from DC Chilvers. 'As you can appreciate, trying to locate someone in the dark and wet weather is increasingly difficult the later it gets, so we're working as quickly as possible to find your daughter and her attacker.'

'So you think Ida has run off and her attacker is somewhere else?' Nathaniel felt strangely relieved that *a* someone had been spotted, that this person might be close by and easy to locate.

'It's a little more serious than that, Mr Munroe. Your brother-in-law was chasing someone he'd seen in the garden. At the moment, no one knows if this is the person who attacked her or an innocent member of the public. Our officers are currently searching the area and conducting house-to-house enquiries.'

'No one told us any of that.' Elise's words were full of tears and Nathaniel went over to comfort her.

'So you could be looking for more than one person?' Nathaniel said desperately.

'Possibly. We're keeping an open mind.'

Elise took Buddy from Nathaniel and placed him in his car seat. 'I need to see Sonny and my father. I need to know what happened.'

'You can't do that, Mrs Munroe. Your father has been taken to the police station, along with Sonny. We'd like you to stay in here while we explain what we need you to do. Save your energy for your daughter, that's the most important thing to do right now.'

'What are you doing with my father?'

Nathaniel could see Elise was becoming dangerously angry; her quiet voice and creased brow were always a sign she was going to erupt. 'My daughter's been abducted and now you're expecting me to sit here while you manhandle my father?'

'Sit down, Mrs Munroe, please. We haven't finished.' DC Chilvers was blocking Elise's way out of the door upon her return to the room. 'No one is manhandling your father. His clothes have been taken for forensic analysis, along with your brother's, and they've both agreed to visit the station to answer some questions, purely for us to get as much information from them as we can, while it's still fresh in their minds. We would like you to do the same. You will also need to find alternative accommodation. Can you stay with relatives or friends?'

'I'm not going anywhere. I'll be staying here and waiting for my daughter to return.'

'Your other two children will need somewhere secure to stay. Do you have any other family they can go to?'

'I want my boys with me,' Elise snapped.

'I'll book us into a hotel and ask my dad and stepmum to come and collect Miles and Buddy – they don't live far away.' Nathaniel looked across at Elise, pleading with her not to make things more complicated than they had to be. 'They'll be better off at my dad's, they need to be settled.'

'Okay, just leave the details with one of us as soon as you know.' DI Davis turned to his DC. 'Can you arrange for an officer to drive the family there?'

Just as Nathaniel's phone pinged, alerting him to an email, another officer knocked on the door and entered.

'Can I have a word, boss?' It was a Scenes of Crime officer. Nathaniel couldn't help noticing all the protective clothing and surgical gloves everyone was wearing.

DC Chilvers followed DI Davis out of the room, passing Nathaniel, who was rooted to the spot and staring at his phone.

'Wait.' Nathaniel handed his phone to the officers, who took it and peered at the screen. 'I've just received an email from Ida.'

Elise moved towards Nathaniel, confused by what he was saying. She snatched the phone and looked at the screen. In big capital letters it read: *WHO AM I?*

CHAPTER SEVEN
THEN

Alistair had been Ida's best friend since they were six years old and he'd arrived at the school as a newcomer. When he was born, his father had wanted to bring him up in his home country of Scotland, but after six years he had decided to move back to London. Alistair's mother, Magda, had grown up there and she missed her family. Her brother Gordon had committed suicide many years ago and she was eager to set up a support group for other people affected by a similar event. That was how she'd met Ida's parents and the connection was soon made, so their children played together at school.

As soon as Ida had decided Alistair was going to be her new friend, all the children who'd ridiculed his Scottish accent decided he was a bit of a novelty. But ten years of solid, loyal friendship had begun to change in more recent months – the inevitable between teenagers of the opposite sex. Alistair had decided he might feel differently about her now. He recalled the temper she'd been in earlier, one of many in the past few days.

Alistair pulled his hood up and made his way home. After they'd had an argument at her grandfather's house and she'd told him to get out, he'd texted and asked her to meet him in the cricket pavilion situated in the park at the back of Ray's house. He wanted to give her the birthday present he'd bought her – a double-coin gold chain. It had cost him all his wages from working at the golf club, but he knew she wanted one and it was her sixteenth birthday.

Alistair had waited for twenty minutes but Ida hadn't turned up, so he'd gone to Ray's house so he could talk to her and explain things. He hadn't been expecting to be chased across the park by her uncle, and he was wondering if Ida had told him what happened between them.

Once Alistair had ditched Sonny, he returned to the cricket pavilion and waited. He dialled her number again and left a message telling her she was being silly. Looking at his phone, he'd had another call from the number he didn't recognise. Whoever it was had been calling for the last hour but not leaving a message, and he hadn't called them back in case it was a scam. But as the signal on his phone improved, it pinged, letting him know he had a message. He dialled his voicemail and listened. It was Nathaniel, asking him if he knew where Ida was, and could he call him back. His phone started ringing, and a brief spark of hope it was Ida lit in his chest, but he was disappointed to see it was the unknown number. He answered it this time, realising who it was.

'Alistair? It's Nathaniel. Where are you?'

'On my way home. What's going on? Where's Ida? She was supposed to meet me in the cricket pavilion.'

'Alistair, did you and Ida have some sort of argument earlier?'

'No . . .' Alistair hesitated, and then decided not to tell him about the harsh words they'd exchanged after school – Ida had been in such a foul mood. 'What's going on?'

'It looks like she's . . . we don't know what's happened to her. She's disappeared. The police need to ask you some questions. I've tried to call your mum and dad, but I can't get hold of them either.'

'Disappeared? I've only just seen her.'

'When? You can't have.'

'Well, it was a couple of hours or so ago now, but I left her at Ray's.' Alistair heard Nathaniel swallow hard. 'Why do the police need to speak to me? I haven't done anything wrong.'

'You need to go to the police station and make a statement. The police will need to talk to you, Alistair. Why didn't you answer the phone earlier? Don't you listen to your voicemail?'

'I didn't recognise the number. I—'

Before Alistair could finish, Nathaniel had hung up. 'Prick,' he muttered under his breath. Checking his phone for any messages, Alistair decided that if it was that serious, the police would have called him by now. He noticed two emails. One was a delivery notice about a book he'd ordered, and the other was from Ida. He smiled, she was fine and there was nothing to worry about, but when he opened it, he stared at the message in capitals that had also been sent to Nathaniel, Elise, Sonny and his mother: *WHO AM I?*

Unable to understand what the message meant, Alistair logged into his Facebook page to see if Ida was online. He couldn't see anything, so he clicked on Ida's name and the screen loaded with some photographs that someone had taken of her. She was smiling and laughing in a few of them, but he couldn't figure out when they had been taken and he knew they weren't ones he'd snapped. They'd been posted that day, just after he left her at Ray's. He stumbled home, not sure what to do or who to speak to. He found the number for the local police station and phoned them but only ended up rambling, unsure what he was calling for, so he hung up. Then he tried to ring Nathaniel back, but a woman answered so he aborted the call. Before he reached home, his phone had pinged with several Facebook notifications, tagging him along with Nathaniel, Elise, Sonny and Magda. The pictures of Ida were all over Facebook, seemingly sent by her.

Alistair tried Ida's phone again and had just put the key in the front door as a police car pulled into the driveway.

CHAPTER EIGHT

At some point in your life you will realise you can't buck against the magnetic force that surrounds us. I found this out very early on in my life.

It was many years ago, when I was still at school. One particularly cold winter, a teacher of ours allowed us to skate on the pond which was situated in the school grounds. The ice was thick and solid, or so she thought. But there was a small patch that was darker, more transparent than the rest; it went unnoticed by her at the time. One boy in the class gravitated towards this area – he couldn't seem to stay away from it, pulled by the curiosity of how close he could get to the middle without falling through the ice. Everything began to slow down as we all stopped to see what was happening. Why did we stop? Have you ever noticed that? There is always a silent pause amongst everyone before anything traumatic occurs.

The crack in the ice caused children to grab on to each other as we all slowed in our frost-filled waltz. Then he was gone, disappearing into the icy water.

The usual panic ensued, as it always does when there is any sort of crisis. Then it was still and oh-so-quiet as we watched the teacher lie down on the ice and slide herself across the precarious slab; the only frantic movement was her arm waving around in the water when she reached the hole, as she tried desperately to find him. Then she went in, but still couldn't find him. She got out quickly, the water being too unbearably cold for her to be of any use in his rescue. Having screamed at us to get help, she went in again, only to reappear moments later.

Anyone with any sense would have known that a couple of minutes in that kind of temperature would disable an adult, never mind a thirteen-year-old boy.

He was dead, gone, absent from this world – he had slipped into the next, and I was fascinated and infatuated by it. I couldn't stop thinking about it. Couldn't stop playing it in my head: his blue face, his dark lips forever emblazoned in my mind as we watched the caretaker pull him from the icy tendrils of his liquid killer.

My obsession with him continued for years. I hero-worshipped him, admiring his phenomenal bravery in leaving his body, choosing to step out of it and into the unknown. The rest of the school was devastated, swathed in the melancholia of tragedy. I wasn't. I wanted answers. Had he felt death creeping up behind him when he got up that morning? Had he known he'd eaten his last breakfast, taken his final walk to school, uttered words during a conversation that he'd never speak again? Where was he now? Could he see himself dead? Was death there, in the physical sense, talking to him through the door? This became my focus for weeks – months, even. And then I realised I wasn't going to get any of the answers because they weren't for me to know. Not yet. They were his answers and for him alone to know. What had I learnt from it? Death is very private and belongs to each one of us in its own way. I wanted to be Death. I wanted to become the one that is there on that special day. I suppose the curiosity was to see if Death is real. He's most definitely there. You can't always see him; he's the black shadow in the corner, the watchman you'll never get rid of, the spirit that never leaves. You waited up to see Saint Nick when you were a child – I began my quest to see Death.

The teacher – Vivian was her name – committed suicide. Even before the incident, she wasn't like the other members of staff. There was something of the misfit about her, as though she couldn't seem to keep it together like the rest of her colleagues. Always late, always disorganised, always making the wrong choices. And her narcissism allowed her to believe the death of her pupil was down to her.

I found her, hanging from the tree in the caretaker's garden, early one morning; body bloated and eyes opaque. Most days I arrived at school well before everyone else, with the excuse, should anyone enquire, that I helped the caretaker in the garden before school started. The truth was, it was so I could buy cigarettes from him. We had a small enterprise going – I bought the fags and sold them to my classmates.

Vivian knew I'd be the first to find her. She wanted it to be me; a final gift from her to yours truly. We were close. I understood her desperate need to fit in and she understood why I didn't want to. I expressed things to her that I didn't feel able to broach with anyone else. You should feel a connection with someone to want to talk to them, and there seemed to be a rare few connections throughout my childhood. They passed through my life like dark angels, sprinkling their wisdom around me.

We smoked, we talked, she said I was mature beyond my years. I know many people would think it strange for an adult to have such an affinity with a child, but we were the same really. Age didn't come into it when we were sitting on our hidden bench amongst the greenery. We were just two souls, two beings, two minds sharing our thoughts. Her soul was lost but I learnt so much from her and she became one of my main markers on how not to conduct one's life.

When I found her hanging there, she was stunning, the most beautiful she'd probably ever been, all the marks and strains of conformity having lifted from her face and body. It was as though she'd finally discovered the answers to all her turmoil; I knew she'd had that conversation with Death that I was so intrigued to know about. This is what fascinates me still, and I wait in anticipation of my own private conversation with Death. Ever since then, I have always leant in close to see if I could hear Death whispering.

As it turned out, Vivian had broken her neck, and she'd been dead for quite some time. By the time I found her, I could feel death's absence; it was cold and still. She sparkled in the early-morning light, tiny flecks of sweat encrusted her body, her hair. She had no clothes on; she'd always told me she wanted to die naked. *I want to go out the way I came in*, she had said – a beautiful, enigmatic pose between life and death. I spent a while with her before anyone else found her, wanting to keep the vision close in my mind. I had no comprehension of Death at the time, that she was more alive than she'd ever been, her spirit still present; I thought she was merely pushing her face through the dimension of another world.

It was the stillness I couldn't comprehend, the silence of the atmosphere; a dark area of the garden which always held the anticipation of something deeper. The trees hung in shadowy coves, encasing their inhabitants in a majestic pattern, and I was caught in her magnificent beauty. Not in a sexual way, you understand. We didn't have that kind of relationship; she wasn't one of those. But a teacher being friends with a thirteen-year-old is inappropriate within the confines of the school gates, no matter what.

No, it was seeing the glamour, the stunning beauty that death had somehow breathed into her, for at that moment, she was more alive to me than she'd ever been. Transfixed in my teenage hypnosis, I was eventually taken away by the caretaker, who assumed I was in terrible shock.

It was almost like Vivian had died and been resurrected, and from then on, I found myself obsessed with death. I have been blessed with many moments such as that, and I have been allowed a glimpse of the true essence of what it means to extinguish your physical form and step into a new realm.

CHAPTER NINE
THEN

DI Davis joined DC Chilvers, who was sitting opposite Sonny in interview room three. Sonny smiled at him but didn't speak. He'd known the officer for years and they'd always had healthy banter, although Sonny was under no illusions he was liked by Davis. There weren't many police officers who were keen on defence barristers or solicitors, and he could see their point, but to him it was just work, like any other job.

'Sonny John Travers. I never thought I'd be sitting opposite you in this capacity.'

'I'm sure you didn't, David, but I'm here answering some voluntary questions, nothing more. I'll let you pretend you've arrested me, if that makes you feel better.' Sonny winked at the officer and rested his elbows on the table, twisting his gold sovereign pinkie ring.

'Quite right. You're free to leave at any time.' DI Davis smiled falsely. 'Let's get started.'

DC Chilvers switched the tape on and they all focused on anything but one another as they waited for the long beep to finish, then introduced themselves for the benefit of the tape.

'Mr Travers, can you tell us what you were doing between the hours of four and six p.m. this afternoon?' DC Chilvers said, leading the interview.

Sonny breathed in through his nose before he answered. 'I came home from work early, waited for everyone to leave the house, apart from Ida, of course, then I set to her with a weapon I found in the shed and cracked her skull open, drove her body to Priory Woods and dumped her in a shallow grave.'

The two officers looked at one another.

'That's what you want to hear, isn't it? I'm the obvious choice out of the family – adopted, only returned three years ago, shady background, recovering alcoholic.' Sonny screwed up his nose and continued to fiddle with his ring. 'The problem you all have, and I know this only too well, is that you would have to prove it in a court of law.'

'Are you admitting to a crime, Mr Travers?' DI Davis glanced at the tape recorder.

'No. And I'm not obliged to answer your questions.'

'Tell us what happened, Sonny. There's a vulnerable young girl missing who should be celebrating her sixteenth birthday this evening. This isn't the time for joking.'

'I wasn't.' Sonny leant back in the chair and tilted his head to one side. His long, slim face, tanned skin and dark blue eyes gave him a look of arrogance before he'd even opened his mouth to speak. 'Okay, I came back from work just before six. The house was in darkness and I thought everyone had already left for dinner. I switched the lights on and that's when I spotted Ida lying on the floor in the orangery. I didn't touch her or move her; she looked in a bad way. I crouched down to check her pulse and couldn't find one. I thought I heard movement coming from the back of the house, so I went to investigate. The security light in the garden had just switched itself off as I reached the kitchen window, so I turned off the lights in the house to get a better view of outside, and that's when I saw a dark-clothed figure making his way across the garden. So, I ran after him, which is when whoever it was hot-footed it out the back and across the field.'

'Then what happened?' DC Chilvers stopped taking notes and looked up at Sonny.

'After chasing the assailant some distance, I eventually lost whoever it was and returned to the house to check on Ida. The police had arrived by that time.'

'But you thought she was dead, so why did you come back in to check on her? Why not call the police?'

'Because, DI Davis, I was pretty certain she was dead, but I needed to make sure before I called the police.'

'You needed to make sure your niece was dead before you made a call to the emergency services? Or you came back in to make sure she was dead before you left the scene? Wasn't it more a case of being interrupted by your father, so you had to quickly get rid of her, return to the house and pretend you'd found her?'

'If that's the case, where is she? How far do you think I would have been able to get with a body and then return to the house in such a short space of time? When I came back in, Ida was gone.'

'You tell us. You were gone from the house for a while, and clearly there was enough time for someone to remove your niece while your father was outside looking for the ambulance. You were the only other person there, apart from Dr Coe, so unless he's not telling the truth, your story doesn't add up.'

'I don't have to answer these questions. Don't make me "no comment" you, David.'

'You can leave whenever you like, pending further investigation. On the other hand, I could take you to the custody sergeant and get you booked in.'

Sonny raked his fingers through his unruly dark hair and linked them behind his head, observing DI Davis. 'You could do that, but you'd have to nick me first.'

'I can do that, no problem.'

'But you're not going to, because that would mean the clock would be ticking and, right now, you don't have any evidence to prove I've done anything wrong.' Sonny sat forward and resumed his earlier position, his elbows leaning on the table. 'I suggest you take my word for it. I found my niece lying on the floor, blood gushing from her head, and chased what was possibly her assailant across the garden and into the park.'

'Who was the person you chased?' DC Chilvers tried to pull the interview back to normality.

'I wouldn't like to speculate. I really don't know. I gave your officers a description, but I only saw the back of him. Tall, lean, wearing black clothes and a hoody.'

'Dr Coe says you returned to the house earlier this afternoon, around 3.30 p.m., and left again. What was that for?'

'I'd left an important file at home. I dashed in and out again.'

'Who was in the house at that time?' DC Chilvers was building momentum.

'Ida was in the kitchen with Alistair, and I believe Ray was in his office with a client.'

'How do you know that?'

'I heard voices coming from that room and the door was closed.'

'But you didn't actually see who was in there?'

'No.'

'Was there anyone else in the house at that time?'

'Not to my knowledge. Like I said, I literally walked in, briefly spoke to my father when he poked his head out of the door, and walked out again.'

DC Chilvers observed Sonny for a few moments. 'Can you tell us how you came to locate Dr Coe and his family?'

'You know all this; it was in the papers.'

Sonny remembered only too well the day he'd first met Ray, even though he'd been blind drunk.

Sonny had spent hours walking the streets, trying to find Ray's house, and by the time he did, he was cold and exhausted, pissed off that there was no answer when he rang the bell. Sonny had slumped in the doorway of Ray's large Victorian house holding an empty bottle of whiskey. This was not that unusual a sight; a well-known psychiatrist who had gained notoriety on a famous chat show where he was the on-screen therapist, Ray regularly took in people like Sonny, often allowing them to stay with him temporarily until they were stable enough to move on. What most people didn't realise was that Ray had been practising the kinds of tests he'd become infamous for since the late sixties. Sonny had spent years researching him and reading everything he'd ever written.

Quite literally, they bumped into each other. Ray was coming out of his gate, on his way out to get some food; Sonny, who had gone off in search of more booze, had decided to go back and ring the bell one more time. He was drunk and staggering along the pavement when they almost collided.

'I'm nobody!' Sonny had shouted as he dodged Ray at the gate, his arms spread wide, as though he was going to embrace him.

Ray glanced at him briefly and walked away; he was used to this kind of behaviour outside his house.

'Did you hear me? I'm no one!'

This sentence caused Ray to stop, and he told Sonny later how his words had resonated, as he remembered Elise saying the very same thing when she was younger, not long after she'd started school and one of the teachers had remarked that her name was made up and utterly ridiculous.

At the time of them meeting, Sonny had been sleeping in a hostel not far from Ray's house. They'd told him to leave because he'd failed to adhere to the rules. When Ray found this out, he was immediately interested in why he'd done this; what had made him decide to jeopardise all the opportunities laid out before him and forfeit a warm bed for a night on the concrete, and a freezing one at that, as the iron fence along his front garden was already sparkling with frost and the daytime had only just slipped into the dark. But much like now, Sonny hadn't wanted to answer any of his questions and had simply asked Ray for help.

'I don't want your fucking change,' he'd snarled as Ray reached into his pocket to give him a card with his details printed on it.

'I had no intention of giving you any. I'm going out to get some supper. I'll be back in approximately twenty minutes. That card contains my address, where we are standing now. By the time you've wandered around, fulfilling your urge to drink, you'll have undoubtedly forgotten where we met. There's a hot shower and a warm bed for you, and a meal, should you decide to accept my offer.'

Sonny remembered wondering about the man standing before him, and how he'd stared at Ray for quite a few moments, looking him up and down, assessing his appearance.

'What are you, some sort of pervert?' Sonny shouted drunkenly, as Ray turned to leave.

'No. If you read the card, you'll see what I do. Probably against my better judgement, I'm offering you a bed and some food. It will cost you nothing.' Then Ray had turned up his collar, shoved his gloved hands deep into his pockets and left Sonny standing there.

'What are we having? Curry or Thai?' he'd shouted after him.

'Fish and chips,' Ray called back.

Sonny had ended up huddling on the doorstep, waiting for him to come home.

'Thought I ought to stay here. Didn't think I'd be able to find it again,' he'd mumbled when Ray returned.

'Come in.' Ray had pushed the heavy door open, and the two men had both shivered at the shock of the heat hitting them from inside.

During those first few months, Sonny had stolen from Ray, verbally abused him and disappeared for short periods only to return, begging for a bed and some food. Ray always agreed. Sonny knew he had faith that he'd eventually come through the other side, and that was what kept him going. When drink wasn't feeding his ego, Sonny was surprised at how much he enjoyed Ray's company, and all the things they had in common. Ray was surprised to learn that Sonny had been a successful barrister once. His ego had got the better of him and he'd accepted a high-profile case where he defended a man who had murdered a young teenager. He won the case and the man went on to reoffend. The media attention was overwhelming, and he had turned to drink, abandoning his wife and family.

Eventually, he stopped stealing from Ray, and only occasionally became verbally abusive when it all got too much for him. Their relationship began to shift from therapist and patient into an amicable friendship.

In return for attending AA meetings, Ray would give him tasks to do during his working hours: making tea, cleaning, answering calls. As he progressed in AA, he added filing and greeting clients – a complete stripping down from what he had once been. Ray paid him, in the form of a free bed and board, all meals included. Once Ray was sure Sonny was following a rhythm, that he felt safe conducting his life with temptation around – for Ray told him this would always be present – Ray began to set him proper hours and the chance to earn money. When he failed to attend meetings and threw himself against the confines of his addiction, being pulled both ways, Ray gave him no tasks, and removed his routine from him.

There were rules surrounding such privileges. Sonny was not permitted to drink alcohol while he was under Ray's roof. But nights spent in the comfort of Ray's home soon became favourable to him. This took time; he would insist on revisiting his old habits only to realise they were just that, and he would find they failed to offer him any joy or comfort. A short-lived euphoria wasn't enough.

Eventually, he told Ray he thought he was his son. Some months later Sonny was back to the work he used to do – his reputation as a barrister having never left him.

Ray had saved him.

When Sonny didn't elaborate, DC Chilvers rephrased the question. 'Did you use an agency, or did you find the Coe family yourself?'

'The internet's a wonderful tool.'

'Can you tell us how you knew Dr Coe was your biological father?'

'My adopted parents gave me the details of my parentage before they died.'

'And what are the names of your adopted parents?'

'Mr and Mrs Smith.'

'Very droll. We'd like the real names and addresses of your adopted parents and any immediate family you have. Do you have a partner, Mr Travers? Any children?'

Sonny knew Chilvers wasn't going to let this line of enquiry drop, but he wasn't about to reveal further details or talk about his wife and family. 'Nadia and I have been separated for some time, and I think you already know that.'

'We do know that, Mr Travers, but we still need all the details. For the tape.' DC Chilvers stayed calm and stared at Sonny.

'This has nothing to do with your investigation, and you are very aware that I know, on a professional basis, that these questions are totally irrelevant and simply designed to unnerve me. I've told you what I know, and I'd like to see my father now and get something to eat.'

The two officers looked at one another.

'It's very interesting to us, Mr Travers, that you haven't enquired about your niece since you've been here.'

CHAPTER TEN
THEN

The vehicle reversed alongside Nathaniel as his dad turned the car in the driveway, and he saw Elise's profile, white and stiff, like marble, as she stared straight ahead, Miles leaning against her and Buddy asleep in his car seat. *Look at me*, he pleaded silently to her. *Turn and look at me, otherwise we'll never get through this together*. But she didn't, and he watched his dad drive them away. He felt a certain amount of relief that they were leaving the awful scene; there were police everywhere, and flashing lights, made more prominent in the dark, heavy sky.

Nathaniel had been asked to go down to the police station and answer a few questions, to verify he'd been at work when Ida was attacked. It was a tricky one, because he'd already lied and now he was going to have to give the police an explanation, and that was going to sound lame. The simple truth was that when he finished work and was free to go home, he would, on occasion, go to a café or bar and tell Elise he was working late. Their fractious home life was too much for him at times, and more recently he'd spent longer periods away. Elise's increasingly temperamental state left him feeling drained and exhausted. Add an eight-year-old and a baby to that mix, and you had all the triggers for a nervous breakdown. The less time he spent at home, the better.

But he realised now that there was no one guaranteed to corroborate his story, apart from the bar staff, and he hoped they'd remember him.

Nathaniel was just about to get into the police car when he heard someone shouting at the back of Ray's house. Nathaniel ran to the side gate and managed to get halfway down the gravelled path, where he was stopped by a police officer.

'You can't go in there, I'm sorry.' The police officer pushed Nathaniel back.

'She's here!' someone shouted further down the garden.

'Let me see her!' Nathaniel pushed against the officer, grabbing the man's sleeves with his fists, then his adrenaline kicked in and he managed to shove him to the ground. He ran, spraying shingle everywhere, and found a small group of people crowded around the old coal bunker that was covered in ivy and lost amidst the rest of the garden.

Someone else tried to stop him, along with the officer he'd shoved in the alleyway, and Nathaniel caught a glimpse of Ida's sheet-white face. Everything slowed, the crowd parted, and people turned to look at Nathaniel as he lifted his face to the rain-filled, dark sky, and his emotions got the better of him. Ida was dead. His daughter's body had been found. The silence wound its way around him like toxic gas.

'There's a faint pulse, I can feel a pulse,' one of the officers said into the darkness. 'Are the paramedics still here?'

Everyone suddenly moved, and chaos ensued, as a couple of people went to fetch the paramedics. Nathaniel tried to break free but was restrained by two officers.

'We still need to preserve as much evidence as possible, Mr Munroe. You can see your daughter once we've got her to hospital.'

Nathaniel wasn't listening. He was staring at Ida, lying on top of the coal in the bunker. She reminded him of the foxes he'd seen dead on the side of the road, discarded like trash. Her face was patterned with blood, stark against her white skin, her eyes open and staring, like she was already dead.

In what seemed like a hazy few minutes, two paramedics carefully placed Ida on a stretcher and carried her to the front of the house and loaded her onto the ambulance.

'Mr Munroe.' Nathaniel turned to see a plain-clothes policeman standing behind him.

'Yes?'

'DS Waterford.' The police officer showed Nathaniel his warrant card. 'What made you come back into the garden earlier?'

Nathaniel frowned. 'I heard someone shouting and wanted to see if they'd found Ida.'

'Okay.' The DS nodded, his hands shoved deep into his suit trousers.

'Why do you ask?'

'I didn't know if you'd come back because you were looking for something. That's all.' DS Waterford turned away and walked back towards the house. Nathaniel made to follow, but thought it was better to stay where he was. It would only get him into trouble.

'Just find the person who did this,' he growled.

'Oh, we will,' DS Waterford called over his shoulder.

Police didn't like journalists or lawyers – that was a fact, even in a situation like this – and Nathaniel knew he wasn't going to get any sympathy, not after the number of unfavourable reports he'd written about them over the years.

CHAPTER ELEVEN
THEN

Elise's mind swirled as she drifted in and out of sleep, making her feel nauseous. She gripped the padded arms of the high-backed hospital chair she'd spent the night in, trying to steady herself against the sensation of moving. Dawn was just breaking through the curtains, highlighting the aftermath of yesterday's awful nightmare, which was all so very real now. Ida had been operated on during the night, to relieve the pressure on her brain, and she was being kept in an induced coma. She was lifeless, a machine helping her to breathe, and Elise knew the reality of the situation wasn't good, but giving up hope wasn't an option.

Elise reached out for Ida's hand, silently pleading with her to squeeze her fingers, respond in some small way, give some sign that she was still present in the world, but there was nothing. Ida lay there, surrounded by machines and covered in wires. If only Elise hadn't worked on Ida's birthday, if only she hadn't been persuaded by a colleague to swap shifts, if only she'd taken Ida out of school that day like her daughter had asked her to. The regret gripped her insides, and visions of what could have been but was impossible now tortured her already-tormented mind.

'Has there been any change? I nodded off.' Elise spoke to the police officer who was guarding Ida's room.

'Sorry, no. I'd have woken you.' The DC whose name Elise couldn't remember smiled sympathetically. She was the second one on guard since they'd brought Ida back from her scan. It was a comfort to know her daughter was being protected.

DC Chilvers had asked to meet Elise and Nathaniel, along with Ray and Sonny, in the family room at the hospital; Elise had refused to go anywhere else in case things changed with Ida. The meeting was to be held at 10 a.m. In the early hours, Nathaniel had gone to visit Miles and Buddy, who were staying at his father's house, to make sure they were okay, and had crept back into the hospital room to bring Elise some hot, sweet tea. They both sat in silence for a while, lost in their own thoughts.

'I wish we'd ignored the leap year, celebrated her birthday another day like we normally do,' Elise whispered into the artificially lit room, as they both stared at the lines on the monitor, the small reassurance that Ida was alive.

'Would it have changed anything?'

'Maybe not.' Elise stood up and stretched out her back.

'The police think the break-in and the assault are connected,' said Nathaniel.

'Well, that's stating the bloody obvious.'

'Did Ida say anything to you about any new friends she'd made recently?'

'I'm just as baffled about who took those photos as you are. Maybe the police managed to get some information out of Alistair.' Elise sat back down, a watchful eye on her daughter. 'There's obviously something she has or had that someone was after. Why else would they ransack her room?'

'We should have been more vigilant about what she was doing online. Neither of us know if she was talking to anyone when she was shut away in her bedroom.'

'Ida wouldn't do that. She's not like other teenagers – she isn't stupid.'

'Someone took those photos and posted them on her account, Elise. Did you find out what Ray was arguing with her about?'

Elise yawned, exhausted but unable to sleep. 'It was something to do with that family tree project she's been doing. I can't remember exactly what Dad said, but she wanted to go into his office and look for some photographs and he told her no. You know what he's like about anyone going in there. He said he'd look for her, but Ida being Ida . . .' Elise stopped herself, suddenly feeling guilty for talking about her daughter like that. She reached for Ida's limp hand.

'She hasn't been contacting anyone she thinks we might be related to? Those genealogy websites have all sorts of cranks on there, claiming they know you.'

'Good point, I'll mention it in the meeting. I don't think she argued with Ray – Miles is exaggerating, they just had a heated discussion about it from what I can gather.'

Suddenly Elise stared at Nathaniel, eyes wide as she felt a flicker of movement from Ida's forefinger.

'What is it?'

'She moved. Her finger moved.' Elise whacked her free hand on the button to call for a nurse as they both watched Ida's pulse rate rising on the monitor.

Both a doctor and a nurse came into the room, but Elise and Nathaniel's hopes were soon dashed when they were told it was probably a nerve twitch, with the escalated heart rate due to changes within her body, and no one could tell at this stage if they were positive or negative. Elise wasn't convinced. She'd felt movement, albeit small, and wanted to believe Ida could hear them, and was somewhere, holding on to her life.

'I'm going to get back to Dad's,' Nathaniel said. 'I want to be there in case the boys wake up. Miles took a while to settle.' He kissed Ida, seemingly unable to look at his wife, who didn't want to be comforted. He was helpless to bring about a miracle, and Elise knew as the fixer in the family he was feeling utterly useless.

'Make sure you're back for the meeting,' she said as he walked towards the door.

'I will.'

Just before 10 a.m., Sonny slowly opened the door and crept in, causing another bout of tears to burst forth from Elise as he embraced her. It was the first time Elise had seen Sonny, and she had so many questions about what had happened. She couldn't help feeling she was looking at a stranger.

'Is Dad with you?'

'Yes, he's just getting us all some coffee. It's been a long night.'

'For all of us,' Elise said.

'Sorry, that was insensitive. Is there any more news on Alistair?'

'No.' Elise fixed her gaze on her almost unrecognisable daughter. 'Do you think it was him you saw running through the garden?'

'I'm sorry, Elise, I just don't know. I'd hate to make a false accusation.'

'Can you remember what he was wearing when you came back from work in the afternoon?'

'I was in such a hurry, I literally dashed in and out. And whoever I saw outside last night could have been anyone – it was raining hard and the light was beginning to fade. I'm sorry.'

'It's okay.' Elise paused briefly. 'Miles said he saw you in the park when he went back to school for basketball. He called out to you.'

'He couldn't have, I went straight back to work.'

Elise watched him for any signs he might be hiding something. Trusting anyone, even her own family, had changed overnight now that someone had tried to take her daughter's life.

Ray walked in before she could ask Sonny anything else, and she decided it was probably best to leave the questions until later, and see what the police had to say.

Ray placed the coffees on the table and Elise stood up and embraced him. She'd never seen him looking so grey and tired. He was a large man, well built and imposing – totally unbefitting what people expected a psychiatrist to look like. He always wore trousers and a shirt, topped off with a panama hat covering the thin blond hair that reached his shoulders. During the winter months, he warmed up with a sweater, a scarf and occasionally a coat when it was particularly cold. Elise had often told him how he looked like a Colombian drug baron.

She recalled now how different she was to her parents, and how for years when she was growing up, she'd believed that's why her father had left. Elise had always felt too grubby, common, unpredictable, and nowhere near as refined in her tastes as they were. Elise had rejoiced in the SodaStream, the *TV Times* and bright orange processed-cheese slices she nagged them to buy her. Ray and Ingrid had owned a decanter, meticulously read the *Telegraph*, listened to Classic FM and ate mouldy, soft cheeses. Even after her parents had separated and she split her time at both their houses, they would prepare a snack in the same way: cheeseboard, celery, grapes, relish and port, all on an antique silver tray, the only food either would allow in the sitting room. Elise just ate straight from the cupboard or fridge as her mother looked on disdainfully. But not once had she ever known Ray to be condescending or patronising towards her, and she had loved him for that.

'You doing okay, kid?'

'Yep.' Elise fought back the tears as Ray squeezed her arms. 'Let's get going before I change my mind.'

Drained and lifeless, they all made their way down the corridor to the family room, though Elise was reluctant to leave Ida. They sat down and sipped their coffees.

Elise stood up and grabbed Nathaniel as soon as he walked in. 'Shouldn't we be doing something? Making some sort of appeal?'

'Let's see what the police have to say this morning, hey? I know you feel helpless but it's best to let them do their jobs. They'll tell us what we need to do.'

'Their way isn't helping Ida, though, is it.'

'No one apart from the doctors can help Ida, Elise. All we need to do now is find out who did this. It's done, there's no turning the clock back, you just have to get used to it. Ida's brain injury is so bad that even if she does wake up – and it's a big if – she'll never be the same again. Do you really want that for her?'

'Don't say that, don't say that.' Elise began to sob, the pain crushing her chest like she was weighed down in a pool of freezing water.

'Come on, Nathaniel, that's a bit much.' Ray put his arm around Elise and tried to offer some comfort, but there was barely any to give.

'Is it? She's better off knowing the facts now. No point getting her hopes up.' Nathaniel sat in one of the armchairs away from the rest of them. He was tired and grumpy, and the last thing he wanted to do was kid himself with unrealistic hopes.

The door creaked open slowly and DC Chilvers quietly walked in. 'Morning, everyone.'

'Will there be someone guarding Ida's room even when we're not there?' Elise had seen the DC leave the room to take a call and hadn't checked she was there when they left, which immediately caused another bout of panic, and she wiped her nose with her cardigan sleeve.

'Yes, we've arranged for twenty-four-hour surveillance. Don't worry, Mrs Munroe, security on your daughter's room is covered at all times.'

The officer's phone rang. 'I won't be a second.' DC Chilvers left the room, murmuring into her phone.

'Where are Miles and Buddy?' Elise's thoughts were scattered, and she suddenly remembered her other two children. She'd spoken to Miles on the phone earlier and he'd been tearful, having wanted to sleep at the hotel in Ray's room but having been told no by everyone. She'd tried to explain why he had to stay with Granddad Nick, but yesterday's events were taking their toll on the exhausted eight-year-old. Elise had felt so guilty saying no, wanting him to do whatever would give him the most comfort, but she knew the children would be better settled in a house familiar to them. The situation had made her even more emotional; as much as Miles loved his dad and other grandparents, he just wanted to be with Ray. Especially now.

'Miles has gone to school and Buddy is with Dad and Karen.'

'Will you bring Miles and Buddy back with you?'

'Yes, later today, but not to this meeting. Miles doesn't need to hear what happened to his sister, he's traumatised enough. We need to keep things as normal as possible for them both. Dad and Karen are taking Buddy out today, and as soon as they've picked Miles up from school, they'll give us a call and see if it's okay to visit.'

'Well, it's not okay, is it,' Elise snapped.

Sonny rubbed her arm, trying to reassure her. 'Come on, Elise, this isn't helping.'

Elise snatched her arm away. 'How do I know Miles is safe at school? What if the person who attacked Ida is waiting for him as well?'

'You're being irrational, Elise,' Nathaniel said. 'I went into the school this morning and explained the situation. You know security is tight there, and even more so now I've told them what's happened.'

'He's my son, and I'll decide what's best for him,' Elise said, standing up.

'Miles is fine, Elise. Now sit down and shut up.' Nathaniel grabbed her arm a little too sharply and pulled her back towards her seat.

'Hey, that's enough.' Ray glared at Nathaniel.

Elise turned to Sonny, remembering what she hadn't asked him earlier. 'Why did you go back to the house yesterday afternoon?'

'I told you, it was quite literally for a couple of minutes. I'd left a file behind – I had an important case yesterday.'

'Did you see Ida?' Elise asked.

'Briefly. She came in with Alistair the same time as me, and when I left they were both in the kitchen.'

'Let's talk about this later.' Ray silenced them both sharply as DC Chilvers reappeared with the senior investigating officer, DI David Davis.

Sonny smiled and stood up, reaching his hand out to DC Chilvers. 'Hello, Alex, it's good to see you again.'

'Mr Travers.' She nodded, barely shaking his hand. 'I hope you all managed to get some rest,' she said to the three of them. 'I know this is a terribly difficult situation, but we're doing everything we can and following all lines of enquiry.'

The DC's tone was stiff, professional, telling Elise she might be delivering some bad news.

'Haven't you charged Alistair yet?'

'No, Mrs Munroe. We'll be questioning him today, but we haven't charged anyone yet.'

'But didn't the photos come from his Facebook account?' Elise's mind was muddled; the photos of Ida had haunted her all night, and she wished she'd never seen them. Under normal circumstances the photos would have been perfectly fine, but no one was sure who had taken them.

'No. They came from your daughter's account, but we can't be sure who posted them, Mrs Munroe. We know your daughter couldn't have uploaded them at that time, but we need to find out exactly who did. It happens a lot, unfortunately. Ida's laptop was found in Alistair's bedroom, but he's insisting Ida forgot to take it with her the previous night when she was there. Jumping to conclusions and making hasty arrests isn't going to help this investigation.'

'Well, it's not like her to leave her laptop anywhere. Can't you just find out who hacked her account?' Elise was becoming hysterical; the thought of her daughter having a relationship with someone they didn't know was filling her with horrors she didn't want to think about. It was easier for her to focus on Alistair, the person they were familiar with and had known since he was a little boy.

'Listen to me, Mrs Munroe,' DI David Davis said while DC Chilvers took another call on her phone, 'we're not going to mislead you in any way; we're just going to tell you the facts, however painful they are, because I think you'll be better equipped to deal with it.' Everyone sat in an uncomfortable silence.

'I'm going to be your allocated family liaison officer, so if you have any questions or information, you need to come to me,' DC Chilvers said, having finished her call.

'Why wasn't Alistair questioned last night if he was arrested?' Elise squeezed her fingers together until her knuckles hurt.

'We didn't arrest him,' said DC Chilvers. 'He was asked to voluntarily answer some questions down at the station. He's going to be questioned today because we couldn't find an appropriate adult to accompany him last night. It's likely you'll be able to return to your father's home later today or tomorrow, but the block of flats is still out of bounds. Are there any other questions you want to ask us?' She looked around the room.

Elise folded her arms to comfort herself, desperately trying to think of all the questions she had wanted to ask, but her mind seemed to have moved to the other side of the room, out of her reach. At last, she came up with something. 'So he was released last night? Why can't Magda or his father, Liam, do it?'

'Alistair's clothes and phone were taken from him last night, and Mr and Mrs King were asked to arrange alternative accommodation with him while some of our team searched their house. His parents felt it was best for him to have an independent appropriate adult, so we thought it would be better to start afresh today.'

'Why?' Elise was becoming more irritated.

'We agreed someone independent would be beneficial. That's all I can say about the matter.' DC Chilvers looked directly at Elise, letting her know the subject was closed.

'There's something I need to draw your attention to.' Everyone immediately looked at Ray, who had been unsettlingly quiet. 'It was something I forgot to mention last night. I had a client with me yesterday. When I received Elise's call about the break-in, I was in a hurry to leave after the session. I'm not entirely sure he left the house . . . What I mean is, I didn't escort him out like I would normally. I'm fairly certain I saw him heading towards the front door, but I can't be totally sure.'

'Okay, Dr Coe.' DI David Davis picked up his pen. 'What's your client's name?'

'James Caddy. He's been coming to me for two years.'

Elise turned to Nathaniel. 'The "strange" man Miles mentioned.'

'The strange man?' DC Chilvers addressed the two of them.

Nathaniel nodded. 'Miles mentioned he spoke to a strange man at Ray's yesterday.'

'Did he say anything else?' DC Chilvers jotted everything down in her pocketbook.

'No, that was it. A funny man with an eye patch.' Nathaniel was concentrating hard on Ray, and Elise could feel things were beginning to get out of hand. Nathaniel and her father had never seen eye to eye about anything.

'You'll need to give us a list of all your clients' details, Dr Coe. Someone should have spoken to you about that last night.'

'Of course. As soon as I can have access to my office, I'll give you the keys to the filing cabinets, so you can look at any relevant cases.'

'We'll be looking at all the files, Dr Coe.' DI Davis looked at Ray over his glasses.

'Are you going to enlighten us on the details of James Caddy?' Nathaniel's gaze was still firmly on Ray.

'I can't discuss my patients with you, Nathaniel, you know that. I will talk with the officers privately.'

'Someone has attempted to kill my daughter and you're worried about client confidentiality?'

'I will talk to the relevant people about the matter. The right people will have the information they need.'

Before anyone could stop Nathaniel, he'd got out of his seat and grabbed Ray by his shirt and lifted him from his chair. 'You'll fucking tell us now!'

Sonny and DI Davis rushed over to defuse the embarrassing scene.

'This is all your fault!' Nathaniel spat at Ray, his voice breaking with emotion. 'This is all your fucking fault.'

'Sit down, Mr Munroe. This isn't helping the situation.' DC Chilvers spoke firmly once Nathaniel had been restrained and was led back to his own seat.

Ray straightened his shirt while Nathaniel shook his head. Elise was silent; it was all more than she could bear.

'We're done here, aren't we?' Sonny said. 'I really must go, I'm due in court this afternoon.' He picked up his phone and keys, ready to leave, as if these scenes were a common occurrence.

DI Davis turned to him. 'We need you to come down to the station and answer some more questions, Mr Travers.'

'Me?' Sonny frowned. 'I really don't have time now – I'll come in this evening. I answered your questions and gave you an account of what happened last night.'

'Sonny, I don't need to tell you how crucial the first few hours are in any investigation. It won't take long, just an hour out of your busy schedule.' DC Chilvers stared at him forcefully.

Ray stood up. 'I'll drive you down there and wait for you. Save you getting a taxi.' He paused, looking at Nathaniel before he spoke again. 'James Caddy is a paranoid schizophrenic. He was admitted to a high-security prison hospital some years ago for the attempted murder of his stepdaughter. He's out on licence.'

'And you just forgot to tell anyone this last night?' Nathaniel shook his head.

Ray opened and closed his hands. 'I was tired and confused. He has no motive. I didn't give him another thought after everything else that happened.'

'What did he do to her?' Nathaniel wasn't going to let it go. 'To his stepdaughter . . . What did he do?'

'I told you, he tried to kill her. That's all you need to know.'

'Come on, let the police do their work.' Sonny squeezed Nathaniel's shoulder.

'Tell me what he did to her, Ray.' Nathaniel was persistent, and Elise couldn't blame him for that.

'You need to calm down, Mr Munroe,' DC Chilvers said. 'I'll get all the details about James Caddy when I get back to the station.'

'I need to hear it from him.' Nathaniel banged his hand on the arm of the chair and then stood up and grabbed Ray again.

'Stop it! Stop it! Stop it!' Elise screamed, her hands pulling at her bedraggled hair.

'If you don't calm down, I'm going to have to arrest you.' DI Davis gripped Nathaniel's arm. 'Is that what you want? Me to cuff you and put you in the police car in front of all the press and photographers standing out there? You need to support your wife.'

Ray sighed. 'James Caddy sexually assaulted his stepdaughter and attacked her with a claw hammer. He doesn't recall the incident; he has paranoid schizophrenia.' He looked at Davis and Chilvers. 'He's been struggling recently, which is why I gave him an emergency appointment.'

A whole new set of thoughts hit Elise like she'd been punched in the stomach. 'Ida hasn't been raped, has she?'

'We don't know,' Chilvers said. 'Ida is in such a fragile state we haven't been able to examine her properly yet.'

'What aren't you telling me?'

Neither police officer answered Elise, focusing their attention on Ray instead.

'Why has James Caddy been struggling recently?' DI Davis moved in front of Nathaniel in case he lost his temper again.

Ray glanced around the room. 'He hasn't been taking his medication and he has a history of cocaine addiction, which exacerbates his condition. He has an alter ego he calls Derek Mantel. The person he claimed to be when he attacked his stepdaughter.'

CHAPTER TWELVE
NOW

Elise slammed the car door shut and let herself into the new home she and Nathaniel had bought in an attempt at starting again, away from all the memories the apartment had stifled them with. No sane person could possibly like the house – it was derelict, and had been abandoned for many years until the owner had decided to live there temporarily. It had been inhabited by an elderly man and no one quite knew his logic. One story Elise had heard was that he was eccentric and owned lots of properties in the area, places he'd never renovated, and as each one deteriorated and he was slapped with a compulsory purchase order from the council, he would move into the next, barely habitable residence. But this was where he met his tragic end in a house fire. Forensics suspected he fell asleep by the hearth in the sitting room while he was smoking a cigarette, and it ignited his clothes. Elise had nearly laughed when the estate agent told them, even though she knew it wasn't funny at all, but it fed her dark sense of humour. He'd been known as such an eccentric character and yet there was no great story to tell about his death.

The smoke had entwined itself around the house, so no one would forget. It had smeared the events of that day up the walls, encasing death inside, and Elise loved it. She wanted to be blanketed in it, to feel the full impact of its acrid, choking smell. It reminded her of Ida, and it was where Elise decided she wanted to be. The chipped black-and-white floor tiles in the hall, the curve of the cracked plaster peeling from the staircase, the smoke-damaged walls in the sitting room that had left a sinister shape by the fireplace, the kitchen with its eclectic layers of paint, and the skeletons of leaves from ferns that had been left to die in the sun on the deep windowsill of the lean-to all represented how Elise felt, and it was like she had found a kindred spirit, a friend. It was them – her and Nathaniel – and from there she could look at it all from the outside in.

In their new home, Death and Elise had swapped the lure of their apartment balcony for the comfort of a gentle drowning, should the mood take her to step into the deep river at the bottom of their long garden and entangle herself in the thick reeds.

Elise had stayed sober for three days now; she was coping and had felt okay until her boss had called her in for a meeting following the latest revelations with the Patons.

'Don't do this, Rick,' she'd pleaded with him. 'I'll be better, I promise. I just went on a bit of a bender at the weekend and things got out of hand.'

'I can't give you any more chances, Elise. I'm being pressured to make a proactive decision because I should have dealt with this before.'

'But if I wasn't known by the public, no one would have any idea what happened. It's only because some idiot filmed it on their phone, sold the story and it was splashed all over the papers.'

'It's got nothing to do with the papers, Elise. Jane Paton has been in to see me.'

Elise frowned. 'Oh, right, and you're just going to take her word for it?'

Rick was silent, and Elise could see he was wondering who she'd turned into now – what sort of person she'd become to be in such denial. And she knew, vaguely, the level of her denial, but it was her protector, her saviour, because letting go meant facing up to a lot of truths she just couldn't bear.

'Elise, she's doing you a favour. She's told the police it was all a big misunderstanding and she wants to drop the charges. You're lucky. I'm not sure I'd be so forgiving if you tried to take my child.'

Elise couldn't believe what she was hearing. Wasn't she allowed a relapse, considering everything that had happened to her family?

'Maybe I'll press charges against her husband for assaulting me. Everyone knows he's a fucking junkie.' Elise shook her head and picked up her bag, ready to leave.

'Mark is a top surgeon, one of the best.' Rick was becoming irritated, and Elise knew she wasn't helping herself, but she was beyond caring and couldn't think of anything else to say. 'Friend to friend, Elise. Go home, have some time off, and check yourself into a rehabilitation centre. You'll have my full support if you do this, and there will be a job for you when you're well enough to return. That is your only option. If you don't accept, I'm going to suspend you. That isn't something you want in the papers.'

Elise had stood up and walked out. Somewhere inside her head she knew he was right, but she couldn't grasp the thought and turn it into something comprehensible, because the major part of her mind was telling her he was wrong. She didn't have a huge problem, she could control this, whatever 'this' was. She was no different to most people who relied on alcohol and various types of drugs to cope with life. She was functioning, she lived her life, for the most part, in a civilised manner – she was employed in a respectable job, she didn't have a criminal record – so what was the problem?

The house didn't offer her any comfort today, which was unusual. Elise normally sighed with relief once she'd closed the door behind her but not today. There was something rattling in the rafters, she could feel it.

Nathaniel walked in just as she'd poured herself a large glass of wine, his face white and drawn.

'What's wrong with you?'

'You better sit down.'

'What?'

'Magda's dead.'

Elise placed her glass on the kitchen counter, trying to take in what Nathaniel was saying. 'How? What happened?'

'I'm not really sure. I was passing and popped in for a coffee. I think she might have committed suicide.' Nathaniel swallowed hard. 'I need to take these clothes off and get in the shower.'

'I don't understand.' Elise frowned. 'Are you telling me you just found her?'

Nathaniel snatched the glass of wine from the table and downed it in several large gulps. 'Well done, Sherlock.'

'Please tell me you've called someone, Nathaniel.'

'No, I haven't, and I don't intend to.'

'You can't do this.' Elise pulled at his arm. 'We have to call some-one – emergency services. Oh shit, what about Liam, and Alistair? You can't leave them to find her.'

Nathaniel grabbed Elise by the arms. 'Listen to me, Elise. After everything we've been through, all the shit that's been written about us in the papers, all the lies that have been told, can you imagine what people will say if I report that I've been to Magda King's house and found her dead? I don't even know if she killed herself – it could be the Suicide Watcher for all we know, or I could be implicating myself in a murder. Sorry, but this is the only way.'

'Why do you think it might be the Suicide Watcher?' Elise's skin prickled at the very thought.

'Because she was sitting at her kitchen table with a bullet through the side of her head.' Nathaniel pulled his top over his head and threw it straight in the washing machine.

'But you can't leave her husband and son to find her. Or anyone else for that matter.'

'Well, I've fucking seen her and I'm okay. Sorry, Elise, but it's tough luck. I'm not putting my neck on the line for anyone, not after all we've been through. Magda is dead, and if she did kill herself, she would have been expecting Liam or Alistair to find her.'

'Are you sure she was dead? Nathaniel, we should call someone, she might need help.'

'Elise, her lips were blue, eyes opaque. She's definitely dead.' Nathaniel pulled the rest of his clothes off, placing each garment into the washing machine and setting it on a hot wash cycle.

'Do you honestly think it's anything to do with the Suicide Watcher?'

'I don't know, but I wasn't going to hang around to find out.'

'Why are you washing your clothes?'

'Like I said, I don't want to be implicated in anything.' Nathaniel swigged some wine from the bottle. 'I'm going up for a shower.'

'What were you doing round there?' Elise followed him up the stairs to the new shower room they'd recently had fitted.

'Just a visit, nothing specific.'

Nathaniel was being evasive and, knowing him so well, Elise was sure he was hiding something. She decided not to press it and left him to his shower.

Having topped her wine glass up, she waited for Liam's phone call telling them he'd found his wife dead. Suicide. A note saying it was over. Given their mutual history, they would be the first he would call.

CHAPTER THIRTEEN

Each person was chosen by me because I wanted them to play a game. Whoever accepted a conversation with me on the train was meant to, and I remember every single one of them. I also recall the ones that declined my invitation, who didn't want to make the connection to what I was offering. They would ignore me by reading their newspaper or would move into another carriage. This didn't happen often – most people will chat to a stranger, probably more freely than with someone they know. Everyone has talked to someone in a queue, in the supermarket or at the bus stop.

One potential participant who ended up becoming a friend, a kindred spirit if you like, instigated a connection with me first. Gerald stepped on to the train and sat opposite me; we had the most interesting conversations.

My first question to him, the one that attracted his attention after we had talked generally about the weather and delayed trains, was if he had days where he felt like he might die. He looked at me for a while, stared at me as though I was a long-lost friend he'd been yearning to find for years. 'Yes, yes I do,' he said. 'Often.'

We talked for quite a few months on that routine train journey he took every morning. Gerald said he found great comfort in our conversations.

He lived this life, you see, one that many deniers follow, as though someone was controlling him, a force bigger than himself, or so he thought.

His theory on this, when asked, was that it had all begun when he'd started school at the age of four. Before that, he'd been – he felt he could recall – a free spirit.

School set him into a routine and he did quite well at his lessons. Talk at home was generally about what he would do with this wonderful education once he'd completed it. There was no question about whether he was going to university or if he would learn to drive when he turned seventeen. His fate was mapped out for him.

And, before he knew it, he'd met someone, got married, elevated his career, bought a bigger house, a better car, tried for a family, and so it went on. The more he had, the harder he worked, and the harder he worked, the more he accumulated.

Every day, he got on the train and made the journey to and from his high-powered job. The job that he had to maintain to afford all the things he never actually wanted. It dawned on him one day that they were what someone else desired and he'd just gone along with it, never once asking himself what he'd like to do.

It's common for deniers to be easily led and I understand, even with my line of thinking, that his story is in no way unique. But he'd begun to wonder, and the wondering made him stand out from everyone else.

In these moments of deep contemplation whilst on the train, he'd started to think about what it would be like if he took his shoes and socks off and walked into the sea and never went home. Other days, he just felt like taking off his shoes and socks and stepping in front of a train. I never got to the bottom of the meaning of the shoes and socks, and I often ponder it. Maybe it just represented freedom for him.

His life was suffocating, stifling, a never-ending perpetual routine that he had conducted without realising it. Going home and telling his wife how he felt filled him with such fear and anxiety, he couldn't talk about it. So I asked him a question, telling him beforehand that he would have just sixty seconds to answer, with the condition it was to be truthful and not what he thought anyone wanted to hear. I asked him what he would do if I gave him a gun with one bullet loaded in it and he had to choose if his wife received the shot or he did. Without hesitation, he said he would shoot himself. Four months later, I asked him the same question again and he changed his answer.

What caused the change in his thought patterns, I have no idea, and I never asked him. Perhaps just being able to tell someone that occasionally he felt like dying was an unburdening and unfurling of further truths.

When I saw Gerald again, he told me he'd purchased a gun that he kept hidden in the drawer of his bedside table. When his wife was asleep, he would get the gun out and hold it in his hands. The weight and the chill of the metal made him feel safe.

CHAPTER FOURTEEN
THEN

Nathaniel wasn't sure if Magda would answer the door. It was, after all, an awkward situation – her son had been questioned over Ida's attack. He had only been asked to come to the station to answer some questions and not arrested, but even so, Alistair was possibly the last-known person to see Ida conscious and the police had found her laptop in his bedroom.

Banging on the door with the palm of his hand, Nathaniel abruptly stepped away and looked up at the windows before turning to leave. Magda opened the door just as he reached the gate. He turned to see an unfamiliar woman, with puffy eyes and dishevelled hair. They'd been friends for years, ever since Magda had taken over the support group. Set up for victims affected by suicide, it was mainly full of people who believed their loved ones had been victims of the Suicide Watcher, and it was where Elise and Nathaniel had previously rekindled their relationship, having seen each other at the group for the first time since they'd been at school together.

In all the years he'd known Magda, he'd never seen her cry or ever imagined she did. She always appeared to be so organised – one of those people who took everything quite seriously but would surprise everyone with remarks that seemed out of character. Liam, her husband, had been her personal trainer, and Elise and Nathaniel had been shocked when they'd met him; he was so much younger than her. They'd imagined a much older man, grey hair, intellectual type, and had giggled about it afterwards. There was no doubt Magda didn't look her age, and was extremely attractive for a woman in her late fifties who'd had a child when she was in her mid-forties.

'I didn't think you'd answer.'

'I almost didn't. I thought it was a bloody journalist.' Magda gave him a wry smile and they embraced one another. 'Come in, I'll make us some tea. Is there any news?'

Nathaniel shook his head. 'How's Alistair? Is he here?'

'No. Liam's taken him to the gym to do some boxing, focus his mind. He's absolutely broken.'

Nathaniel wanted to show some concern, to say he was sorry to hear that, but to be honest he didn't really care about Alistair's welfare.

'It's not like you to miss out on some training,' he noted as he followed her inside. When Magda wasn't at work, Nathaniel always knew her to be in the gym working out.

'I've been overdoing it and put my back out. Thought I'd give it a miss.'

'This is difficult, isn't it? Maybe we shouldn't talk about it. I'm sure you're feeling as awkward as I am.'

'I don't feel awkward about anything.' Magda placed the filled kettle on the stove and lit the gas. 'Maybe talking about it is the best thing for us all. We might piece together what happened.'

'I guess so.' Nathaniel couldn't help feeling rattled. It wasn't Magda's child lying in a hospital bed, fighting for her life.

'You know Alistair wasn't arrested or charged with anything?'

'I know. The police said they took him in for questioning.'

'Nathaniel, I've always said, blood or not, if one of mine did anything wrong, anything at all, I'd shop them.' Magda got the teabags from the cupboard along with two mugs. 'I honestly don't believe he has. I genuinely think he waited in the cricket pavilion for her. I'd know if he was lying, I just would.'

Nathaniel nodded, taking a deep breath.

'I know my boy, Nathaniel. He loves Ida, she's his best friend.' Magda primped her curly red hair, as if it might be out of place.

'Maybe he loves her too much, hey?' Nathaniel couldn't make sense of it all – Ida's laptop in Alistair's bedroom, the photos on her Facebook account.

It was the wrong thing to say – Magda's face became tense, her blue eyes sharp, and she began to distract herself by tying her hair up into a ponytail with a band. An awkward silence descended for a few moments and Nathaniel wondered if their friendship would withstand this kind of pressure.

'He's a good kid,' she insisted. 'And anyway, he wouldn't do anything to jeopardise the promising future he has in front of him.'

Nathaniel nodded. 'Is he still going to fight at the weekend?'

'Yes. This is a huge boxing match for him. It could lead to bigger things. His heart isn't in it right now, but we've told him he's got to carry on regardless. I'm sure that's what Ida would want.'

The observation about his daughter jarred Nathaniel somewhat. 'I'm sure she would.'

'How's Elise? Any change with Ida? What about the rest of the family?'

Nathaniel peered out of the window, hoping to find some inspiration, some words to describe what state they were in.

'No change with Ida. And as for us lot, I'm not sure.'

'Sorry, silly question. You know we'll have Miles and the baby for you, give you all a break? Miles loves Alistair, and I know he'd like to see him.'

'Thanks, they're with Nick and Karen – trying to keep things as normal as possible. I'd better get back. Miles has an interview at the police station this afternoon.'

'Nathaniel, my son isn't violent. I sat with that boy and questioned him just as much as the police did and there's no way he did anything to hurt Ida.'

Nathaniel stood up and pushed his chair in. 'Look, Magda, I understand this is difficult for everyone concerned, and it must be hard to see or even accept that someone so close to you could do such a thing . . . but I think that's the point, Magda. You're too close to be able to have an objective opinion about it all.'

'Sit down a minute, Nathaniel.' Magda got up and poured hot water in the mugs. 'When your mother died all those years ago, what was the initial conclusion? What did it all look like?'

Nathaniel was a bit surprised by her questioning, which seemed to have appeared from nowhere.

'You know what happened, I've told you before.' It wasn't a memory Nathaniel wanted to dwell on, especially at a time like this. Visions of his mother, Anna, swirled in his mind along with Ida, blood pouring from her head, stirring his nausea again.

Being a latchkey kid, Nathaniel had found his mother, dead on the bathroom floor, one day after school. She should have been at work; she ran a launderette situated amongst an unimpressive array of depressing shops near to where they lived. Nathaniel had burst into the bathroom that day, desperate for a pee, and there she was, leant up against the bath. He didn't connect her with the mess up the tiles on the walls and across the floor, not to begin with, not until quite some time afterwards. He'd thought she was having a joke with him and had laughed at first. They had always played tricks on each other, having a giggle together.

A few minutes later, his older brother Richard turned up and screamed the house down, as if he were tearing the walls in two. Nathaniel remembered staring at him, wondering where the noise was coming from because it didn't seem to be anything to do with his mouth. Then Richard stopped, and the echo resonated in his ears, the buzz, the ringing from his scream crawled around Nathaniel's lobes, across the back of his neck, and that's when he knew it wasn't a prank. Nathaniel had sat on the edge of the toilet, watching her, expecting her to suddenly draw breath, explain what had happened. He stayed with her until the pointless ambulance arrived, quickly followed by his – at the time – feckless father.

'Well, you all thought it was suicide, didn't you?' Magda brought him back into the room. 'The point I'm trying to make is, it wasn't necessarily what it first appeared to be. Your dad knew that too, and that's why he asked for her case to be reopened.'

'I think the police had their suspicions; they wouldn't have just reopened it based on my dad's opinion . . . Anyway, what has this got to do with Ida?'

'I'm just saying, things aren't always what they seem,' Magda said.

'Very cryptic.' Nathaniel finished his tea and got up to put his mug in the sink. 'What really made you take over the support group, Magda?'

'You know why . . . because of my brother, Gordon.'

'Did the police reopen his case? You've never talked about it.'

Magda searched his face, trying to work out what he was looking for. 'What's going on, Nathaniel? Why have you come here?'

'What led you to believe Gordon was a victim of the Suicide Watcher?'

'I think you better leave, Nathaniel. You're under a lot of strain. Let's not fall out.'

'I read the article in the archives about how your brother died. He didn't die from a gunshot wound, he died falling from some cliff-tops when he was on holiday. It's not anything to do with the Suicide Watcher, is it?'

Magda stood up. 'It's irrelevant how my brother died, and actually none of your business.'

'Why did you tell us Gordon was shot, a possible victim of the Suicide Watcher? You went into quite a lot of detail for someone who was lying.'

Magda breathed in deeply. 'Have you ever thought I might find it easier to lie about his death? That I want to be like you and Elise – have some sort of answer? Rather than have my parents wondering for years after, why we were all so bloody awful, so bloody unbearable, that he felt the overwhelming need to kill himself? The verdict was misadventure. I didn't want my family to know, so I made sure the papers printed it as an accident. I lied, big deal. I didn't want my family ever wondering if he'd done it deliberately – he'd tried to kill himself before.'

Nathaniel nodded, completely unconvinced of her explanation, which sounded practised, as if read from a script.

'Whatever, just go home,' Magda snapped, irritably.

Nathaniel stepped into the hall and made his way towards the front door, briefly glancing at the side table as he passed. Then he stopped and turned around. Magda quickly tried to manoeuvre him towards the door and an awkward scuffle ensued.

'Why is there a parcel addressed to my daughter sitting on your side table?'

CHAPTER FIFTEEN
THEN

Elise and Sonny sat in the room where the police had sent them, blowing on insipid tea that had been brought for them from the machine. They were waiting for Miles to finish his interview, and Elise was wondering where Nathaniel was and what had been so important he couldn't get back to be with his son.

'I still don't understand why one of us couldn't go in there with him. He's just a little boy, he doesn't know any of these people.'

'Elise, with anything like this, immediate family members are suspects. The police will be looking at all of us.' Sonny shifted uncomfortably in his seat.

'They asked me why you have a different name to Dad.' Elise blew on the steaming tea, desperate to dampen her dry mouth. She hadn't eaten for days and had been taking zopiclone on an empty stomach. It had left her feeling slightly ragged around the edges.

'I assume you told them?' Sonny placed the plastic cup on the table.

'Of course. I thought they wanted to talk to Miles about James Caddy – show him some photographs, see if he can identify him? I wish they'd hurry up, I want to get back to Ida.'

'They'll be asking him about everything, trust me.' Sonny leant forward and rested his elbows on his knees. 'Elise, there's something I need to tell you. Something you need to hear from me.'

'What? What is it?' Elise sat up, anticipating alarm at anything that was said these days.

'It's difficult to know where to start,' Sonny said.

'Is it something to do with what happened to Ida?'

'No, but you might not understand if you hear it from someone else.'

'You're worrying me now. Just tell me.'

Sonny looked up at the door and took a deep breath. 'I had been asked by a colleague to represent a difficult client. He thought I was best placed to deal with her. She was seventeen at the time – she'd stabbed her older sister with a penknife. They'd got into an altercation one evening and things had got out of hand.'

Elise was quiet for a moment. 'Did she die?'

'No.' Sonny frowned at Elise, causing her to wonder what was wrong with her question. 'So, the girl, the sister, she was charged with attempted murder. Throughout the trial, she was evasive and difficult to represent. She thought I could work miracles without knowing all the facts.'

'Why did she do it?' Elise was suddenly absorbed in someone else's life, giving her a small amount of respite from her own troubles.

'To this day, I'm still not entirely sure. We had to be so careful how we dealt with her because she was a young seventeen, uneducated, and no one wanted to be accused of putting suggestions in her head. There was no talk of abuse – the two of them seemed to have a good relationship apart from the usual sibling spats – nothing obvious that might have pushed her into such a rage. Sometime near the trial, I asked her again, but more directly, why she stabbed her sister multiple times.'

'What happened?' Elise sipped the tea, waiting for Sonny to tell her more. There was a brief moment when she wanted to leave the room; the story was peculiar, forced somehow, and Sonny seemed to be acting differently. Or maybe she was viewing him from another perspective, she wasn't sure.

'She just laughed and said her sister owed her a tenner and she'd asked her for it too many times.'

'That was it?'

'That was it. Then I realised it was the first time anyone had asked her why. The most obvious question, and none of us, not even the police, had put this to her. We were all so busy tiptoeing around her.'

'What has this got to do with anything we're talking about?'

Sonny took another deep breath and shifted in his chair. 'Just before her bail hearing, I went to her cell, so we could discuss her plea – she'd changed it from guilty to not guilty and I couldn't understand why. Long story short, we got into a bit of a wrestle. She took my ballpoint pen from my book and stabbed me in the hand. I grabbed her wrists to stop it going any further and we grappled for a few seconds. I left the cell and went to get some first aid. My hand was bleeding quite badly by this time. When I got back, there were police officers running everywhere and I was cautioned and taken into custody. The bitch had torn her knickers, roughed herself up, made her wrists look worse and called for help, saying I had sexually assaulted her.'

Silence descended. Elise hadn't liked how he'd referred to the young girl. It was a flash of a person she didn't recognise; she'd never heard him call anyone a bitch before.

'I take it they believed her?'

'Everyone is entitled to make an allegation and receive a fair hearing. There was no CCTV in the cells – I shouldn't have gone in there unaccompanied and I was seen leaving in a hurry. I had to prove it was to see to my hand and not because I'd committed a crime.'

'But I can't understand why they would believe someone with her background over a well-respected barrister like you.'

'By this time, Elise, I wasn't liked – not by my colleagues and especially not by the police. I was arrogant and obnoxious. I'd won some big cases and believed I was invincible.'

'Even so, surely no one would believe someone like that?'

'Why wouldn't they? I had made the mistake of comforting her on a couple of occasions when she was upset – two police officers gave witness statements to that effect. My sexual history hadn't done me any favours. I was married but known for shagging about, sometimes with girls like her. Drunken nights after work.'

'What, teenagers?' Elise was beginning to feel even more uncomfortable; she hadn't known any of this about Sonny.

'Yes, Elise.' Sonny stood up and walked over to the door and peered out of the small square window. 'You're judging me. They weren't all that young – I didn't seek them out, if that's what you're thinking.'

'Of course I'm going to think that. So would you, if your sixteen-year-old daughter was lying in a hospital bed.'

'I certainly wouldn't be here talking to someone I thought might be guilty of attacking one of my children. I'd want them dead.'

Elise looked up sharply, startled at Sonny's tone. 'Yes, I would want you dead, you're right. What makes you think I'm suspicious of you? Or anyone else for that matter?'

Silence engulfed the room as Elise waited for Sonny to respond.

'It doesn't matter what I say. Ultimately, you'll make up your own mind.'

'Tell me why you think I'm suspicious of you.'

'In my experience of dealing with this kind of thing, mothers are suspicious of everyone. You suspect me, Ray, even Nathaniel. Don't tell me it hasn't crossed your mind.' Sonny turned from the door and stared at Elise. 'The police think I did it, they're watching to see if I make any mistakes; arresting other people to lull me into a false sense of security. I know how it works.'

'What happened with the girl?'

'I was found not guilty and she admitted afterwards that she'd lied.'

Elise rested her head in her hands, exhausted and nauseous, her mind jumping from one question to another, interrupted by flashes of Ida's face smiling at the unidentified photographer. Now the images were scorched into her burnt-out brain.

'You're right, I was suspicious. What am I meant to think? It's not like we grew up together, is it? I don't know you like I would any other sibling.'

'Would that make any difference? You'd still be suspicious of me. I was the first to find her – that puts me at the top of the list.'

'I guess so.'

Sonny sat down again, just as DI David Davis entered the room with DC Chilvers.

'Where's Miles?'

'Mrs Munroe, we need to speak to you for a moment. Where's your husband?' DI Davis placed a file on the table.

'I have no idea. What is it? Has Miles identified someone? Is he okay?' Elise said, beginning to panic.

'Miles is fine, he's still being interviewed. Mrs Munroe, earlier today we arrested Alistair King based on a confession and some forensic evidence to corroborate his statement. He's admitted assaulting your daughter and we've charged him with attempted murder.' DC Chilvers's blunt words hit Elise in the face like shards of glass.

'What?' Sonny looked at the two officers, but they ignored him, focusing their attention on Elise, who had begun to shake uncontrollably. 'A confession? Alistair?'

'Yes. He claims they had sex a few days prior to the attack and she accused him of rape. On Monday the 29th, he skipped lessons and broke into your apartment so he could destroy any incriminating evidence, and he stole Ida's laptop with the intention of deleting anything that might prove his guilt. Upon leaving the block of flats, he bumped into Ida and she agreed to walk with him to the cricket pavilion in the Maryon Park, so they could talk. We believe Ida may have dropped her phone before they left, which was why you discovered it near the apartment. After they'd been to the cricket pavilion, they went back to your father's house where an argument ensued, and he struck her on the back of the head with a heavy object.'

'No. No. This isn't right.' Elise stood up, tears rolling from her sore, red eyes. 'Alistair wouldn't do that to Ida. He loves her.'

DC Chilvers looked at DI Davis. 'At this time, we're still looking at evidence and corroborating what he has said.' DC Chilvers turned to Sonny. 'Your description of the person running from the garden matched the clothes Alistair King was wearing that day.'

Elise staggered backwards, bile reaching her throat as DC Chilvers managed to grab her before she hit the floor, guiding her back to her chair.

'Try and sip your tea, Mrs Munroe. You'll feel better.'

'Has she been sexually assaulted? Do you mean he raped her?'

'No, and there's no evidence of that. It was the one and only time, and Ida became cross with him because she didn't want their relationship to change. He thinks she regretted it and accused him of forcing her. He says they argued about it at your father's house and he lost his temper.'

'Has anyone called Nathaniel?' Sonny said, reaching across and taking Elise's hand in his.

'Would you like me to call your husband or do you want to do it?' DC Chilvers said.

'What exactly did he do to her? What did he hit her with?'

'Come on, Elise,' Sonny said. 'Don't upset yourself with questions like that.' He squeezed her hand before she could pull it away.

'We have only just received this information and we're still waiting on some forensic reports.'

'I want to know exactly what he's done to her. You said there's forensic evidence to support what he's saying?'

The two police officers looked at one another.

DI Davis linked his fingers together before giving a considered response. 'It's probably best we wait until all the facts become clear and Forensics can tell us more, Mrs Munroe. Your brother is right – speculating will just upset you.'

'I want to know what evidence you have.' Elise's voice was rising. 'I've known Alistair since he was six. He's stayed with us, been on holiday with us, he's part of our family – and you're telling me he's tried to kill my daughter?'

DC Chilvers addressed Elise directly. 'We found significant amounts of unidentified spatter on his clothing, which would suggest he attacked her – enough to corroborate what he's saying anyway, should he change his plea.'

'It "would suggest"? What does that mean?' Elise began squeezing her fingers together, wanting to feel some pain.

DC Chilvers took a deep breath, trying to find the right words to explain it. 'When your father's clothes were tested, Forensics found blood spray, conducive to someone breathing out. So when he lifted Ida off the ground, the breath that came from her mouth contained particles of blood that were expired on to Dr Coe's clothing. Alistair's clothes had significantly more, which would indicate spatter from the blow to the head. We're still waiting for the results to confirm exactly what the staining is.'

'That wasn't what I meant. You used the words "claimed" and "suggest". Are you saying you're not sure he's telling the truth? Are you still looking for other suspects?'

'In a case like this, especially when a teenager makes a confession, we never stop looking at the entire picture. Alistair hasn't told us exactly what weapon he used and where it is. This is an important fact we need to establish to prove he's telling the truth.'

'But why would he confess to something he hasn't done?' Elise couldn't understand any of it. She thought she knew Alistair like he was one of her own children. There had never been any thoughts he might be unhinged. In fact, he was the one person she had dismissed when Ida had been attacked.

'People do, I'm afraid.' DC Chilvers handed Elise her tea. 'It can be for notoriety, infamy, that kind of thing, and sometimes they do it because they feel guilty about something else, that they might have failed that person in some way, so they admit to the crime as a way of punishing themselves.'

'Sounds to me like you don't think he's guilty.'

'We keep an open mind throughout an investigation, Mrs Munroe. Everyone is still a suspect until we reach a conviction,' said DI Davis, glancing briefly at Elise. It was then that she realised it wasn't just all the people around her who were under suspicion. She wasn't exempt because she was Ida's mother. They were all guilty until proven innocent.

Elise looked up and focused her gaze on Sonny. Everything appeared to slow down, the floor and walls seemed to be moving towards her.

She was certain Alistair wasn't guilty at all.

CHAPTER SIXTEEN
NOW

Nathaniel threw a pile of tabloids on to the bed. It was a few moments before Elise stirred and pulled herself into a sitting position.

'Did you know it's exactly a year since Buddy has been gone?' he asked her.

Elise shrugged, making him even angrier than he already was. It was almost like she'd regressed to being a child.

'Still not long enough for you to sell yet another story to the bloody press. This is low, even for you,' Nathaniel snapped at her.

Elise moved her messy blonde hair from her face and pulled back the quilt, swinging her legs out of bed.

'Hung over?'

'Nathaniel, you once said to me that to deal with the press was to be their friend. So, that's what I do now, give them a story before they make one up.'

'You had no right to sell a story about my mother.' Nathaniel walked around the bed, cornering her so she wouldn't storm off to the bathroom like she usually did when they argued.

'It wasn't just about your mother. It's not always about you,' Elise said. 'It's stopped them finding out about Buddy, hasn't it?'

At the mention of his son's name, Nathaniel sat down heavily on the bed and, as predicted, Elise went straight to the bathroom. Moments later he heard her switch on the shower.

The previous day, they'd had a call from a social worker informing them that a decision had been made to place Buddy into adoption – find him a permanent home. It hadn't appeared to have had any impact on Elise, but Nathaniel felt like someone had placed his body under a guillotine and sliced him in half. It didn't matter what he said or offered to do, social services were adamant the decision was final. It reminded him of that desperate day when they'd taken Buddy away – up there with one of the worst days of his life.

A year ago, Jed – that was the social worker's name – had visited to tell them the news. Nathaniel could see his lips moving but the words didn't seem to be sinking in. Buddy was going to be taken to a foster home until the situation could be assessed again, in twelve months' time. It was in Buddy's best interests, Jed had said. Then Nathaniel heard Elise say she'd been sober for five days and he wanted to punch her in the face for being so pathetic and sounding so childish. They'd been here so many times before, and it was only ever three or five days at the most, and then she tended to replace the drugs with alcohol.

Nathaniel could recall all the times he should have done something during that year. He knew the social worker's visit was inevitable. Then there were all the incidents they didn't know about.

'Buddy stays with a childminder when I'm at work,' he'd explained, 'and the rest of the time he's with me. I don't ever leave him alone with my wife.'

'Don't do that, Nathaniel. Don't talk about me as if I'm incapable of looking after him.' Elise was slurring now, having tanked herself up before the social worker arrived. The irony was, she didn't even want Buddy. Nathaniel had never been a violent man, but the last few years with Elise, his temper was a constant spark immediately inflamed at the smallest irritation.

'We know that, Mr Munroe, but our main priority is Buddy and we need to know he's safe at all times. There have been too many concerns for his welfare.'

Nathaniel looked away, remembering all the other incidents social services didn't know about – on one occasion Buddy had fallen out of his high chair and on to the tiled floor; Elise hadn't been watching him and it had resulted in a broken arm. Then there'd been another time when Karen, his stepmother, had been babysitting, and found strips of zopiclone under his cot mattress – Buddy had been sick, and she had made the discovery whilst changing his bedding. Elise had protested that she'd had to hide the tablets where no one would think to look because she was being constantly nagged about them, completely missing the point that their son could have found them, with catastrophic consequences. They'd had to rush him to hospital to check the cause of his sickness, which luckily hadn't been anything to do with the drugs.

Nathaniel's father and stepmother had threatened to report everything to social services if he didn't do something about it.

Aside from all this, there had been the issue of Elise stalking the Patons and her public outbursts. They'd been given too many chances already.

'I'll leave,' Nathaniel told them. 'I'll pack my bags and take Buddy right now. He can live with my father too, until I get a place to live. We can get a court order like there was for Miles.'

Lauren, the younger social worker who hadn't spoken other than to say hello, stared at the coffee table, unable to look at Nathaniel. Buddy turned his attention to Nathaniel and began to crawl towards him.

'I'm sorry, Mr Munroe, but it's too late,' Jed said. 'We've tried to speak to you and your wife on numerous occasions about this matter and nothing has changed.'

Nathaniel shot a glance at Elise, who had said nothing. Her face was blank, indifferent and cold. He scooped Buddy into his arms and stood up.

'I'm going. I'll leave now and promise I'll never come back. Please don't do this.' Nathaniel was struggling with his emotions; everything was closing in around him and he knew he was running out of time. 'I can stay at my father's tonight and sort a place to live tomorrow.'

'It might be an idea to take him back to his real, biological parents. I can give you their details.'

'Don't you dare . . . don't you dare do this.' Nathaniel leaned towards Elise, making her flinch and causing Buddy to start crying. Nathaniel was seeing her as if for the first time. All the realisations that should have been apparent months ago were hitting him with sharp clarity, but now it was all too late. Everything had been clouded as they were pulled together by what had happened to their daughter, and he hadn't been able to see what his father had been telling him all along.

'Buddy doesn't belong to us!' Elise screamed. 'You want to fight? Fight for the child who's living with the Patons!'

'We've had all the fucking DNA tests. He's our son.' Nathaniel's aggressiveness caused Buddy to launch into a scream.

'Okay, this isn't helping matters. We have a court order to remove the child and we have to follow it through.' Jed stood up and moved towards Nathaniel, who in turn stepped back and reached for his phone.

'Wait, please. Let me call my dad. I need him here.' Nathaniel's hand shook as he dialled, telling Nick to come over urgently. 'Please just wait for my dad to get here. That's all I ask.'

'Nathaniel, we've had this conversation before. Your son is suffering. He's not developing as he should for a child of his age.

Cognitively, he's below average and lacking in communication skills.' Jed followed Nathaniel into the kitchen. 'Trust me, this is for the best under the circumstances. It's not forever and there'll be visitation rights. We've found him a really nice family with lots of experience. He'll be absolutely fine.'

'But he'll be frightened without me.' Nathaniel's voice broke, his emotions choking him as he looked at Buddy's face, red cheeks and wet eyelashes where he'd been crying. 'I can't believe this is happening.'

Nathaniel knew they were right; he'd looked it up on the internet and seen the effects a post-partum depressive parent could have on a child. Admittedly, Elise had recovered from that, supposedly, but she'd been left with an addiction to prescription drugs of which she was in complete denial.

Buddy's only word was 'no', an appropriate one for the negative situations that were forever in their lives. Even when he meant yes, he said no. He didn't respond to anything other than raised voices, which he cried at. Nathaniel knew that, eventually, Buddy wouldn't respond at all. Now Nathaniel was full of regrets at not having left Elise before – stupidly, naively in some ways, believing that if he just kept Buddy away from her, social services would back off.

'How long do I have?'

Jed closed his file and placed it into his bag. 'I'm afraid we need to get going soon.'

'Today?'

'There's nothing more I can do, I'm sorry.'

'Where are you going?' Nathaniel turned to see Elise walking out of the sitting room, towards the stairs.

'I'm taking a shower.'

'Aren't you going to say goodbye to our son?'

Elise stopped on the stairwell but didn't turn around. 'It doesn't matter how many times you say it, Nathaniel, he will never be my son.'

No one spoke for a few moments, and the atmosphere was full of tangible thoughts. Jed looked at Lauren and Lauren looked at Nathaniel.

Jed broke the silence. 'The best thing you can do now is work towards helping us with Buddy.'

Nathaniel rocked Buddy in his arms, kissed his soft head and wrapped his large fingers around one of his tiny hands.

'Just give me a minute with him, please,' Nathaniel almost roared at them both. He was so angry with himself – with Elise for dragging them into this mess. He walked over to the front window and watched his father pull up and get out of the car. Buddy pointed, recognising his granddad, oblivious to what was about to happen, his small hands banging on the glass.

Nick let himself in with the key Nathaniel had given him in case of emergencies. 'What's going on?'

Nathaniel kissed Buddy and handed him to his father. 'I need to go and pack some of his things.'

Upstairs, Nathaniel sorted through Buddy's clothes and favourite toys, his heart feeling like it would drop from his chest and on to the floor. In the drawer, he found the blanket they'd wrapped Buddy in when they'd brought him home from the hospital. He picked it up and smelt it but all he could remember was the time he'd come home from work, when Ida and Miles had been at school and he'd found Elise, heavily pregnant with Buddy, standing on the ledge of their roof terrace, leaning over the edge, arms spread-eagled, the waist-high glass the only barrier holding her back. Fear had gripped him and he'd run across the terrace and grabbed her forcefully by the arm, pulling her on to the floor.

'I just wanted to see what it would feel like,' was all Elise had calmly said.

Nathaniel had countless nightmares after that – dreams of Buddy falling from Elise's belly, like oil in a lava lamp. He was well aware their problems had started way before anything had happened to Ida, and yet it was all so obvious when he thought about it.

All the times she'd stood on the edge of that terrace and now he was beginning to wish he'd taken the opportunity to push her over the edge. After all, he knew the simplest way to murder someone was to make it look like suicide.

CHAPTER SEVENTEEN

You think you're different to all those participants invited to play my game, don't you? Protecting yourself from tragedies by thinking the old adage: that it won't ever happen to me. I even hear people say it when they win the lottery. Why do you think you're exempt from change, that you have complete control over your lives? You're so contradictory! You moan that you have to put up with whatever you're dealt with, when it's obvious the way life is to be lived is a choice. And then you complain when things change for you. Madness! You've mistakenly thought all these tragedies happen to other people. Do you think a bomber cares who you are when he blows up a bus – how many children you have, how successful you are, how old you are, what you are yet to achieve, who will be devastated by your death, how many people rely on you? No, because they don't care. In fact, the more you have to lose, the better.

Embrace the unexpected – it's always there, you just can't see it. Something or someone is always watching you: the mugger, the killer, the stalker, the friend . . . ready to step in and change your life at any moment. It could be you; it can always be you.

There are a lot of people who have studied my case who have been reported to say I have made mistakes and that's how the authorities became suspicious about the deaths. None of this is true. When there appears to be an inordinate amount of suicides, similar to one another and situated in one area of the country, it's bound to raise suspicion. I wanted *people to wonder if there was someone else involved. Otherwise, what's the point of it all?*

There's no suicide note, that's the first clue. Most people leave letters to their loved ones before they take their own lives. Instead, mine leave an obituary that I have asked them to write during the time I was building a relationship with them. You might ask yourself why anyone would do this, but if you tell someone it's therapeutic, that it helps them view and make changes to their lives in an objective manner, they'll do it. I am new, refreshing; they want to be my friend, to please me. The most obvious evidence of all, which was probably never public knowledge, is that a pathologist would be able to see the direction of the bullet, the way the gun fell from their hand and see, quite clearly, they didn't pull the trigger themselves. This wasn't noticed until much later; a change in attitudes and an advance in science, I suppose. None of this is important.

Magda, one of the first survivors of my game, understood me, and I had a feeling when I went to her home that she would work it out. And, at that time, I wanted someone to. No one had come even close and I was beginning to lose interest. I began searching for a different type of participant. I wanted someone who was going to volunteer, be fully present and choose to live by winning the game.

There is nothing but a splintered silence when the gun goes off, as though you've blasted through some palpable atmosphere. No feeling of Death's presence, as I'd been hoping and expecting. On one occasion, I saw a dark shadow cross over someone's face; that was strange, and I couldn't explain it. They wept, most of them, disappointing me further, as I realised they weren't who they'd portrayed themselves to be.

Magda didn't cry; she didn't even flinch and showed no signs of fear. Instead, she looked me straight in the eyes as she pulled the trigger. There was a slight look of surprise on her face when she became aware that the gun was empty. I think she suspected that, but couldn't be absolutely sure until she'd pulled the trigger.

Magda is the only one I revealed my identity to, but she won't ever tell anyone who I am because she confided a secret that she would not want anyone to know. A year before I met her, she killed her brother and made it look like an accident.

We exchange letters on a regular basis. She is eternally grateful for being able to confess such a burden, and my response to it is something she will never forget. Her guilt no longer carries the heavy weight it once did, and as far as I'm aware, she now lives life as she was supposed to. Some people deserve to die, and that's the truth of it.

CHAPTER EIGHTEEN
THEN

DC Alex Chilvers was listening to what Nathaniel was saying but she wasn't taking any notes, and he wasn't sure if family liaison officers were supposed to do that or were trained to retain information to keep everything informal.

'Do I need to speak to someone else about this?' he asked her.

'Not unless you want to. Nathaniel, we're following all leads, questioning everyone who's ever been involved with Ida, and we have an extensive, highly experienced team dealing with it all. I promise I'll look into what you told me.'

'What did I just tell you?' Nathaniel wanted to know exactly how much she'd listened to.

'When you visited Magda King's house, you found an item addressed to Ida. It's odd but not unusual for teenagers to do this sort of thing. As Mrs King told you, Ida occasionally had things delivered to their address because she was worried you'd disapprove of what she was spending her allowance on. It was just a piece of doll's furniture.'

'Have you seen those bloody doll's house projects?' Nathaniel was tired and unsure if he was overreacting, but everything looked out of place and magnified now that someone had attempted to murder his daughter. He had thought the project was strange when Ida and Miles had started it. They'd found a book in Ray's library – *Nutshell Studies of Unexplained Death* or some such nonsense. It was filled with models of real-life crime scenes, made using small dolls and furniture – not dissimilar to the one they'd found in Ida's bedroom the day she'd gone missing. That's how it had all started. When they'd seen this book, the children had wanted to build one of their own and Ray had indulged them by putting a doll's house in the summer house at the bottom of the garden. Nathaniel hadn't liked it – there was something about the whole idea that had given him the creeps – but Elise had laughed and told him he was being ridiculous. They'd ended up having a furious row about it and Nathaniel had been left feeling like he was overreacting.

'Nathaniel, if Ida was aware of your disapproval, it might explain why she was having things delivered to her best friend's house.'

'If that was the case, why didn't she just have them posted to Ray's? There's something off about it. You will look into it and not just take Magda's word? She was hiding something, I could tell.'

'Of course.' DC Chilvers stood up. 'Nathaniel, why don't you give Buddy to me and go and get some sleep. I can look after him for a while.'

'No.' Nathaniel pulled a sleeping Buddy closer to him. 'Thank you, but I need to keep busy. Sonny should be back with Miles soon.' Nathaniel looked at his watch; they should have returned by now. Ray had a flight booked to Norway, something he couldn't rearrange, and Sonny had offered to drive him to the airport. Miles had wanted to go with his uncle and grandfather, not wanting to stay in the large old house knowing Ida wasn't there. Nathaniel couldn't blame him, he already couldn't stand it. It seemed macabre, sinister to him, that they were staying in the house where Ida was brutally attacked, but Elise had insisted they go back there because for some bizarre reason, she felt safer at Ray's. She had been hysterical there, though – the news of Alistair confessing and then the police releasing him too much for her to take in. She'd had a desperate need to keep Miles with her, suffocating and frightening the boy with her devastation. Nathaniel had no choice but to call their GP, who had prescribed Elise more sleeping tablets. When she'd awoken from her drug-induced sleep she'd been angry about Alistair's quick release and gone straight back to the hospital to be with Ida.

Alistair had withdrawn his confession after telling the police, in great detail, he had hit Ida with a rolling pin he'd found in the kitchen and then washed afterwards. This long-winded account didn't match the forensic evidence, which showed that she had been attacked with some type of heavy sharp object. The blood spatter on him had come from a fight Alistair had been involved in with another boy earlier that day, when he'd punched him in the face. The blood didn't belong to Ida.

Eventually, Alistair had broken down and confessed he'd wanted to punish himself for upsetting Ida, for arguing with her, because he loved her so much. Nathaniel hadn't been entirely convinced, but the police seemed to be quite sure about it; there was no forensic evidence linking him to the attack. They were back at the beginning, searching for a new suspect, leaving them feeling that crucial time had been lost.

Nathaniel didn't want to go to the hospital with Elise and keep vigil over Ida. As harsh as it sounded, he saw no point, and he didn't need a constant reminder of what had occurred. He wanted to accept what had happened, not convince himself there was any hope.

Now the house was too quiet, leaving room for Nathaniel to imagine sounds he didn't want to think about – the cracking of his daughter's skull, her body hitting the floor, Ida's traumatic moments there.

DC Chilvers followed Nathaniel into the kitchen and took over as he tried to make coffee one-handed, with Buddy sound asleep, his head resting heavily on his father's chest.

'The cold case team are reopening the suicide cases again. I'm not sure if anyone told you?'

'What's that got to do with my daughter?'

'Well, nothing at the moment, but you and your wife both lost family members in the same way. We need to find out why your daughter was attacked, what the motive might have been. Maybe there's a connection.'

'It's a pointless exercise.' Nathaniel walked past DC Chilvers and closed the double doors leading through to the orangery, blocking it all out.

'What makes you say that?'

'How can you prove who killed themselves and who didn't? I've given it a lot of thought and I know I couldn't do it. I couldn't shoot myself, no matter what. I think the people who are genuine victims of the Suicide Watcher must have been drugged or tied up.'

Nathaniel's mind drifted to a time that he'd forgotten about until recently – a time when his mother had been in a bad way.

The irony that the group meetings Nathaniel attended should be where he'd find another woman just like his mother wasn't lost on him. He'd clung to Elise, quite desperately, because she was alive and his mother was dead. As time moved on, though, Elise had become stuck within the walls of her past and the details of her mother's death – lost in a pool of self-pity he suspected hadn't been as prominent until she began attending this group, unless she'd hidden it quite well. She wanted to analyse it, work out the whys and wherefores. Every occurrence, everything she experienced, every little foible she noticed was to do with what had happened to her mother. This was a subject they disagreed on. It was difficult discussing or reasoning with any addict rationally, because their view of the world was like a camera lens smudged with Vaseline. Had Nathaniel found out about Elise's addiction and neuroses when they had just been friends, he would never have embarked on anything more serious, but he had fallen in love by that time.

'No one knows what anyone would do in that situation.' DC Chilvers's voice came back into focus. 'Murder is murder and needs to be proven one way or another. Someone else may have pulled the trigger, and if so, we need to find out who. Which cases were suicide and which were murder.'

'Have you interviewed James Caddy yet? Are you any closer to making an arrest?' Nathaniel's tiredness was making him agitated and impatient. Nothing seemed to be happening. After all the time-wasting with Alistair, Nathaniel had been sure everything would speed up, but other people were still being questioned, making him think the police weren't entirely sure of what they were doing.

'I know it's frustrating, but we tend not to make arrests until we've gathered plenty of evidence, especially with someone like James Caddy, who has a history of mental health problems. Once you nick someone, the clock starts ticking. And they invariably cock up after a murder – are seen somewhere they can't explain or dispose of items they shouldn't have.' DC Chilvers handed Nathaniel a cup of coffee.

'So, you do have someone other than James Caddy in mind?'

'There are a couple of people we're interested in, yes.'

'Is Sonny one of them?'

'No more than anyone else. Why do you ask?'

'You don't like him, though.'

'Just because I don't like him doesn't make him a killer. He's a good barrister.'

'And?' Nathaniel hadn't ignored Elise's ramblings about Sonny when he'd put her to bed, but he was finding it hard to think that Sonny was guilty of anything. He and Nathaniel were so close, more like biological brothers than brothers-in-law – they had hit it off pretty much as soon as they'd met, and at the pub one evening Sonny had told him about the incident at work when he'd been accused of assaulting his young client. Nathaniel had been slightly perturbed when Sonny had begun the story, but his telling of it was so plausible, Nathaniel had been convinced he was telling the truth. Nathaniel had reported on such cases many times during his career.

'And nothing. Like most coppers, I struggle with the morals of someone who can defend a client they know is guilty.' DC Chilvers filled a cup for herself. 'There's no evidence pointing towards your brother-in-law, and he has an alibi.'

Nathaniel gave some thought as to whether he felt something beyond what Elise had told him.

'I guess we should be suspicious of everyone around us. It's usually someone you know, right?'

'It is, usually, but it's not always the case. We're a little concerned about some of your father-in-law's patients. The situation with the children sometimes being in the house while his patients were in therapy there changes this type of case.'

'In what way?'

'Well, it gives us a broader outlook of what might have happened that day. That said, we try not to focus on what might seem obvious; we have time to explore every avenue. It's not like it used to be, years ago, when corners were cut just to get a conviction because of public pressure. You know that, being a journalist.'

'Quite. The problem with that, from my point of view, is if it does turn out to be one of Ray's clients, a good barrister will advise them to go for diminished responsibility.'

Nathaniel left the detective to her coffee and went upstairs to settle Buddy into bed. He'd been sleeping in a room with Buddy and Miles, wanting to be near his children, since Elise was staying at the hospital.

When he went back into the kitchen, DC Chilvers was still in there staring out of the window.

'Everything all right?' he asked her.

'Yes. When Sonny told Ray who he was, he had the relevant tests done to verify it, didn't he?'

'Not that I'm aware. As far as I know, Ray knew who he was. It was he who set up the surrogacy deal, although Christ knows why. From what I can gather, Ingrid was a headcase. Elise thinks it was having Sonny that escalated her mental health issues . . .'

Something dawned on Nathaniel that he should have realised a long time ago if he hadn't been so wrapped up in his own life. Elise was, of course, her mother's daughter. All their children had suffered because of her mental instability, and it was only getting worse. Her rejection of Buddy was increasing rapidly.

He forced himself to refocus on what they'd been talking about. 'Sonny looks like Ray, don't you think?'

'You've completely lost me . . . Surrogacy?' DC Chilvers said. 'Your wife told one of our officers that Sonny was adopted.'

'I guess it's easier than telling people about the surrogacy. Sonny is biologically Ray's and Ingrid's, it's just that they had him for a couple who couldn't have any children. They were clients of Ray's, I think.'

'So what you're telling me is that your wife's parents sold a baby to another couple?'

Nathaniel frowned. 'Well, it's not as crude as that, but yes, I guess so.'

DC Chilvers nodded, as if she was matching up other facts in her head. 'We'll need to speak to your father-in-law about this, and Sonny of course.'

'Hey, listen, Sonny is a good person. He's done a lot for our family.'

'I've learnt from most cases that the best thing to do is not trust anyone.'

'You probably shouldn't tell me that.'

'If it were my daughter, I'd be looking at everyone.'

'Even your own family?'

'Especially my family,' DC Chilvers said, just as the telephone pierced the atmosphere, startling them both.

The last person Nathaniel was expecting to hear on the other end was Ray.

'What's happened? Your flight cancelled?'

'No. I need to tell you something before I get on the plane.'

'You're making me nervous now, Ray. What's going on? Are Sonny and Miles there?'

'Stop panicking!' Ray sounded sharp and exasperated. 'Sonny and Miles are on their way back to you now.'

'So, what's the problem?' Nathaniel was trying to appear calm but was waiting for Ray to confess something about Ida.

'I need you to talk to Elise before the press get hold of the story. Because they will, if they haven't found out already.'

'Go on.' Nathaniel was losing patience.

'I'm on my way to see Ingrid, Elise's mother. She's alive and living in Norway. I'm on my way to see her.'

Nathaniel frowned. 'Elise's mother is still alive, and you knew about it?'

'She's one of the survivors of the Suicide Watcher.'

CHAPTER NINETEEN
THEN

Staying at home was stifling Nathaniel, especially with the recent revelations – Ray had left him with news and he had no idea how he was going to tell Elise, and Nathaniel was angry at his father-in-law for being such a coward. Always the coward, always running away.

The details of the attempted murder of his daughter were leading to all sorts of secrets that had been kept quiet over the years, and he couldn't think clearly. The press was hounding them constantly about Ida's attack, speculating and making ridiculous assumptions, so after visiting Ida in the afternoon, he arranged for his father to take the children out for dinner and slipped out through the back gate and across the park to attend his weekly group, something he needed now more than ever. After his conversation with DC Chilvers, he hadn't been able to stop thinking about his mother and her early demise.

One of the teachers at his primary school had asked him once if everything was okay at home; she'd clearly noticed something wasn't right.

'My mother is euphoric,' Nathaniel had said. 'Euphoric.' He'd liked the word and the way it sounded in his throat. It was a good word, a strong word, but Nathaniel had no idea what it meant then, and in the wrong context it wasn't so positive. The teacher had frowned at him, when he had expected her to laugh or smile.

'Mother is always saying she's euphoric,' Nathaniel said, worrying he'd upset the teacher. *Anyone asks, tell them I'm euphoric*, his mother would say.

But, of course, she wasn't. The irony and sarcasm were lost on them as children. Nathaniel caught her once, when he and his brother were supposed to be in bed. He had heard a deep, sporadic humming; on and on it went. Eventually, even though they were always forbidden to get out of bed unless they were ill, he'd got up to investigate. Their dad wasn't around, and his brother was fast asleep, so Nathaniel had taken it upon himself to check that their mother was all right. He'd found her in the kitchen, crying her eyes out over a mug of tea, gripping it with both hands as if her life depended on it, which of course, to her, it did. It was so strange for Nathaniel to see her like that, her normally beautiful, smiling face, crumpled in such agony.

'Help me,' she said. 'Someone please help me.'

Nathaniel had run to the telephone in the hall and dialled the emergency services, just as he'd been taught to do if there was anything wrong.

'They want to know what kind of emergency it is,' Nathaniel called to his mother from the hall, placing the receiver briefly on the telephone table. She slowly joined him in the hall, told the person on the switchboard it was all a misunderstanding, and placed the phone back on the hook.

Quietly, without saying a word, she made Nathaniel a hot drink, took him back to bed, climbed in behind him and went to sleep. He didn't question her; he was just glad she'd stopped making that awful noise.

In the morning he thought she was dead. He couldn't move her heavy arm from around his small body, she was holding him so tightly. And because she'd been crying the night before, in what Nathaniel had thought was pain, he decided she'd died from whatever it was that had been ailing her. Of course, she hadn't. He'd found out afterwards when he'd called his father and asked him to come round, she'd taken some sleeping tablets and they hadn't worn off.

After Alistair had been released, there had been a fraught and difficult conversation with Magda. She was passionate in her belief that her son had been pushed into confessing something he hadn't done. By the end of their lengthy talk Nathaniel didn't know what to believe, but the two of them had agreed to move forward the best way they could. Even after he had spoken to DC Chilvers and been convinced of Alistair's innocence, Nathaniel couldn't get past how self-indulgent the boy had been, and how seriously his little charade could have jeopardised the investigation. It made him question Alistair's so-called love for Ida. But Nathaniel would never admit any unfavourable thoughts he had about Alistair to Magda. There was a certain amount of manipulation in Nathaniel's amicable attitude – he was willing to be nice to anyone so he could get to the truth. Magda had conveniently avoided the allegation that Ida had made against Alistair.

The group in the room fell silent when Nathaniel walked into the hall; people he'd thought had become quite friendly with him looked at the floor or began rummaging through their bags. He searched around for his old friend Ted, but he couldn't see him. Magda walked over to him and quietly welcomed him into the room.

'Just carry on as normal.' She squeezed his arm.

'I'm just trying to work out why my daughter seems to have been hiding so much from us,' Nathaniel said, staring directly at Magda.

There was a heaviness to his last words as he looked at his old friend. He knew Magda so well, but he had an overwhelming gut feeling she was covering something up.

'I don't know, Nathaniel.' Magda held her hands up, as if surrendering something.

'Don't worry about it.' Nathaniel didn't want to draw attention to their altercation, making it appear important. 'It was nothing, and I overreacted. I'm just not sure what to do with myself. What am I supposed to be doing?'

'Anything you feel like,' Magda said, her face softening. 'This lot will be okay, they just don't know what to say to you.'

Nathaniel sat down in his usual place and wondered whether to say anything, but the awkwardness was lifted when the lady next to him, a woman called Sue, reached across and said how sorry she was to hear about his daughter. The words he'd heard several times over the last couple of days but had never thought would be uttered to him.

'Thank you . . .' Nathaniel looked up to see the rest of the group engaging with him.

It was the only place he felt comfortable in, and it had been for some time; he wished there was more than a weekly session. Everyone who attended had lost a wife, husband, mother, father, brother, sister or child. Some people had been going for years, but the odd one or two came for a few months here and there and then left again. It was a casual place to come and talk – not just about what had happened to their family members but anything they wanted to share. They would all sit in a big circle and discuss any news or revelations they'd had since the last group session. This was the very place Nathaniel had met Elise again.

There had been one huge similarity between Nathaniel and Elise, and that was that they'd both believed their mothers had died from suicide. Now he knew Ingrid was still alive and an alleged survivor of the Suicide Watcher, and Nathaniel wondered if they'd have seen each other again if Elise had known this years ago.

Nathaniel and Elise had been best friends at school, and then gradually they'd grown apart, bumping into each other at the group talks six years later. The group considered themselves the leftovers – the results of what happens when a family member decides to kill themselves. As far as they were aware, they were the only group whose family members were possible victims of the person who was known by the media as the Suicide Watcher. About ten years ago, someone had sent an anonymous letter to the police telling them about the game, but no one knew who it was. The letter had got into the hands of the tabloids, and from that they had coined the name 'the Suicide Watcher'. It had caused a flurry of people to call in saying they believed their loved ones had been coerced into playing the game, but no one could pinpoint any common denominators.

Allegedly there were a few survivors – would-be victims who some-how escaped the bullet – but as yet there were no confirmed victims, and as far as they knew none of the survivors themselves had ever attended these meetings. Not that they *would* know, Nathaniel thought; he had a theory that their survival depended on continued secrecy. He often pondered the members of the group, wondering if they knew more about the cases than they made out. He'd even considered one of them might actually be the Suicide Watcher.

There were too many descriptions of this enigma, and fabricated assumptions about the mystery. To Nathaniel's mind, that meant the Suicide Watcher or any potential survivors were ever further from being identified. Whenever a potential story emerged regarding the Suicide Watcher, journalists appeared immediately, like cockroaches. Nathaniel wondered if this would cause people with information about the cases to retreat, possibly in fear for their own lives.

Aside from these sessions, the group would often be invited to attend various talks and therapy seminars. The media watched them, like they were insects trapped in dirty, ragged net curtains, in the hope there would be a confirmed victim of the Suicide Watcher. They were also desperate to see one of them fall, and, being a journalist, Nathaniel was only too aware of this fact. The families of the suicide cult, their story was long forgotten but so easily recalled by members of society who really knew nothing about it.

Other than these tragedies and their decision to expand themselves as a family, Elise and Nathaniel had nothing in common. Especially now the entire subject had been talked out with no sign of resolution to any details either of them had disagreed on, making things worse. When they first rekindled their friendship, they'd spent many evenings after the meetings talking animatedly over dinners and copious amounts of wine. Now they barely talked at all. Nathaniel had wanted her so badly when he'd met her again, but the feeling had faded away.

Magda brought Nathaniel back into the room by squeezing his shoulder, encouraging him to stay in the present, listen to others in the group. But he felt so different to everyone now. He'd stepped into another realm, surrounded by a darkness that no one wanted to be touched by, and he just couldn't concentrate. It was during this distraction that Nathaniel noticed someone familiar standing by the entrance, staring right at him. At first, he thought it was a journalist he'd seen before or someone he'd worked with, but as he continued to hold the man's gaze he realised it was an old friend who'd become a stranger after they'd had a fight. He'd changed somewhat, but it was unmistakeably him. Steven Bridges, that was his name. One evening, Nathaniel had caught him in Ida's bedroom and thrown him out. They'd never seen nor heard from him again.

CHAPTER TWENTY
THEN

The plane was a large cylindrical pod. Ray imagined that this was what sitting in an oil tanker must be like. He suddenly felt incredibly small and insignificant, and yet so much of his life he'd felt enormous, hugely important – such was his ego. All the events he'd experienced had been so exposed, giving him a sense of fame. Ray realised the cause of this inflation was because he'd stayed within the parameters of his own small world, and that had made him feel this false importance – had magnified it in such a way that he believed all eyes were permanently on him. But he soon came to realise that people forget the true facts of a story and so they can be altered in any way you like, especially when you're the one it happened to.

A heat, not unlike the feeling of nausea, began to rise in his throat and then sank back down, burning his gullet – the clicking of belts causing him to feel even worse. He preferred it when people were shoving bags in overhead compartments, when he still had the option to get off the plane.

Thinking of disembarking wasn't helping Ray's situation. Techniques he advised his patients to use seemed ridiculous now that he was immersed in his own panic. He recalled a few long-term clients' expressions of despair and began to fully understand why they felt that way.

Instead, he resorted to what he always told everyone not to do when facing their fears – have a drink. Ray beckoned over a steward and ordered a large brandy, only to be told he would have to wait until after the seatbelt light had been extinguished. The attendant offered him some assistance, but he waved him away impatiently, the panic inside making him feel isolated from everyone. He began to look around at the people he might, quite possibly, die with. He didn't even know them, and why would he? But it seemed so bizarre to face death amongst strangers, although he guessed so many people did. There was some comfort with this thought, though; dying with loved ones seemed so much worse. He'd never thought about it until now – hadn't ever had cause to, because it was the first time he'd made it on to a plane since 1986.

He calmed himself with a thought he dwelled upon regularly – his age. Pushing himself into the back of his seat, it dawned on him that if there weren't a purpose to his travels, he wouldn't be remotely concerned about dying. He thought about not seeing Ingrid again before his life ended, and then thought about how everyone had thought she was dead for all these years. He'd had no choice; her existence had to be kept a secret, it was vital to her survival. Regardless of his safety on this journey, there was no guarantee he would see her again. He had received what he suspected might be a suicide note from her shortly before Ida was attacked. He'd saved Ingrid once before, all those years ago, and he had been naive to think she wouldn't attempt it again. He'd made everyone believe she'd committed suicide – it had been better for Elise that way. But the media would be churning up any dirt they could possibly find about their family, and it was inevitable that Elise would discover the truth soon enough. He couldn't face it, especially with everything that had happened. He'd failed Elise once again, and in the process had been unable to protect Ida. He was hoping Nathaniel would talk to

Elise – as usual, Ray was shunning his responsibilities. There it was: he was a coward. The guilt tipped in his stomach as the plane ascended.

While the flight was mercifully short, the anticipation of leaving the airport had been quite a trauma, as the plane had been delayed, prolonging his agony further. He didn't know why he reflected on this now. Probably euphoria. There was a slight elation that he'd managed to board the plane and endure the journey without too much stress – a small achievement to most, but a triumph for him nonetheless.

When the exit door opened, he felt like a peanut being released from a can; the freezing cold air, not unpleasant, smothered his face and hands, penetrating his clothes.

It took him a little while to descend the steps; he had been cooped up in a self-induced ball of stress for almost two hours and, being of an age, he didn't so easily straighten out like he used to. Reaching the tarmac, Ray stood for a few moments absorbing the winter sun, relishing his freedom, the ground beneath his feet, as passengers trundled past. Right now, they were dishevelled, pale, and crumpled from their travels; some of them exhausted, they looked worn and very much second-hand. In a week's time, most of these people would look quite astonishingly different. Regardless of the Norwegian temperatures, it was still a holiday. He had always wondered why no one could maintain this persona throughout life. His mantra to clients had always been to treat life like a holiday. Now he wondered if he'd ever followed that theory himself.

Swapping his bag to the opposite hand, he made his way into the airport. The large throng of people he spied through the glass doors worried him slightly, and he could feel his pulse begin to race as he wondered how he would spot Ingrid through the crowds – if she was even there. He had written and told her he was coming, and emailed his flight details. But Ray had followed this ritual many times before, contacting her in some way to let her know when he'd be there, and then he would fail to arrive. He had never asked if she had waited for him each time, so he was guessing it was too much to ask that she should be there now.

Two hours later, the clinically clean airport was practically empty, apart from a few people reading or sleeping on the many seats scattered around. Ingrid hadn't arrived to collect him, so he decided it was time to search for a taxi. The wait had enabled him to settle into his surroundings. Ray didn't usually thrive in unfamiliar territory; his claustrophobia would never allow it.

He was sitting outside in the frosty night air, a quiet, low hum of noise surrounding him as he waited for the train he had been told stopped in a small town outside Oslo, where he could get a taxi to his destination.

Ray felt a calm relief at being in different surroundings, an unfamiliar terrain, that he hadn't been expecting; the unusual buildings, white snow and frost rested his eyes and calmed his nerves. But for the first time since he had parted from his wife all those many years ago, he felt isolated, lonely and quite insignificant, realising they'd had more years apart than they had spent together, though not many days had passed on which they hadn't had some sort of contact. He had loved her unconditionally from afar – that's just the way it was, the way it had to be.

Ray had simply lied to all their family and friends, told them Ingrid had committed suicide and her body was being sent to Norway for the funeral. He organised a memorial in England, to make it look real, and then the story had expanded as if it were a snowball Ray and Ingrid had rolled down a hill. Ingrid had tried to take her own life before, so those who knew her had thought it was inevitable. No one asked any questions, just took the good word of a doctor. As time went on, a few people had mentioned the Suicide Watcher and Ray had just let them believe what they wanted to.

Ray had never asked Ingrid what had happened that day – she had insisted they not talk about it. She couldn't talk about it.

There were times over the years when she had come to England and they would spend a few days together. The fact that people thought she was deceased seemed, in a very warped way, to work for Ray and Ingrid. There was nothing in her grasp she could hurt.

After Ingrid left, Ray had sent Elise to live with his brother Mac and sister-in-law Estelle. When he finally returned from Norway, he continued with his life for a few months alone, and then he insisted Elise came to live with him. His brother had been devastated, and had accused him of stealing their daughter, of using them for another one of his social experiments, and they hadn't spoken since.

The irony was, Ray could see the Ingrid in Elise. His daughter should never have had children – she lacked the genetic maternal instinct to care, and her children had become her competition. That she had gone on to work in midwifery had been quite disturbing to say the least, but apart from her dependency on drugs, she was good at her job.

After the short train journey, Ray managed to get a cab from the station. When the taxi stopped at the bottom of a track on a very precarious corner, Ray presumed the driver was taking a breath, ready to turn up the steep, narrow ascent. It wasn't until he stared at him through the mirror that Ray realised he wanted him to get out. So he paid the fare and staggered up the hill with his bag, wishing he had worn a thicker coat.

Halfway up, Ray paused for a rest, and turned to look at the spectacular view. He noticed the taxi was still at the bottom of the track, and the driver, phone clamped to his ear, was staring up at him. Then he pulled away, narrowly missing another driver who angrily beeped his horn; muffled shouting ensued.

Ingrid was sitting in the glass extension to the side of the property. Ray saw her feet and legs before anything else – still slender, just as he remembered them. They were resting on the chair opposite, next to the wood burner, where he was soon seated.

It was as though all the years apart had never happened. They didn't even talk about his journey; there was no need for either of them to fill the silence. Just comfortable, as it always had been, always was between them. They picked up where they had left their last conversation on the phone; there was never any need to explain themselves to one another, they had always connected wherever they were in the world.

After Ray unpacked his case, showered and changed into some clothes Ingrid had warmed on the radiators, he joined her for some food. She had been expecting him after all; the table was laid out with cheese, fruit, fresh bread and wine and a pot full of stew – simple foods. Ingrid handed him a plate, which he took and placed back on the table. Ray couldn't eat, he just wanted to sit and absorb his surroundings, relax in his temporary home, observe the face he'd missed but never forgotten for so many years. Ingrid was still beautiful, even more so now she'd aged; her hair was shoulder-length, lighter in colour – silver, almost – making her eyes shine a deeper blue. Everything about her was softer, a shade lighter; she'd always worn hard colours, deep shades that made her look pale, but now she could be mistaken for a different person. A surge of energy poured into Ray's chest as he reached across to touch her cheek. Ingrid would always be his quixotic paramour; they had always belonged to each other. Ray had lived, fulfilled, his whole life just to share these small pockets of time with her, a collection of moments in comparison to the life he'd lived alone, but that made it even more worth it. Desiring this time, anticipating it, had kept him alive; without it, Ray believed he'd have died many years before.

'How is Elise?' Ingrid said, placing the wine glass firmly on the tablecloth, pressing her fingertips on the stem.

It was a few moments before Ray spoke, linking the words in his head, assessing the best way to say them, and Ingrid spoke first.

'You don't have to pain yourself. I know what's happened to Ida. I'm just disappointed you didn't tell me.'

'I couldn't find any point in telling you until now. I couldn't bring myself to tell you, I suppose. How did you know?'

'I read it in the papers, it's all over the news. My granddaughter.'

Ray poured them both some more wine.

'Did you tell Elise you were coming here?'

'I told her I was coming to Norway but I don't know if she was listening. She didn't say much about it.'

'I'm not surprised. If you've told her about all the other times you've been planning to visit and never made it, I shouldn't think she took much notice.' Ingrid smiled, a look he'd not seen for so many years. 'She doesn't know about me, does she? You haven't told her?'

'No. I've tried so many times, but we always end up talking about something else.' Ray tore off some bread but took little interest in it, recalling all the lies he'd told Elise over the years; wondering how many things she knew weren't true.

'I suppose all this time has passed. A few more months isn't going to make much difference.'

'You could come back with me. Give her time to get used to the idea and then you could meet her?'

'I don't want to do that.'

'Ingrid, Elise needs you. I think having you in her life could be the answer to a lot of her problems. I'm no help to her.'

'She has lived without me all these years and she will continue to do so. What makes you so sure she would want to see me again anyway?'

'I think you could have a good relationship now.'

'Let me sleep on it. I have commitments here . . . things I need to sort out. I can't just leave,' Ingrid snapped. She was getting tetchy; she had never liked being advised what to do. 'You know how difficult it is for me to leave, my reasons for coming here in the first place. That hasn't changed.'

'It won't be long before the press discover you're still alive, if they haven't already – that there is no record of your death. Don't let Elise face that alone.'

'I said I'd think about it and I will. There is little point getting involved in her life if we have to part again.'

'Fine.'

Ingrid's face softened. 'No regrets.' She reached across the table and touched Ray's hand, and he was surprised at the sudden show of affection.

'No regrets, my darling.'

CHAPTER TWENTY-ONE
THEN

Having seen Steven at the group, Nathaniel had arranged to meet him the following day but had decided not to tell anyone. He wanted to work some things out for himself first – he felt so ostracised from the investigation, so cut off from knowing the facts of what had happened to Ida that he needed some space to think. He couldn't help feeling like the obvious answers were right in front of him, loosely laid out within his day-to-day life, but he couldn't see them.

Sitting opposite Steven in a café, Nathaniel realised why he hadn't recognised him immediately – his left eye was completely blacked out, no white left, as if his pupil had burst and leaked. He'd also grown a beard, which was auburn against his darker hair. Nathaniel could see he was nervous; his forehead glistened, and he continually raked his fingers through his hair. The movement began to irritate him. Someone else he knew did that, but he couldn't recall who.

'So, why were you at the support group?'

'I told you, I'm just doing a bit of research, for a book I'm writing. I've been discharged from the army.' Steven pointed to his injured eye. 'And I'm looking for material.'

Nodding, Nathaniel observed him again as Steven told him what he was writing about. He was trying to be casual, leaning back in his chair then pushing himself forward, linking his fingers together and resting them on the table – a sign, Nathaniel thought, that he was desperate for Nathaniel to be okay with him.

'Why didn't you answer my message?' Nathaniel had tried to contact him, and many others, when Ida was attacked – just a long shot that someone might know something. He hadn't realised until he recognised him that he had been one of the few who hadn't answered.

'I've been off the radar for a bit, to be honest . . . I quite literally came back the day before I bumped into you.'

'Oh?'

'I went away for a few months; a digital detox, shall we say.' Steven laughed but Nathaniel didn't laugh with him; none of this was funny.

'You know Ida has been attacked . . . you know what happened?'

'Yeah, sure, of course I do. I'm really sorry . . . it's awful, I don't really know what to say, to be honest . . . To be honest, mate, I was worried about getting in touch after what happened the last time I saw you . . . we didn't exactly part on good terms.'

To be honest, to be honest, to be honest, Steven tagged these words on to every sentence and Nathaniel began to analyse what they meant. When was he not being honest? He thought about asking him but decided against it. He could see Steven was uncomfortable, which was nothing new; he was used to people not knowing what to say, cutting themselves off. What few friends they did have had drifted away gradually over the last few years, unable to cope with the perpetual trauma of their lives, the complex layering of sad events, wanting it to end, not knowing how to help. It had started when Elise had suffered a miscarriage quite late on in her pregnancy, and she had stopped being popular when she developed her addiction. She pretty much became incapable of maintaining relationships. Nathaniel's friends became hers too; it was the only way she could make friends, as long as he tagged along.

Nathaniel seemed to attract loners, and one of them was sitting in front of him now, trying to justify why he hadn't been in contact with them, but Nathaniel wasn't buying it. As far as Steven was concerned, he hadn't done anything wrong that night. So if that was true, why was he making excuses now?

The whole meeting was awkward, stilted, none of the easy chat they'd once shared when Steven used to come over. Maybe it was because it was always at their apartment and large amounts of alcohol would be consumed in a short space of time; a flurry of excitement that they had a guest to stay, a new face, someone who wanted to share their company.

'That night . . . in Ida's bedroom . . . you know it didn't mean anything. I would never have hurt her.'

'What were you doing in there?'

'I was watching her sleep, that's all.'

'Bit weird, isn't it?' Nathaniel remembered grabbing Steven by the back of his T-shirt and dragging him from the apartment. They'd wrestled one another at the bottom of the stairs until Nathaniel had managed to throw him out of the front door. His rucksack and phone had followed from the top-floor window.

'Look, I don't want to argue. I was pissed and stumbled into her room by accident.' Steven raked his hand through his hair again.

'War wound?' Nathaniel said, looking directly at Steven's damaged eye. 'Can you see out of it?'

'Yes. And no, I can't see out of it.' Steven looked down, not wanting to talk about his eye. 'That's why I was discharged from the army.'

Nathaniel tightened his fingers around his cup of coffee. He wanted to ask Steven about Ida – if he knew anything. Was he in the country when she'd been attacked? How much did he know about it? Did he have anything to do with it? But he knew accusatory questions would make Steven walk out, and he needed to think carefully about what he was going to say next. The thought of accusing him of anything landed with a heavy thud in his mind as he realised how ridiculous it all was. The man had been in the army, always being posted all over the place.

Nathaniel knew Steven hadn't meant any harm that night; it was a ridiculous idea. He'd seen enough paedophiles in his job to know when he was talking to one.

Nathaniel opted for telling the truth. 'Do you know, I had this crazy notion . . . Well, after what happened that night – I thought you had . . .'

'Something to do with the attack on Ida?' Steven finished Nathaniel's sentence and it sounded like Steven was asking a question he wanted him to answer.

'We hadn't seen you, hadn't heard from you, for ages . . . and then you appear at the support group.'

'I was in the army, mate. You know I was posted away a lot.'

'I know, but when something happens to your child, you look at everyone differently, even the people closest to you. Especially if there's history.'

'That's understandable. I bet you've looked at every single person who has ever said hello to you, right?'

They ordered more coffee, the atmosphere easier now they'd addressed Nathaniel's worries, and Steven explained that he was just back in town, and talked about where he'd been, the countries he'd travelled to, what led to him accepting a long-term posting abroad, changing his direction in life. But there was still something peculiar about Steven's whole demeanour. Nathaniel nodded at everything he said and agreed to catch up with him again soon, but just as Nathaniel stood up to leave, Steven grabbed his arm, forcing him back.

'I see your father-in-law has a new lodger?' Steven's question felt like a threat, a spontaneous punch in the face after their previously amiable conversation.

Nathaniel sat back down in his chair, slightly alarmed. 'I didn't know you knew Ray.'

'Come on, everyone knows Ray.'

The two men stared at one another for a few seconds, the air having become quite contentious once more.

'How did you know he has a lodger?' Nathaniel said, but then quickly realised who he was talking about. 'Oh, you mean Sonny. He's lived there for years.'

'Yeah, I know Sonny John Travers. He was my barrister. Went out of his way to lose my case.' Without any warning, Steven stood up, banging his chair against the wall behind. 'Perhaps you should look a little closer to home, you fucking wanker, instead of accusing innocent people. The coffee's on me.' Then he slammed a note on to the table and walked out.

CHAPTER TWENTY-TWO

Once upon a time there was a house, a particularly banal-looking 1970s building, one of many clustered on an estate; which, during the mid-1980s, was becoming quite an unpopular structure.

Within the rounded curve of the dead-end road I would sit and watch this one particular house, which stood out from the rest. Even though they resembled a pack of cards fanned out across a table, this one was different. I was drawn to it because of Anna, the woman who lived within. She was a mesmerising manifestation; a rarity amidst the usual. She was to be my next participant. Unconsciously calling me to join her, I could hear her whispers through the walls.

The ink-black hair, which shone like the deepest fathoms of the ocean, hung down on either side of her face. She had soft, small features with gently rounded cheekbones, all accentuating her green eyes, which I had the pleasure of discovering were flecked with gold.

The most memorable of my participants, she was a symmetrical being to me and I was fascinated with her, by her, for her.

The day I entered the house, she'd been crying; her eyes were red and there were smudges of black make-up beneath. It did not detract from her beauty, and the pull I felt towards her was even greater.

Once we had spoken, there was a quietness throughout my stay and it was as though she'd been expecting me, like we were old souls, familiar to one another. There had been an initial look of surprise when she first saw me and then she silently, submissively allowed me to take her towards her next path.

Let me explain something to you. When you hold someone at gunpoint and tell them they are, without doubt, going to die – shoot yourself or be shot – they become hysterical. They are unable to see the beautiful transitional journey upon which they are about to embark, a gift from me to them. And they are most definitely going to die, but I never actually said when, did I?

But Anna was different, this masterpiece before me, and I spent many years in her company before she died, watching the transition of life within her being.

The inevitable was about to occur, although neither of us knew when, and she embraced it, without panic or fear or expectation. It was a moment filled with relief, a palpable peace that I have never known before or since. From that moment, I fell in love with her. Prominently, in a lascivious way, you understand. I longed, thereafter, to watch her again through the window. The only time I've ever seen someone's true emotions are through the glass when they're pondering, alone and unwatched. Within her face was a magical beauty that I will probably never encounter again.

It wasn't the wrong time for her to go – it was ultimately her decision and I'm not sorry – but the strong essence of her stayed with me for a long time after. It's still with me now, but it's taken on other forms. There is a familiarity with any love affair as it matures over time. She is and always will be my quixotic paramour; I understand she now belongs to another.

CHAPTER TWENTY-THREE
THEN

Elise wasn't with Ida when she died. A new day was just breaking, and Elise had wandered down to the hospital café for a hot drink to keep herself awake. She'd been distracted by the piles of morning newspapers that had just been delivered – the top one's headline read: SURVIVING VICTIM OF THE SUICIDE WATCHER REVEALED.

The man behind the shop counter had given Elise a copy when she'd asked if he could cut the wrapping tape holding the tabloids together. He recognised her – everyone did, and she'd barely paid for anything since the news had broken about Ida. She wished they'd treat her normally, rather than handing freebies to her that were tainted with her family tragedy.

The shop assistant didn't say anything when she took the copy, just smiled at her sympathetically.

When she sat down with the newspaper, she hadn't been expecting to see her mother's name printed in big black capital letters on page four. She returned to the front page, suddenly realising the large photo there was of her mother, exhaustion having clouded her sight.

Controversial psychiatrist Dr Ray Coe is being questioned about his possible involvement with the Suicide Watcher cases. In the late 1980s, Dr Coe led family and friends to believe his wife, Ingrid Coe, had committed suicide and was a possible victim of the infamous killer, but a source has revealed the seventy-nine-year-old is very much alive. The news comes as the police's cold case team reopens the unsolved murders, following a vicious attack on Dr Coe's grand-daughter at his home less than a week ago.

It is unknown how many Suicide Watcher victims there have been. Suspicion was first cast in 1988 when a man in his early thirties was found dead at his farm in the Oxford countryside. Left-handed and an experienced rifleman, John Tilney was found with a single bullet wound to the side of his head and gun residue on his right hand. He had a seven-year-old son, Benjamin, who disappeared the same night. Police officials believe he is also dead, but his body has never been found.

It is as yet unconfirmed where Mrs Ingrid Coe has been residing all these years and the police are eager to locate her . . .

Elise skipped paragraphs until she found the piece about Ingrid's so-called death. It was like reading, verbatim, what Ray had told her all those years ago. Elise returned to the front page and then back to the article inside. There was a small passport picture printed at the bottom, with Ingrid's head pushed towards the camera as if she were peering at an onlooker. Even though it was black and white, there was no mistaking the sharp blue eyes, identical to Elise's, and the blonde hair. She remembered the picture from when she was a child.

Picking her phone up from the table, Elise began to dial Ray's number but quickly changed her mind and hung up. Was Ingrid alive? If so, he must have known all along, and that's why he was in Norway now, because the story was going to leak. He was with her mother in Norway, Ingrid's home country, preparing her for what was to come.

The day she'd heard the gunshot coming from the bathroom blasted through her mind again, always so readily there whenever she thought of her mother. The time had read 16.43 on her Swatch, the timepiece Ray had bought her as a birthday present. She never wore it on her wrist, just carried it around with her, using the stopwatch to time everything. Ingrid had tried to take her own life before, had even fired a gun at the mirror in the bathroom, but she'd never gone through with it. That day, outside the bathroom, Elise had timed the minutes until her mother would emerge, but that day she never came out.

There was a feeling lurking within her now that maybe she'd known all along that Ingrid was still alive.

Elise folded the newspaper, collected her coffee and made her way to the lift, too fatigued and upset to walk up the stairs. She was completely unaware of the commotion that had occurred in the last hour while she'd been away from the ward, and all was still again by the time she wandered back in.

One of the consultants came out of the family room further down the corridor, a pained look on his face, and she knew straight away he was looking for her.

'Mrs Munroe.' He walked towards her, hands held out. 'I am so sorry.'

'What's going on?' The consultant had mistaken the tears falling down her face as a sign that someone had already spoken to her.

'There was nothing more we could do.'

Elise pushed past him and ran to Ida's room, where she was stopped by DC Chilvers.

'I'm sorry, Mrs Munroe. Your daughter has been taken for a post-mortem examination. We need to preserve as much evidence as possible.'

'But I haven't given my consent.'

DC Chilvers frowned. 'We don't need it. This is now a murder enquiry.'

CHAPTER TWENTY-FOUR
THEN

Ray sat in the airport lounge waiting for Sonny to collect him, as various people came and went amongst the orange chairs. Staff members enquired after his welfare, because he'd sat there overnight, but he assured them he was fine. He had slept in the airport seats many times, in those previous years when he'd bought a ticket and never boarded the plane. This time, it had nothing to do with being fearful of boarding; that particular phobia seemed to have been conquered.

The fear had been mild at first: elevators, crowded shops and public transport were all places he could manage, but as he'd grown older it had become more intense. Then, on a small jet to the Channel Islands with his parents when he was twelve, the turbulence had been terrifyingly extreme. He'd developed claustrophobia, and it had kept him company for so many years now that he'd petted and fed it like a dear old friend. A psychiatrist with a disorder – one of many, he told himself. He also believed that claustrophobia had saved his life once. Saying this out loud to himself one day, he realised the utter ridiculousness of it, although he still believed it was partly true. It had been 1982, 1983 maybe, he couldn't recall the exact year, but he could clearly remember staring through the enormous glass windows and watching the aeroplane he was supposed to have boarded turn and line itself up on the runway, regret beginning to pinch his skin as he realised he'd wasted yet another ticket. Another chance to spend time with one of the most important people in his life.

Ray had turned from the window and faced the multitude of empty orange chairs – not unlike now, the endless empty rows still giving the sensation of nuclear warfare having wiped out the entire population. Maybe it had been an exaggerated premonition that day, because as he began his deflated walk from the airport, his hand luggage weighing even heavier on his shoulder, one of the cylinders in the engine of the plane caught fire and it crashed back on to the runway. The sound it made when it hit the tarmac rattled the glass in the airport; the odd scream erupted from the few looking in that direction. And then there were a few moments of eerie silence before the whole situation turned into mass panic.

When the pathologists finally started the arduous task of doing the post-mortems, they found that it wasn't the crash that killed the passengers, it was the toxic fumes from the burning material on the seats within the plane – it had incapacitated many travellers and most of them died from inhalation. The whole tragedy was to change the design and safety of plane interiors forever.

That day had a monumental effect on the course of events his life would follow. If he'd boarded the plane he was supposed to get on, everything would have been very different. He often wondered what his parallel life looked like – if, of course, one existed.

The day after arriving in Norway, Ray had woken up to find a letter saying she'd read the papers and it was time for her to go. He'd waited for her, tried to contact her, even looked in places he vaguely knew of, but no one had seen or heard from her. Ray knew it was time to leave and be with the people who needed him, especially after he received the sad news from Sonny that Ida had passed away. As soon as the plane had landed in the UK, Ray had been so grief-stricken he was unable to call and tell anyone he was home, and instead had sought sanctuary in the airport.

Now he watched Sonny walking towards him across the terminal, until he was standing in front of him.

'Please tell me you haven't been sitting here all this time and you did actually go to Norway? Why didn't you call me? I would have picked you up.' Sonny looked concerned, and it reminded Ray of how roles had reversed so quickly in the time they'd known one another.

Ray now wanted someone else to give him the answers for a change. Ray was tired, and uncharacteristically weak.

'This isn't like you.' Sonny sat down next to Ray, the chair optically reducing in size as his tall frame descended. He was calm but imposing, something Ray thought had become more prominent a few months into his sobriety. 'Elise badly needs your support.'

'I stupidly thought if I didn't leave the airport, you'd come and tell me Ida had woken up and everything was okay.'

'I wish I did have news like that for you . . . but no, I'm sorry. The consultant said her head injury was too extensive for her to recover from.' Sonny leant forward, resting his arms on his knees. 'Ray, the thing is—'

'I've been giving some thought to the work I've done all these years – not the TV stuff, or any of that, but the clients who have come to me. Patients, I suppose.' Ray was talking at Sonny as if he weren't there.

'Ray, can we talk about this later?'

'I've realised that for forty-five minutes I engage with a stranger, listen to their deepest thoughts and emotions, and the truth of it is, I don't really care. Because dead on the three-quarters of an hour, I stop them, they pay me and leave.'

'It's a service, Ray. We all need to make a living. I'm a barrister, I get paid to defend criminals I know are guilty. Get over it.' Sonny stood up, clearly expecting Ray to follow.

'That's different.' Ray pulled his coat around himself and folded his arms, deep in thought, wanting to avoid whatever it was Sonny wanted to say.

'Ray, I really need to get you back to the house. The police want to talk to you.'

'I've seen a lot of clients who've lost children. I even counselled a couple whose child was never found, dead or alive. For years, one or the other came to see me. We would go over every possible scenario about what had happened to their son. Eventually, I began to have a lot of thoughts about why they couldn't move on, that they were wasting their entire lives pondering on what might have been and ultimately missing out on so much with their other children. Everything was halted . . . why would they do that when their son's life had presumably been cut short through no fault of his own?'

'I have no idea. I don't even know what you're talking about.' Sonny rubbed his forehead with the palm of his hand. 'We need to go.'

'I shouldn't have lied, Sonny. I've protected my patients over my family. I've been too confident in my abilities and assumed I was totally in control.'

'What are you talking about?'

'I put my family in danger.'

'You're being ridiculous, and I'm not going to indulge you in this self-absorbed crap. We need to get back to answer some questions. The police think you're in Norway with Ingrid. You can't just drop a bombshell like that and disappear. That is where you went? To see Ingrid?'

'What do they want to talk to me about?'

'I'm not sure, you'll need to speak to them about it.'

'How did Elise take the news that Ingrid is alive?'

'How do you think? She read about it on the front of a newspaper. You should have told her. It doesn't affect me like it does her. I had a different life somewhere else.' Sonny sat down again. 'Ray, your client, James Caddy, has been arrested.'

Ray looked down at his lap, clenched his jaw and linked his dry fingers together. He knew the moment he heard the news that Ida had been attacked; he had known there could only be one person who had murdered his granddaughter that day. Ray knew Ida would have talked to James when he was leaving his office, engaged him in a conversation. Ray and Ida had the same mind – Ida was a female version of himself and, as a teenager, he would have been curious too. She had always made him feel like he was reversing time, watching himself grow up; they shared so many interests.

Sonny stood up, ready to leave, and Ray followed him out of the airport.

'I've told them.' Sonny accelerated on to the main road out of the car park, bringing Ray back to the present.

'Told who what?'

'I've told the police about my past. It's best to be up front.'

'Yes, it is,' Ray replied quietly.

'The thing is, Ray . . . The thing is . . .' Sonny took a deep breath and abruptly swung the car into a layby.

'What are you doing?' Ray grabbed the door handle to steady himself.

Sonny laid his head back on the seat and exhaled.

'Spit it out, lad,' Ray snapped, fatigue and stress affecting his normally patient demeanour.

'There's something I haven't told you . . . another reason I was on your doorstep that night.'

Ray stared at Sonny, seeing a stranger amidst the all-too-familiar face.

'I'm not the surrogacy child. I'm not your son, and the police will match the DNA and find out we're not related.'

'Don't you think I know that, Sonny?' Ray hissed through gritted teeth. 'I know exactly who you are.'

CHAPTER TWENTY-FIVE

It was 1976 when I met Cheryl. If you saw her in the street or on the station platform you would assume that she was uneducated, shallow and unambitious. Whenever I saw Cheryl she always looked dishevelled, like her clothes were doing her a favour. Her shoulders slumped forward, her face expressionless, indifferent. It was strange how someone could just stand out amongst a mass of people.

It was raining heavily outside, and I ran into a carriage where I was surprised to find Cheryl reading a book. Dirty blonde hair hung limply around her face; food stained the front of her clothing.

Cheryl was a playwright, I discovered during our third conversation. Not a successful one, but a few pieces of her work had been staged. Like many women of her era, she was pulled down by children and a husband she didn't care for anymore.

Most of the time, Cheryl only travelled on the train during the school holidays, so she could get away from her children. She rarely got off at any of the stops, just rode as far as she could go and back again. She was crass, abrasive, and said whatever she was thinking with no care of offending anyone.

'I want my life to change but I keep putting it off.' Cheryl said this quite often, as if she were validating the excuse for herself.

'What changes would you make?'

'That's easy. I'd leave my family — just disappear one day and live a solitary life somewhere in the country.'

Cheryl made her choice and changed everything shortly after that. Beyond that harsh, rough exterior was a lot of fear, and she cried at the end – they usually do. We all leave the party eventually.

The funeral was interesting in the way that a lot of people attended but none of them seemed to have much to say about her – they were all of a similar ilk, with quite a lot of potential but no inclination to do anything about it. What was there to say about Cheryl? She drank tea, she smoked, tried to control a chaotic house and wrote plays on the train. That's all her friends and family knew about her. Even her husband didn't know who she truly was and couldn't remember the person she had been when he'd first met her.

It was her brother who helped her become posthumously famous through her work. I read an article about it in the newspaper some years later. Cheryl's husband had boxed up all her notebooks and given them to her family. Her brother discovered some very gritty stories she'd written about the estate where she lived and they were published. That would never have happened if I hadn't met her on the train. It is of no consequence to me where you are when you achieve greatness.

CHAPTER TWENTY-SIX
THEN

The children had set up trestle tables inside the old summer house situated at the bottom of Ray's garden, and Elise was shocked to see the changes that had been made in the room. It was another punch in the gut – the realisation of how little attention she'd paid Ida and Miles the last few months. Elise and Nathaniel had tried to recreate something similar on the garden terrace of their apartment, but nothing would ever match what Ray did for the children. It was their own fault; they were so wrapped up in their work, in themselves, taking for granted the fact that Ida was a teenager and could take care of herself – and Miles a lot of the time. She recalled Ida shouting at her the morning before she'd disappeared, and how even then Elise hadn't taken much notice of her. She'd put it down to a teenage strop, told her they'd have a nice dinner for her birthday and sent her off to school.

Elise peered at the carefully constructed scenes Ida and her brother Miles had painstakingly put together. Both her children spent more time here than they did at home with her and Nathaniel. She could understand the fascination; she loved the old Victorian villa with its expanse of private lawns. Ray was far more interesting than their boring old parents who worked all the time – and who, when they weren't doing that, didn't have time to listen or play because they were too busy doing grown-up things that they deemed far more important. Ray, being a semi-retired psychiatrist, was far more exciting to her children. He knew how to engage with them and hold their attention.

The children loved him; he told them things that other adults tried to hide. One example being the doll's house Elise was scrutinising now. It was based on a book Ray had told Ida and Miles about, but Elise couldn't remember the name now. Doll's houses and furniture, along with figures, were used to reconstruct crime scenes, a well-used technique for teaching students who were studying forensics. Ida and Miles were in awe of the book, so Ray had helped them build their own house and they'd spent the last few months carefully filling the rooms with tiny items, all leading to a murder scene. Elise didn't know whose murder or what scenario they were reconstructing – she hadn't taken the time to ask.

Elise wandered around the cold room, fascinated by the detail in the miniature rooms they'd created and how much work the children had put into them. She was about to leave the summer house when one of the rooms she'd walked past made her turn back for a closer examination. It looked like the orangery attached to Ray's. To imitate the glass and wood frame, Ida and Miles had fashioned it from cellophane and lollipop sticks. Inside, the room contained a small doll lying on the floor, her dark hair plaited against her head, just as Ida wore hers. The entire scene was weird and felt very different to the others, although Elise could recall only too well Miles shouting, 'You be the victim, Ida, and I'll be the one that finds you dead in the house! Please Ida, please!' He'd begged and begged, excited by their gruesome little game.

She stared at it for a few moments but decided she was being paranoid, brushed it off and pulled the door closed behind her.

Elise stood on the damp grass thinking about the times they'd laughed at the macabre project, seen it as a game, and now she couldn't help feeling as though it had encouraged the children to create some kind of reality. Elise shook the thought away as she saw Ray walking across the garden with a cup of tea.

'They've spent hours out here, working on this bloody project.'

'And a fortune.' Ray smiled. 'Ever since I showed Ida that book.'

Elise didn't say how odd she thought it all was, because if she said it out loud, that would somehow make it all real. Even though it *was* real, and Ida's body was now lying in a mortuary.

'It's freezing out here,' Ray said. 'Why don't we go and sit in the kitchen?'

'You can. I just want to be outside for a bit. I need some air.'

Ray turned away from her and Elise expected him to go back to the house, but he didn't. Instead, he walked up the steps to the summer house and pulled open the door.

'It's quite amusing, like a tragic set of plays suspended in time.' Ray peered into the rooms, reminding her of a scene from *Alice in Wonderland* where Alice looked through the windows of the house she was too large to fit in.

'Did you notice if Miles was awake?'

'He was awake when I got home – said he'd had a nightmare – but he was fast asleep when I checked on him just now.'

Elise was slightly rattled that Ray had heard her son and she hadn't – guilty that she'd relied on the zopiclone to knock her out.

'It's not unusual for Miles to have nightmares. It's to be expected, especially now.'

They stood looking at each other for a long moment, and then she said, 'Why are we skirting round the subject?'

'I'm not skirting around anything, Elise. If you want to talk about your mother, we can.'

Since Ray had come back from the airport, there had been no proper explanation of what had happened all those years ago. Ray said only that they'd had no choice and Ingrid had to get away. Elise could glean more information from the media about her mother than she could from her father. Various articles repeated the same story, that Ingrid had possibly been a patient of Ray's before they'd started a relationship, and she had suffered from mental health issues. Others suggested a personality disorder, that she was a threat to her child. But as Nathaniel told her, they were just journalistic speculation. The only people who could tell her the truth were her mother and father.

'What else are you hiding, Dad? What did the police want to talk to you about?'

'Nothing, sweetheart. Nothing at all. You must understand how things were in those days. Your mother was suicidal most of the time. I had to do something to protect you. She would have succeeded eventually – you must remember what a mess she was?'

'The psychiatrist who couldn't fix my mother. Or me. Or himself, it would seem. Why can't you just tell me the truth? The thing I now have to live with, Dad, is the fact that when you took Ingrid away from me, she survived. So *I* must have been the problem. You allowed me to believe she was dead – and worse, a victim of the Suicide Watcher. How could you do that?'

'Elise, listen to me. Your mother was suffering from postnatal depression, and it was unheard of when you were a baby. Unfortunately, other mental health issues complicated everything and she just didn't get better. You can understand that, with all the issues you've had to deal with. I did what I thought was best at the time. I had to protect you,' Ray said, grabbing her arm to show her he meant it.

Elise pulled away from him. 'You better hurry up. You're due at the police station again in an hour.' She left the summer house, emptying her cup on to the grass, and began walking back to the house.

She didn't want to hear his nonchalant explanations, or about how familiar he was with the parenting of her children, reminding her how she'd failed at various times during their childhoods. And here they were with Buddy, a baby who had come about as a last attempt at repairing her and Nathaniel's marriage. She knew her emotions towards Buddy weren't normal. To her, he was just a little stranger, an imposter in their family unit. She'd caught herself feeling angry towards him, as if he were somehow to blame for what had happened to Ida. But, if she was honest, Ray's explanation about her mother had touched a nerve, and made her shockingly aware of her own frailty.

The children were always told about everything that was going on, although Ida had been at an age where she asked too many questions and didn't like a lot of the answers. Elise had never lied to them or protected them from other people's actions; Ray had always taught her they wouldn't thank her for it when they were older. She wondered if this was why they had always felt so free to explore the macabre. Though they didn't see it like that; to them, it was just a normal part of life. Bad people did bad things to others, something Elise had also been told when she was growing up.

When she was only eleven years old, Elise had to come to terms with the death of her mother, who had allegedly blasted herself into oblivion on the other side of the bathroom door. The bathroom door in their 1970s house, where Elise's mind was forever trapped. Whatever she was doing, her mind was always outside that room, where one of the marbles she'd been playing with had parted from its group and rolled across the carpet runner, on to the hard wood before clonking its way down the steps, exactly at the point she imagined the gunshot had sounded, causing her narrow frame to flinch and settle. At 16.43. Elise had often returned to the house afterwards and sat outside the bathroom door where she believed Ingrid had taken her own life. All she remembered afterwards was Ray arranging for her Uncle Mac and Aunt

Estelle to pick her up so she could stay there while Ray went away. Mac was a relaxed version of her father and Estelle a clipped Frenchwoman who only seemed to ever smile at Elise. She'd stayed with them for almost two years until she was able to live with Ray again. Elise had never got to the bottom of why Ray was estranged from his brother and sister-in-law.

After Ingrid's death there was no 'it'll be okay', no words of comfort at all from Ray, or anyone for that matter, and no one explained what had happened. All she knew was her mother was being taken to Norway, so her family could give her a burial. A fake one, an utter farce, so it would now seem.

This was the tragedy she'd grown up with. It was whispered about, apparent in the eyes of people who knew them; they were the victims behind the glass. But Elise didn't want to hide it in the cupboard, so if anyone asked about her family, she openly told them her mother committed suicide, as if she were telling someone Ingrid was a doctor or a scientist. Now they had a different tragedy to deal with, a real scenario, and Elise wished that Ida's death were fake instead of Ingrid's. She wanted it so badly she thought her heart would explode. Their children were intrigued by sinister news and stories that neither she nor Nathaniel had discouraged them from reading. Now they had become the stories people would read about, as their lives were splattered like roadkill all over the media. There had been articles written suggesting Nathaniel had been having an affair, and others that accused them both of attacking their own child. The stories about Ray were even worse – fictitious claims he was involved in some weird cult, or saying he'd conspired with a patient to get rid of his granddaughter, or another that suggested he was involved in illegal surrogacy deals. Now Elise was wondering how much of it was the truth.

Miles was awake when Elise looked into his room. He was staring at the bed opposite, where Ida usually slept. Elise climbed in behind him and pulled his warm little body into her arms and kissed the back of his head.

'Ida told me she was going to die on leap year.'

'Don't be silly, Miles.' Elise squeezed him tighter, but he wrenched himself from her grip and turned to face the wall.

'I don't want to live with you and Dad anymore. I want to stay here with Granddad Ray.'

CHAPTER TWENTY-SEVEN
NOW

Mark Paton stood at Elise's front door holding his son, Louis, in his arms. Louis had obviously been crying quite a lot, because he was gulping air in staggered breaths.

'Can I come in?' Mark's T-shirt was stained but Elise didn't think about what had caused it, so shocked was she to see him there. Her heart lifted at the sight of Louis, her Buddy, who looked so familiar to her. If Elise hadn't been so distracted, she'd have noticed Mark had also been crying, but she mistook his red-rimmed eyes for tiredness.

'Sure, come in. Everything okay?'

Mark didn't reply; he simply walked past her and abruptly turned around. 'I think I need a coffee, or a drink?' Mark lifted his free arm up to wipe his nose on the sleeve of his hoody, his fingers wrapped around a handgun. Elise's eyes widened, and she turned towards the front door, stopping just as she reached it, an instinct to protect the little boy suddenly overwhelming her.

'Don't do that.'

Elise slowly turned around to see Mark holding the gun to Louis's head. 'No!' she shouted, causing Louis to flinch, and a new bout of crying ensued. 'Please, Mark, don't do that.'

'Come away from the door and get me a drink.' Mark's face crumpled. 'You've got to help me, Elise.'

'Okay, Mark. I'll get you a drink if you put the gun down and let me take Louis?'

Mark's foot was tapping the floor; he was agitated and jumpy. 'You can have Louis, but I'm not putting the gun down.'

Elise was stunned, and began to shake as she took a now-screaming Louis into her arms, frantically thinking how she was going to get them out of this situation.

As she headed towards the kitchen, she wondered if she could text Nathaniel – her phone was on the worktop – and then she felt what she assumed was the muzzle of the gun in the middle of her back.

'If you try anything or call anyone, I'll shoot both of you.'

'It's okay, it's okay.' Elise was saying this more to herself than anyone else. With a shaky free hand, she found a glass in one of the cupboards, her brain racing, thinking who might call round. She found some whiskey and poured it into the glass, passing it to Mark as Louis returned to his staggered breathing.

'Do you have a sitting room in this shithole?'

Elise led Mark into the lounge and chose to sit in the chair by the fireplace. Mark briefly glanced at the black, charred wall in the opposite alcove and sat by the door.

'Mark, what's happened? What's this about?' Elise put her hand on Louis's forehead and kissed his hair. That smell – the smell she remembered from the hospital – was faint, but she still recognised it.

'Daddy?' Louis held his arms out to Mark.

'Just sit with me for a minute, sweetheart.'

'Touching.' Mark swigged his drink. 'You know, I thought you were such a mad bitch. I was convinced you were cuckoo when you started harassing us, telling us we had your son. Completely crazy. I didn't think for one second that you might be right. That was until yesterday, when I found out what a fucking liar my wife is.'

'Mark, I don't know what you're talking about.'

'Do you know what she said to me?' Mark started waving the gun around, making Elise even more nervous. '"He's not yours, anyway."'

'This isn't making any sense. Who's not whose?'

'That isn't Louis sat there. That's your son.'

Elise was quiet for a moment, stunned at what she was hearing. 'How do you know?'

'I found a contract between Jane and your father, paying her a lot of money to take your son and swap him with ours.'

'You're lying. My father wouldn't do that.'

'Well, he has.' Mark was talking animatedly, in a sarcastic tone.

'Mark, whatever is going on between you and Jane is none of my business. You shouldn't be here; you're going to get me into so much trouble.'

'You're the lunatic who made our lives a misery and now you don't believe me when I tell you that's your son?' Mark stood up and walked to the window, reaching up and touching the livid scratch on the back of his neck. 'Do you want me to tell you why she did it? This'll make you laugh. Jane said she'd been having therapy with your father because a work colleague raped her. What she really means is, she was shagging someone she worked with. I know how you women work – you make a mistake, feel guilty and then lie to cover it up. In a nutshell, she was spouting all this to your father and, for whatever reason, he offered her a lot of money to swap your baby with hers, so she wouldn't be reminded of the bloke she'd been shagging.'

'But why would my father do that to us?'

'I don't fucking know – some experiment, knowing the good old doctor. Your old man has previous for all that kind of thing – I mean, he's been nicked before.'

Elise didn't answer him.

'That's not the best of it. Apparently, it's all my fault.' Mark said, a sarcastic smile appearing on his face. 'We don't have any money – we're in debt because I have an addiction. That's why she took that money from your father.'

'There's clearly been some sort of misunderstanding. I'd love to believe that he's my son, I was so convinced of it.' Elise remembered all the times she'd doubted herself, had pushed her head through the bubble and realised how wrong she sounded. 'But I think someone is playing games with you. Mark, put the gun down and go home. I'll follow along with Louis and we'll say no more about it.'

Of course, that wasn't what Elise was going to do, if he agreed to it. She was going to call the police immediately and tell social services what had happened, so they could protect Louis and possibly Jane.

'I might be drunk, off my head, whatever, but I'm not stupid. Stay there.' Mark suddenly decided to leave the room. Elise looked out into the hall at the back door, but knew it was locked and it was too risky to try to get out.

Mark came back seconds later with the bottle of whiskey and filled up his glass.

'There must be more to all this, Mark. You've got it wrong. Even if my theory is right and I have your son and you have mine, it'll just be some mix-up at the hospital when they were born.'

'I've seen the contract, Elise, I can read,' Mark said in a sing-song voice.

'Okay. Why don't you call Jane, ask her to come here and we can talk about it all?'

'She won't answer.' Mark took a large gulp of whiskey and touched the scratch on the back of his neck, checking his fingers afterwards to see if it was bleeding.

'It's worth a try though. Get this mess straightened out.'

Mark put his glass on the floor and refilled it one-handed. 'Jane won't answer the phone, because I shot her in the face.'

CHAPTER TWENTY-EIGHT

The first time I played the game – fulfilled the actual role of Suicide Watcher, as the media has dubbed me – was on 6th August 1976.

As you might have guessed, it was hot outside, sunny but humid, a dark blue tint to the sky, threatening a turbulent change.

My participant and I had talked about the game. Well, on the surface, the way people in denial like to discuss things. Kathy was her name – just a word, nothing particularly interesting about it. But names are important to me; they had to be right, fit for how I was feeling at the time. And when I met her on the train and discovered she was called Kathy, I liked how it felt and sounded in my mouth when I repeated it. The next day might have been a different story.

I met all my participants on the train. I used to watch people on buses, but experience showed me that a different class of people travelled on them in comparison to the trains. The seats are too close to each other on the buses, there's no privacy, people want to listen in to your conversations, join in. Not that I had anything to hide, I was just forging friendships, no harm in that. The carriage formations on trains used to give you a certain amount of privacy, unlike today. Most recently, when I've been on the trains, people are absorbed in their phones or laptops, with glazed and vacant expressions. In the days when I used trains, people read books or newspapers, or simply gazed out of the window. Now their ears are stuffed with headphones, blocking themselves off from the world.

Book readers are the easiest people to strike up a conversation with. Over the years I have found them to be inquisitive people, open to looking at life from a new perspective. They travel in their minds and are able to visualise someone else's life, another person's story. They are my favourite kind of people. They want to talk; to share what they are reading. Then they give me a name, are prone to volunteering personal information and then, after some time, they often talk of invites to their homes.

My reasons for choosing Kathy are inconsequential to her participating in the game. Willingly, in her subconscious mind, she wanted to kill herself and I helped her do that. They say experiencing anything for the first time is the most memorable. This isn't true in my story. Kathy was an anti-climax, a disappointment, like the long-anticipated excitement of someone new who never quite meets your expectations. The obituary she had written for herself was nothing of note . . . 'Kathryn Moss née Harding was thirty-four . . . married to Mark . . . produced two sons . . . got divorced and enjoyed reading . . . has no plans other than to be happy . . .'

'And didn't think enough of herself to stay', was what I wanted to add. I learnt, from that first experience, what I needed to change about parts of the game.

That was why, when I asked her the question – shoot yourself or be shot – I was so surprised at her answer. There was nothing outstanding in Kathy's features that made her physically special, but she was interesting to talk to. Initially she'd had some intriguing ideas, but being faced with adversity showed her for the liar she truly was. Choosing to be shot at the end told me that in all the months we had been friends, I had allowed her to become a different person outside her family. She could be someone else, a fictional character who didn't really exist, like the people in the books she read.

Just before the end, she cried and begged. In my naivety, I hadn't been expecting that, because we had talked so often about dying. She'd even told me about the times she'd felt like taking her own life, and she had even attempted to do so when she was much younger. When she truly faced death, she panicked, allowed her ego to step in. It's simply the feeling we all experience, of not wanting to miss out on anything, a bit like having to leave the party early.

Kathy's children found her when her ex-husband dropped them off after a day out. The obituary she willingly wrote for herself, and which I left on the table, was taken for a suicide note. I read about it all in a newspaper a few days later.

It was the life afterwards I discovered to be more intriguing. I hadn't foreseen this curiosity. A life led poorly, as in most cases, never interested me, but what lay after death and the change it brought about in others was fascinating. Even some of the people remotely connected to the deceased were affected. It was like dropping marbles on to the floor and watching them scatter.

It's easy to observe people when they're grieving – send some flowers, offer your condolences, attend the funeral as a friend. The shock of losing someone close can have positive and profound effects on a person. Kathy's ex-husband accepted redundancy, sold their properties and emigrated with his children. He would never have done that if Kathy had still been alive. He would have continued living to exist.

It turned out that suicide had many facets to hide behind. No one saw the common denominator. That was me.

CHAPTER TWENTY-NINE
THEN

For the first time in fifteen years, Ray smoked a cigarette, one he'd managed to pinch from the police officer who was standing in the exercise yard with him. Ray had to wait there for a doctor, so they could assess him before his questioning could be resumed.

When he'd stepped into the interview room, his claustrophobia had got the better of him and he'd begun to panic. Ray could tell by the look on the officers' faces and the sergeant's tone of voice that they thought he was faking it. One of them had asked him how he'd managed to get on an aeroplane if he couldn't sit in an office with the door closed. Nonetheless, they allowed him to wait outside.

Ray had thought he was going to the police station to answer some questions about Ida, but once seated in the interview room they'd wanted to talk to him about something entirely different. Details from his past he wished he could change, because he knew how it would look on paper.

Pacing the yard now, Ray began to feel his anxiety rise as a couple of other people joined them in the small area to have a cigarette. They were bricked in on all sides and there was mesh over the top to stop anyone attempting to scale the wall.

After the doctor at last arrived and gave Ray the all-clear, he returned to the interview room where the two detectives, a DS Colburn and a DC Everett, adhered to the doctor's advice and kept the door open as they attempted to question him for a second time. Ray felt more violated than when the police had taken his clothes for forensic analysis the day he'd found Ida. The questions were relentless and tiring because Ray had nothing to say, knowing it wouldn't change their opinion. He had conducted some strange experiments in his time, but he didn't believe until the last few weeks that he'd ever put his family in danger. It was starkly obvious now.

'Dr Coe, can you tell us about this document?' DS Colburn slid the familiar papers across the desk.

Ray put his glasses on and examined the file. 'Am I under arrest?'

'No, Dr Coe, but we strongly urge you to answer the questions. Do you want me to call the duty solicitor?'

'If you arrest me, I'll arrange my own legal representation, thank you.'

'Can you tell us the details of the alleged surrogacy that took place in 1979?'

Ray shifted in his seat, uncomfortable and defensive at being asked questions that had nothing to do with his granddaughter's murder.

'That is a legal contract between myself, my wife and couple X, as stated there.' Ray pointed to the sentence he was referring to. 'It was different in those days – they were friends of ours. There's no law against having a child for someone else.'

'It depends if it's surrogacy or trafficking.' DS Colburn linked his fingers together and rested them on the desk. 'Dr Coe, who are the couple marked as "X"?'

'I could never disclose that. It would be breaching doctor-patient confidentiality.'

'This has nothing to do with your profession, Dr Coe.' DS Colburn glanced up at the clock on the opposite wall.

'And this has nothing to do with my granddaughter's murder, but I'm still answering your questions.' Ray was becoming agitated. 'Don't ask me about their identity again.'

The two officers looked at one another, happy to leave that line of questioning for later.

'Dr Coe,' said DS Colburn, 'can you explain to us how and where insemination took place? Your wife was the surrogate, so who was the donor?'

'I became the donor when it emerged that the male X was infertile.'

'So what you're telling us, Dr Coe, is that you and your wife conceived a child and sold it to another couple?' DS Colburn lifted another document from the pile and placed it in front of Ray.

'Yes, that's pretty much how it happened.'

'Dr Coe, in front of you is a document dated the twenty-fourth of April 1988, signed by you, your brother Mac Coe, and his wife Estelle Coe.'

Ray lifted it up and looked at the piece of paper carefully. He knew exactly what it was, had recognised it immediately, but he was buying himself some extra time, thinking about what he should say.

'What can you tell us about that document, Dr Coe?' DS Colburn was much more confident in his line of questioning now that Ray had basically admitted the allegations they suspected him of.

Ray folded his arms. 'No comment.'

'Isn't it true, Dr Coe, that when your wife allegedly committed suicide, you arranged to sell your daughter, Elise Coe, to your brother and his wife for the sum of twenty thousand pounds?'

'No comment.' Ray sat back further in his chair and stared at the open door.

'Dr Coe, isn't it true that your brother and his wife had discovered the previous year that they couldn't have any children and you agreed to help them out?'

'No comment.'

'Isn't it also true, Dr Coe, that after faking your wife's death you gave Elise to your brother and his wife, in return for twenty thousand pounds, and left the country?'

'It wasn't like that.' Ray banged his hand on the table, startling the officers.

'This contract states that your brother and his wife were to become Elise's legal parents. Sounds pretty final to me.'

'My wife was very sick at the time. I was doing Elise a favour, I had to protect her from Ingrid. It was inevitable she was going to commit suicide and I was protecting my daughter.'

'In what way, Dr Coe? By telling an eleven-year-old her mother was dead?'

'I was scared Elise would come home and find her one day – or worse, Ingrid would kill her. I needed her safe and I knew Mac and Estelle could give her a better life while I was away. I intended to have her back as soon as I came home. Once I got my wife back to her native country of Norway, I knew she would recover. I was right, and I returned home.'

'The facts are, Dr Coe, you set this up as a social experiment, easily manipulating desperate, childless people into buying your children from you because you wanted to see how they would grow up without your wife's influence. It was so easy that you decided to continue this operation and set up an illegal service. Isn't that true, Dr Coe?'

It was a few moments before Ray answered. He was trapped in a corner with no way of escape. It wasn't as crude as they were making it out to be, but he knew how it all looked on paper.

'Yes, yes, it's true. What are you going to do? No one got hurt. My wife and I made a childless couple very happy, and Elise was settled with Mac and Estelle for the time she lived with them. Anyone I helped thereafter was extremely grateful for everything.'

'Your brother and his wife no longer have any contact with you and haven't done for some years.'

163

'No comment.'

'Can you tell us where your wife is, Dr Coe?'

'No comment.'

'You recently visited your wife in Norway and she has since disappeared. Isn't that true, Dr Coe?'

'No comment. I'd like to leave now. It's my right to leave.' Ray stood up.

'You can try to leave, but then I'll caution you and take you to the custody sergeant and get you booked in.' DS Colburn held Ray's gaze until he sat down again. 'We believe,' DS Colburn went on, 'that you went to Norway to see your wife with the purpose of stopping her reporting anything incriminating about you.'

'That's ludicrous! Are you suggesting I killed my wife? Don't be so ridiculous, man. What reason would I have?'

'Does the name John Tilney mean anything to you?'

'No. Why would it?' Ray looked at the photograph of the man that DS Colburn pushed across the table in front of him. 'Never seen him before.'

'John Tilney's seven-year-old son, Benjamin?' The detective pushed another photo across the table.

'No comment.' Ray folded his arms and refused to look at the many photos that were placed in front of him, answering 'no comment' to all the names.

'We believe, Dr Coe, that you groomed these people and then shot them.'

'Do you know who I am? Please be serious.'

'I know exactly who you are, Dr Coe – a cold-blooded serial killer. Is that why you had your granddaughter murdered, because she discovered who you really are?'

Ray shook his head in disgust.

'A short while before the day of the incident, Ida had been in your office looking for photos. She discovered some private documents, and when James Caddy called you for an appointment, you saw it as an opportunity to pay him to kill her. The trouble was, he didn't quite manage it, so you came back to the house and tried to suffocate her.'

'No!' Ray banged his hand on the desk. 'Sonny was the first person to find her, I wasn't even there.'

'We found blood spatter on your sweater that matches Ida's. Can you explain why that might be, Dr Coe?'

'I've told you this already. I lifted Ida into my arms when I found her, and she coughed.'

'Can you tell us why we found bloody smudges, consistent with finger marks, on Ida's right cheek?' The other detective pushed a photograph of Ida's face across the table. 'Ida's blood was found on your fingertips.'

Ray shook his head, desperately trying to think. 'I placed my hand over her mouth to see if I could feel her breath on the palm of my hand. I promise you, there was nothing sinister about it. Anything that James Caddy has done is nothing to do with me.'

'We've got James Caddy in custody now and he says you offered him money to kill Ida.'

'He's lying. James Caddy is a paranoid schizophrenic; he'll say anything if he thinks he might be in trouble. Can't you see that?' Ray was becoming very emotional. 'I've answered all your questions regarding my granddaughter. I'm not speaking to you about it anymore. Not until I have legal representation.'

'Dr Coe, I'm arresting you for the murders of Ida Munroe, John Tilney, Benjamin Tilney, Kathryn Moss and Cheryl Fitzpatrick. You do not have to say anything, but it may harm your defence if you do not mention when questioned something you later rely on in court. Anything you do say may be given in evidence. Do you understand?'

'This is utter madness. I will admit to the so-called trafficking, but these murders have nothing to do with me. Nothing.'

'We'll be continuing our investigations and you may be charged with further offences. Like I said at the beginning, we're from the cold case team, reopening suicide cases that occurred between 1976 and 1988.' DS Colburn signed off the interview and switched off the recording. 'Just because a crime was committed historically, Dr Coe, doesn't mean you can get away with it.'

'But this is ludicrous. My daughter needs me.' Ray stood up, so he was face to face with the officers.

'Your daughter needed you, Dr Coe, after you told her she would never see her mother again. We are trying to ascertain if any more of the suicides during that period were actually murder.' DS Colburn stared directly into Ray's dark grey eyes.

'How do you know those people didn't want to die?'

The DS looked perplexed. 'Explain what you mean.'

'Whether they did it themselves or not, they agreed to be killed. A little helping hand doesn't make it murder,' Ray said in a loud whisper.

'Are you confessing to the crimes, Dr Coe?'

'No, I'm simply asking you to look at it logically.' Ray sighed. 'I can tell you where my wife is.'

DS Colburn breathed in deeply, exasperated with Ray. 'If that is the case, Dr Coe, why didn't you tell me when we started the interview?'

'Because, my dear man, it's your job to work it all out.'

CHAPTER THIRTY
THEN

It was the first time Elise and Nathaniel had been to the apartment since their nightmare had begun, and it was as though someone had poured hydrochloric acid on to their lives. Discovering Ingrid was still alive on top of everything else had been a tipping point for Elise. She was angry with her parents, and while she was trying to process everything, Nathaniel had persuaded her it would be better if they returned to their own home. She knew it was partly because he was struggling to stay in the house where their daughter was murdered, and she understood his reasons for wanting to return. She didn't know where she wanted to be right now; sitting on the moon wouldn't have made any difference to the way she was feeling. Strangely, Elise couldn't help turning her anger towards Buddy, blaming his existence for the monumental changes that had shaken their lives. The little baby who was now screwing up his face and hands, getting ready to wake up as Nathaniel carefully placed the car seat on the tiled kitchen floor, reminding her of the wriggling chrysalises she used to find in the garden at her father's house. She stared at him briefly, astonished at how perfect he was, considering the abhorrent way she had thrust him into the world.

There was no denying it – Elise hated him. With every hour that had passed since Ida's death, the weight of his existence had become heavier. There was no going back, no changing her mind, and it had all just dawned on her a little too late that, actually, she hadn't wanted any more children; she just wanted the one she'd lost. It was clear to Elise that if she hadn't agreed to have another child, they'd still have Ida. That was the forfeit.

When Ida was born, aside from the shocking earthquake that sent a tremor through her world, Elise had been filled with awe and wonder, an overwhelming, all-consuming, engulfing love for the little person she'd created. It was so overpowering Elise thought she'd be sick from it; she had been totally in love with this small baby.

She longed for those days when she thought about the situation they were dealing with now, which had descended on their home like a dark cloak, and smelt and felt like death.

'You okay, love?' Nathaniel said.

Another stupid question, but that didn't surprise her – Nathaniel had been asking them since Ida had died. His father and stepmother had come over and were currently in the sitting room with DC Chilvers, discussing everything, but Elise had no inclination to talk to anyone. The small imposter decided to settle, giving Elise a rare moment of quiet, so she made some tea and went up to the roof terrace, ignoring Nathaniel's fussing.

Elise pulled a chair out from the garden table and sat in view of the shed they had bought Ida and erected in the corner of the terrace. Ida had painted it not in bright colours as you would have expected of a teenager, but a delicate sky-grey matte – neat and understated. She had insisted on having large pot plants out the front of it, and they had grown so much the shed was only partly visible through the foliage. Very quickly, the shelves of the shed were filled with jars of insects and wooden boxes with glass tops containing various moths and butterflies, collected on long walks and now frozen in time. Ray would often go on these walks with Ida, and spent a lot of time in the shed with her, the two of them perched on little stools drinking hot chocolate.

Elise sighed, swallowing down more tears. Ida wasn't here anymore, and Elise couldn't help feeling that she wasn't either.

Everything had changed, of course it had, but it wasn't just the fact their home contained more police officers, whom she detested, and various family members who wouldn't normally visit. It was like they'd moved properties and Elise had forgotten about it – everything seemed strange and unfamiliar. They'd become the family she had always pitied, the people behind the glass whom everyone stared and pointed at, always remembered for one thing only – they had a murdered daughter. Nathaniel had thought it would be good for them to return to the apartment, part of some strange acceptance, but it was just making her feel worse.

Back inside, Elise moved slowly to Ida's bedroom and stood looking through the open doorway, acutely aware of her daughter's empty desk chair. Voices in the sitting room had quieted and she could see DC Chilvers staring at her through the gap in the door at the end of the hall. A look of pity on her face – of course Elise would fail as a parent; she was bound to follow in her mother's footsteps.

Elise purposefully slammed the door to Ida's room. And that's how she wanted it to stay. Closed, forever casting darkness across the corridor until Ida opened it again.

Nathaniel bumped into Elise in the hallway. 'What's going on?'

'I'd like everyone to leave, including you. Take that with you as well.' Elise pointed at the baby. 'I want to be left alone.'

'Why don't you go and lie down for a bit?'

Elise took a deep breath. 'Nathaniel, go and stay with your dad and take the children with you. This isn't your problem.'

She saw the pain that whipped across his face and she liked that he was hurting. She wanted to cause suffering to everyone she could. It wasn't in her nature to be unkind, but after years of bottling up feelings and putting them on the shelf, she needed to lash out – a nasty cocktail of hormones, drugs and sleep deprivation.

'Don't do this, Elise. Ida is my daughter too,' Nathaniel quietly retorted.

'But I gave birth to her, it's different for me,' Elise snapped, spitefully.

'Come on, love, everybody is upset.' Nathaniel's dad, Nick, joined them in the hallway, his wife, Karen, standing behind him.

'Go and play happy families in your own home, Nick. You don't need to be caught up in any of this awful mess. All of you, please leave.' Elise's rage was beginning to engulf her, so she took herself into Ida's bedroom and closed the door. The stark reality of her daughter's absence hit her like a sharp gust of icy-cold air, taking all the rage out of her body. She tiptoed carefully over to Ida's desk, where there were various items with some kind of importance. A foil-wrapped chocolate from a Chinese restaurant they'd taken Ida to – her first grown-up meal for her twelfth birthday. There was a crude pencil case she'd made in Textiles. Elise unzipped it and lifted the felt bag to her face, so she could smell all the fruit-shaped erasers it contained. She tipped them out on to the desk, remembering the sweet strawberry scent that hovered around Ida when she was doing her homework. A lone marble dropped on to the table and rolled off the desk and on to the chair, eventually landing on the carpet with a whisper of a thud. Elise carefully bent down to retrieve it, the ache of her body reminding her of the traumatic time she'd had giving birth to Buddy.

She held the battered glass ball up to the light, recalling how Ida had discovered it on the beach, which had caused much excitement. She had spent the rest of the day making up stories about where it had come from – children playing on boats near remote islands, or a shipwreck spewing it out.

Of course, both then and now, the sight of the marble made Elise feel nauseous, reminding her of the past.

The dynamics had been perfect that day, and after all these years Elise could still remember it so well; she had never before been able to get a marble to hit each step, all the way down, without it rolling off one of the open slats and falling to the floor below. A simultaneous moment of joy and devastation.

A feeling that she now understood to be freedom would float around her whenever she let the marbles loose from the confines of their bag. She was forbidden from leaving them on the floor, especially near the staircase – the dangers were clear – but occasionally she would allow one, carefully observed, to roll away from the group. It made her feel exposed – alone, in a strange way – like a baby bird briefly left by its mother, open to the horrors of prey. But Elise had liked that feeling. She was that marble and she could still hear the sound of it clonking its way down the steps. Her mother had always been the marble that rolled off the back of the slat, landing straight on to the tiled floor beneath. The sound still followed the gunshot in her head, like the familiarity of the next song on an album.

Now it was Elise tumbling down those stairs, rolling away, falling from the life she knew. It was always hovering in the background.

In her head, during meditation in her therapy sessions, she would visit the place outside the bathroom door, the marbles tucked away, giving her hope; all restrained in a small bag, banging against one another, clamouring, squashed, to then so suddenly be free and sprayed across the carpet. That was her mother that day – free from her constraints, blasting herself into oblivion on the other side of the bathroom door at precisely 16.43, or so Elise had believed, while she waited patiently outside. Not content with being released from her marble bag, Ingrid had sought a new kind of freedom, one she could never find beyond the front door of their house.

For years after, Elise wondered why her mother had left her behind. That was when she truly understood loneliness, at the young age of eleven, and she had believed ever since that this emotion hit you once, like being scarred from a burn, and it would always be with you, reignited at certain times in your life but never as severe as the first. And there Elise had stayed, in her head, at the top of the stairs in Ingrid's house, waiting for someone to come and collect her.

Returning the marble to Ida's desk, a piece of folded paper caught her eye. It was weighty when she picked it up, and she unfolded it to reveal a small oval mirror, with gold gilt edging. Across the middle was a large crack, causing the top piece of glass to slide underneath the other part when Elise held it up. A note on the piece of paper read: *For the doll's house. To be placed in the hall.* She recognised the handwriting, and everything slowly started to shudder, like a giant drill sliding into the earth.

Elise left Ida's room as quickly as her body would allow, walked up the staircase to the roof terrace and into her daughter's shed, where she found the doll's house missing.

'What's wrong?'

Elise turned to find Nathaniel behind her. 'Where is Ida's doll's house?'

'Tolek has it – said he'd fit the electrics for her,' Nathaniel said.

'Was there anything inside?'

'Not that I'm aware of. I didn't check. Tolek collected it a couple of weeks ago.'

Elise began to shake. Turning around, she looked at the empty space where the beloved doll's house had been. 'Get it back, Nathaniel. Get the doll's house and put it back exactly where it was.'

'I'll ask Tolek if he's finished with it and then I'll collect it. Just calm down.'

'Get it back now!' Elise screamed as she pushed past him and made her way down the stairs.

'Okay, I'll sort it out. There's no need to get in such a state about it. I'll call him now.' Nathaniel walked off in search of his phone.

Slightly calmer, Elise wandered into their bedroom, where she found the little stranger had been settled into his Moses basket, and she picked him up and took him up to the roof terrace. He was screaming full pitch by the time Nathaniel discovered Elise standing on the ledge with the low glass surround bearing her full weight. As he approached her, Elise pulled a screaming Buddy from her chest and held him over the balcony, in mid-air, three floors up.

CHAPTER THIRTY-ONE
THEN

Completely broken, Nathaniel dropped to his knees, his voice shuddering with tears as he begged Elise not to hurt Buddy, hoping somebody downstairs would realise there was something wrong and come and help him.

'I can't go on, Nathaniel, I can't live without her, without Ida.' Elise was sobbing uncontrollably, and he was finding it difficult to hear exactly what she was saying.

'Let me help you, Elise. Please don't do this. We can and we will get through this.'

Elise closed her eyes and shook her head, still holding a now strangely quiet Buddy over the edge, making Nathaniel clutch his head in despair. He wanted to run and grab them both but he was so frightened she would step over the barrier and jump. Slowly and carefully, Nathaniel pulled his phone from his back pocket.

'Nathaniel?' It was DC Chilvers, summoned without him having to dial. She came up behind him and helped him to his feet. 'Go inside, please.'

'I can't leave them . . .' Nathaniel said, shaking with fear.

'Trust me. I know how to deal with this. Go and call your doctor. Please, Nathaniel.' DC Chilvers squeezed his arm.

Reluctantly, Nathaniel went inside and somehow managed to call their GP. He stood in the hallway, not wanting to alarm the others. About ten minutes later, Elise appeared at the top of the stairs without Buddy, and for a moment, until he heard him crying again, Nathaniel had the horrifying fear she'd gone through with her threats, but DC Chilvers came down the steps holding their baby.

Nick came out of the sitting room holding an empty coffee cup, oblivious to what had just occurred. 'Everything okay?'

There were a few silent moments before anyone answered, and Nathaniel was too upset to find any words.

'Everything is fine,' DC Chilvers said to Nick, who had been joined by Karen. 'No harm done. Elise is just a little overwrought and needs some sleep.'

Nathaniel relieved her of a screaming Buddy and somehow managed to calm him down.

'What's going on, son?' Nick moved towards Nathaniel. 'Do you want us to take Miles and Buddy back to ours for a day or two?'

'Thanks, that might be a good idea,' Nathaniel said, staring at Elise, who was leaning against the stair rail, focusing on the floor. He had an overwhelming urge to embrace her and throw her at the wall at the same time.

To stop himself doing anything he might regret, Nathaniel left the apartment and went across to Tolek's to fetch the doll's house, in the hope it might calm her down. The moment their neighbour answered the door, Nathaniel broke down, he was so exhausted with grief and despair. Tolek led him into his sitting room and poured them each a large whiskey. Nathaniel allowed the viscous, golden liquid to heat his cold and empty insides, and took a deep breath for what felt like the first time that day. They talked for a while and Nathaniel felt better for offloading.

'I better get back.'

'It's probably not the right time, but I've been meaning to talk to you, make sure we're on the same page?' Tolek said. 'You haven't told anyone about our "project"?'

'No, I haven't said anything. We're on the same page. Although the police have my computer, so it's only a matter of time before the police unlock those files.' Nathaniel tipped his head back and stared at the ceiling. 'What a fucking mess. How did we get here?'

'Just sit tight,' Tolek said, squeezing his friend's shoulder as he got up to fetch the doll's house.

Nathaniel swallowed hard at the sight of the structure Ida had been so fond of and spent so much time renovating. He had picked it up at an auction and remembered her excitement when she'd first seen it. That had led Ray to tell Miles and Ida about the *Nutshell Studies* and they'd been fascinated with doll's houses ever since. Nathaniel decided now they would get it all working and filled with furniture in Ida's memory.

'Thanks for this.' Nathaniel lifted it up awkwardly.

'I'm sorry, but I haven't had a chance to fit the lights. I'll come over sometime and do it for you.'

Nathaniel walked across the hall and set the structure carefully on to the floor, so he could find his door key. The catch on the doll's house roof had come loose and some papers were poking out of the gap. Frowning, Nathaniel placed his keys back in his pocket and lifted the lid. Inside, he found a pile of letters. He flicked through them briefly, scanning various paragraphs, tripping over some of the words. The handwriting was unfamiliar to him, but the content made perfect sense.

CHAPTER THIRTY-TWO
THEN

Nathaniel wasn't surprised as to why he would suddenly be asked to go to the police station the next day to answer some questions. DC Chilvers had been quite terse about it on the phone when she'd told him.

'Can't you ask me the questions now, or another officer come here to do it?' Nathaniel asked, buying himself some time.

'No. They want you to go down to the station,' DC Chilvers said before the line went dead.

Nathaniel didn't have a problem answering questions, it was battling the press that were camped outside their apartment that bothered him. None of that lot were in the mood to be cordial with them. The shock and numbness from Ida's death had begun to wear off, and the full force of the reality was beginning to hit them all. The rot was setting in and people were starting to accuse them of killing Ida. Nathaniel had known it would happen – he'd seen it with so many high-profile cases.

From what Nathaniel understood, the police were expecting to charge someone later that day. Nathaniel had wondered if Ray was the one about to be charged – it wouldn't surprise him, knowing Ray's unethical past. The thought immediately made him feel guilty, despite the fact he didn't like the man; he knew how much Ray loved Ida.

DC Chilvers had arranged for her colleague, DC Greg Aster, to collect Nathaniel and drive him to the station, but other than general talk, the officer didn't say anything.

Nathaniel was greeted by another officer and was struggling to remember all their names. 'There's nothing to worry about, Mr Munroe, we just want to ask you some questions. I'm DS Brand and this is DC Aster, as you already know.'

'Has this got something to do with the man you've arrested?'

'Take a seat, Mr Munroe. Can we get you some tea or coffee?'

'Just water thanks.' Nathaniel's mouth was dry already.

They all took their seats in the interview room and waited for the recorder to stop buzzing.

'Mr Munroe, where were you on Thursday the third of March between eight and nine a.m.?'

Nathaniel took a moment to think; the days had all blended into one blurred mass of time. 'Oh, that was a couple of days ago, sorry.'

'That's okay, take your time.' DS Brand sniffed and rested her hands on her lap.

'I went to my support group as I always do on a Wednesday evening – it's a support group for families affected by suicide. Magda King runs it. I bumped into an old friend and arranged to meet him for coffee the following morning.'

Both officers just stared at him, waiting for him to continue.

'It was the morning that . . . Ida . . . well, when Ida died . . . but I wasn't aware she'd passed at the time.' Nathaniel stared at the table, wondering why he hadn't remembered not being at the hospital when his daughter had died.

'Can you tell us where the café is and the name of your friend?' DS Brand was rearranging some paperwork on the table, distracting Nathaniel slightly. His heart was beginning to race. Something was wrong here.

'I can't remember the name of the café, but it's a greasy spoon on the Eastleigh Road. I hadn't seen him for years, so we decided to go for coffee.'

'What is the name of this friend, Mr Munroe?'

'Steven. Steven Bridges. Am I in some sort of trouble? Has he accused me of something?'

DS Brand removed some photographs from a folder and slid them across the table. 'Can you tell me who the man in the picture is?'

Nathaniel looked at the photographs of himself sat in the café with Steven. He swallowed hard. 'That's Steven Bridges.'

'Can you tell me who this man is?' DS Brand removed another photo from the folder, a mugshot. Things were getting serious and Nathaniel was now wishing he'd mentioned his suspicions about Steven earlier. The police had asked him for a list of people, anyone they'd known over the years that they might be worried about. Nathaniel had put Steven's name forward but hadn't told them about the fight they'd had.

'That's also Steven Bridges. When I said he was an old friend . . . Well, what I meant was, he was an old friend years ago, but we had a disagreement. He disappeared, we haven't seen him for years, until Wednesday when I spotted him at the group.'

'What did you have a disagreement about?' DS Brand closed the folder.

'It might be something and nothing. I caught him in Ida's bedroom when he was over at ours one night. He was standing in the doorway and told me he just wanted to watch her sleep. We'd all had a lot to drink and I lost my temper and threw him out.'

DC Aster looked at DS Brand.

'Mr Munroe – can I call you Nathaniel? Do you know a James Caddy?'

'No. I only know he's a client of Ray's and might have something to do with Ida's murder.'

'Have you ever seen James Caddy?' DS Brand removed the photos of Steven from the desk.

'No. But my son, Miles, gave a good description of him.'

'Nathaniel, you were seen at a café yesterday morning with James Caddy. He's currently being questioned in connection with your daughter's murder.' DC Aster placed some different photos in front of Nathaniel.

Nathaniel looked at the pictures. It was unmistakeably the same man – one of his eyes was as black as the depths of the sea – but it was Steven, not this James Caddy. Nathaniel and Steven had known each other for years.

'What? I don't understand.'

'Nathaniel, can you tell us why you were seen drinking coffee with James Caddy, who you claimed you didn't know, at the time of your daughter's death?'

'I thought it was Steven. It's Steven Bridges. I've known him for years.'

'Nathaniel, this is not Steven Bridges, this is James Caddy.'

Nathaniel looked through the photos again. 'I don't know what to say . . .'

'Mr Munroe, the laptop we retrieved from your home was searched. We found a locked file containing images of teenage girls. We also found correspondence from your computer to James Caddy's email account. Can you explain this please?'

Nathaniel had had a feeling that document was going to get him into trouble. He'd deleted it, but knew he'd have to get rid of the entire laptop for it to disappear. Something he hadn't been able to do because the apartment was a crime scene and out of bounds.

'No, you've got that all wrong. I can explain it. I'm a journalist. I was setting people up for a story. I had no idea who I was talking to on there. Speak to Tolek Nowak, our neighbour at the apartments, he'll corroborate my story – we were going to meet these paedophiles and secretly film a documentary. I promise, the only reason we accessed those sites was to make those disgusting perverts think we were like-minded.'

DS Brand nodded but he could see she wasn't buying it.

'Your daughter, Nathaniel, had been happily chatting to James Caddy online. He was the one who hacked her account and posted the photographs of her, along with the email messages.'

'Ida wouldn't do that. She wasn't stupid.'

'Nathaniel, your friend James took those photos. She must have met him at some point.'

'No. You're lying.' Nathaniel was letting his arrogance get the better of him; he was tired and pissed off.

'Mr Munroe, you have pornographic images of teenage girls on your computer. Can you tell us how they got there?'

'I'd like a solicitor please.'

'Did you download them?'

'No comment.'

'Mr Munroe, did you conspire with James Caddy to groom your daughter for sexual gratification?'

'That's disgusting. No comment.'

'Nathaniel Munroe, I am arresting you on suspicion of downloading illegal images. You do not have to say anything, but it may harm your defence if you do not mention when questioned something you later rely on in court. Anything you do say may be given in evidence.'

CHAPTER THIRTY-THREE

There are many days when I spend vast amounts of time in the compartments of my mind. Where else would I be? It has very little bearing on my life, being in the physical world. I much prefer being internal. It's a practice not dissimilar to meditation. I am still perfecting it, but I have become quite good at entering my head whilst still focusing on the present. The only way I can describe it to you is like a library filled with thoughts, memories, sentences – anything I might want to recall at any time. My mental records, I suppose.

Yes, I do talk to people in my head, but I am not a schizophrenic, you understand. They do not guide me, rule me or dictate how I think. They are individuals I call on for conversation. Intellectual stimulation, if you like. There is a lounge area within my library, and occasionally I invite a participant to sit and converse about various topics.

It must be interesting talking to me. I'd like to be able to do that from an objective point of view. I've tried it several times and it will take practice, a further advancement of my mental training. Try imagining you're sitting opposite yourself, and then, when you've completely detached yourself from yourself, you may be able to have a conversation. Training myself to talk to my subconscious self is quite difficult, and it is one of my more intriguing challenges.

One of the psychiatrists I used to see asked me to do this. They don't listen, just take notes that are of no importance. Why would they be? I don't want to be fixed. I like myself; even my objective inner being likes me. There, I made a little joke – quite an achievement for an alleged psychopath.

Strong emotions for anything are usually connected to a conscience. Apart from, I think, the passion to love. Love in its true sense is for my pleasure; I have no care whether it is reciprocated. We come, we go, we love one, we then love another, that's just the way it works. It's not complicated, it never has been. It's the deniers that encase these emotions and then wonder why they corrode and erode as though some ethereal force was raining down on them. Oh, the deniers are very good at blaming everything on each other. And if that fails, they make excuses; blame it on their circumstances or surroundings.

Why do we talk of love? Why can we not just be? Because deniers, if they were to be truthful, want to share their mistakes with another. 'Let's mess it up together, then I can pass most of the blame on to you.' And they call me the psychotic one . . . the irony is killing me.

Briefly, I'd like to return to Gerald, the man on the train. He was such an important factor in a concentrated period of my life. I learnt things from him, you see. Then the teacher became the pupil for a short time. The information I imparted to him seemed to flourish within him, like a growing bulb; I watched that transition, the knowing which appeared in his eyes. Everything suddenly made sense to him and his approach to life changed – a quite astonishing transformation.

One such day, he didn't get off at his usual stop; he remained in the seat beside me. I noticed he'd removed his shoes and socks. I made no comment; after all, it was no concern of mine. When the train moved away from the platform, the large station sign passing the window, he breathed a deep, satisfying sigh. I'm not sure whether it was relief or pleasure. Perhaps these two emotions are the same? There shouldn't have been anything remarkable about the fact he'd disposed of his shoes and socks, but that day it felt different, like the end of something, moving into a new era.

I continued reading. We had grown used to our comfortable silences; mostly everything had been said that needed to be. He was a travelling *companion, one whose company I quite enjoyed. There was no denying I was intrigued to see if he was going to get off at the same stop as he usually did. He didn't. When I stood up, he remained seated. I offered the novel I had just finished. He took it, thanking me with great pleasure, as though I'd given him an item of enormous worth. I suppose it was, depending on your desires.*

'Aren't you getting off?' I enquired.

'No,' he said, quite calmly.

'Where are you going?'

'I don't know . . . wherever it stops at the other end, I suppose.'

Sitting back down in my seat, I removed a flask from my holdall and offered him a cup of coffee. I travelled with him for the entire journey. The man with no shoes or socks.

CHAPTER THIRTY-FOUR
NOW

The church was almost full, apart from a couple of empty rows at the back. Magda's family was small, but she had many friends and acquaintances. Some of the people from the support group were there. Ted, one of the long-time members, whom Nathaniel got on particularly well with, was there, and put his hand up in greeting.

After the service, everyone stood outside, making small talk, discussing whether they would go to the wake, which was being held at a local pub near to where Magda had lived. Suicides were always the same. Nathaniel could see people were torn between wanting to celebrate the life lost and an underlying feeling of anger and disappointment that she took her own life. No one knew what had caused Magda to commit suicide. Liam, Magda's husband, had called Nathaniel, trying to make sense of it all. He said she'd been a bit edgy a couple of days before. He and Nathaniel had then had a very uncomfortable conversation – Liam was so desperate to know what had happened with Magda that he asked Nathaniel all sorts of questions about his own mother's suicide, given the similar circumstances.

Nathaniel couldn't stop thinking about Magda's death and the argument they'd had not long before she died about her brother, Gordon. He found himself listening for gossip amongst the congregation about the fact that it appeared the two siblings had both ended their own lives. The police were still investigating Magda's case, and hadn't ruled out the Suicide Watcher.

'It seems a bit ironic, don't you think?' Ted had joined Nathaniel and was busy buttoning up his coat and pushing his hands into his pockets.

'Ironic how?' said Nathaniel.

'That Magda ran a group for victims of suicide and then she . . . well, you know.'

'Yes. I was thinking just the same thing. Have you seen Elise?'

'No, can't say I have. Are you staying on for the wake?'

'No. You?' Nathaniel was distracted, searching through the crowd of people for his wife. He'd moved out a few days ago to give them both some space and he'd tried to ring her several times to check she was okay, but she hadn't returned his calls. Arriving late for the service, and therefore being the first one out of the church, Nathaniel assumed he would see her when everyone spilled out.

'No, lad,' Ted replied. 'Not my thing – pubs. I've paid my respects, I'm off home.'

'Sorry, Ted, I'm just trying to find Elise. She should be here, and she hasn't returned my calls.'

Ted frowned. They'd talked before about Nathaniel's troubles at home, so Ted knew things were a bit fraught. 'Could she have gone away for a few days?'

Nathaniel focused on Ted, suddenly realising he wouldn't know about the recent events because he hadn't seen him that week. 'No . . . Well, not that I know of. I've left her . . . I'm staying at my dad's for a bit.'

Ted nodded. 'I see.'

Nathaniel knew what Ted was thinking. Ted's wife had taken her own life – another suspected victim of the Suicide Watcher. It was one of the stories in the group that had had quite an impact on Nathaniel.

Ted had no relatives left, apart from distant ones he'd never met; a few good friends kept him company and he them, but some of them had recently died. Every day Ted would walk his dog around the local park; ablutions and necessities aside, this was the only activity he repeated daily. Recently, he had begun to calculate his life, almost hour by hour – the times all mapped out, lists pinned to his kitchen wall, but each day different to the previous one. Tuesdays were the same every week but different to Wednesdays, and he followed this schedule rigidly. Nathaniel found it all quite fascinating. Ted felt it offered him enough variety to urge him from his bed each day; something he'd previously struggled to achieve. That was all he wanted out of life – to feel at least a small amount of anticipation; enough to make him want to exist.

Nathaniel recalled when Ted had first told him about his wife, who had killed herself when their daughter was just a baby, in much the same way as the others: the signature bullet in the side of her head, her fingers awkwardly clasping a handgun, distinguishing her, attaching her to the Suicide Watcher. Ted had become aware very quickly that he had to formulate a routine so he could be a father to his daughter, of whom he was understandably very protective. Until she turned fifteen, he had barely let her out of his sight. Just after her fifteenth birthday he agreed she could go and stay with an old school friend who had moved away many years ago but had remained in touch. Ted drove her to the station, saw her safely on to the train and waved goodbye to her from the platform. About halfway through her journey she died; her heart just stopped beating. An undetected defect, adult cot death – or as it's more commonly known, sudden adult death syndrome. Nathaniel had felt sick when Ted had told him, and guilty that he should think he was the only one who'd ever suffered. He could see now that Magda's funeral had drained Ted.

'I'll give you a lift home if you like.'

'Don't let me stop you, if you're staying for a bit.'

'No. I want to get back . . .' Nathaniel hesitated, wanting to tell his friend he had a visit with Buddy at his foster home, but he felt too embarrassed and ashamed.

'Let's swing by your place on the way to mine. Check Elise is okay.'

It was dark when they arrived at the house. Not one single light illuminated the windows and Nathaniel began to feel nauseous. Something was very wrong, and he wished now that he hadn't assumed she'd gone on a bender. Normally, these heavy excursions resulted in her calling him – or, on a particularly bad night, the police, because she'd been arrested. But he hadn't heard anything from anyone.

'Have you still got a key?' Ted stared through the windscreen at the dark building, its dirty white render illuminated by the sparse street lamps. 'I'll go in, you stay here.'

'No, I can't let you do that.'

'It's fine, Nathaniel – better I see what's inside than you. I've seen it all before, and, trust me, it's much harder when it's personal.' During Ted's working life he'd been a coroner, so grim scenarios didn't faze him.

'I'm going in and that's the end of it.'

'I'm coming in with you, then.'

They both got out of the car, Ted insisting on leading the way. As soon as they unlocked the front door and opened it, there was a faint putrid smell that reached their nostrils, as though they'd released the lid on an out-of-date can of food.

'Oh shit.' Nathaniel turned and went outside to empty his stomach.

'Stay there.' Ted closed the door on Nathaniel so he couldn't go back in. Once the nausea passed, Nathaniel paced the driveway, watching the windows light up throughout the house. His mind was frantically searching through the last few days. What conversations had taken place between him and Elise? How had they left things? Why hadn't he bothered to check on her? Where had the days gone?

After what seemed like the passing of another day, Ted appeared. 'It's okay, Elise isn't in there and neither is your son.' Ted had assumed

Buddy was still at home, not knowing about the foster care. 'But there's someone in your sitting room. A man. It looks like he's shot himself. You're going to have to call the police.'

Nathaniel frowned. 'A man? I need to see who it is.'

'It's not good, lad. The contents of his head are decorating your sitting room wall.'

Nathaniel went through into the lounge, where he indeed found a very unpleasant scene. Even though he'd blown the back of his head out, the face was intact and Nathaniel recognised him immediately – Mark Paton sat in one of the armchairs, a bottle of whiskey at his feet, a glass by his left hand and a gun in his lap.

CHAPTER THIRTY-FIVE
THEN

After Nathaniel was questioned, he was taken to a cell where he eventually lay down on the hard, thin mattress and tried to get some sleep. DS Brand's voice ran through his head, the sound merging with the underlying smell he couldn't identify, beyond the harsh whiff of urine and disinfectant.

Due to exhaustion, he finally managed to get a short, concentrated window of sleep. He dreamt he was in a restaurant, quite an ostentatious place. It was full of square tables for two and they were all empty apart from one situated in the corner, where Ida was sitting waiting for him. She looked older, like she'd grown up since he'd last seen her. He knew it was her, but he couldn't be completely sure. There was a natural wave in her chestnut-brown hair, which was longer now, reaching her shoulders, and a sparkle in her brown eyes. But there was a sadness hovering in the background. She was wearing a long gown, a dress he hadn't seen before, a creamy white colour that reminded Nathaniel of a meringue – it had that kind of sheen to it. She was beautiful. Had always been beautiful. It reminded him of the better times they'd all shared, when the three of them would go to a posh restaurant to celebrate a birthday or a milestone and she would feel so grown up, excited to be going out for a proper meal. Nathaniel suddenly realised it was just the two of them – no Elise, Miles or Buddy.

In his dream, he found himself looking around for his younger son, who had begun to cry. He started looking under restaurant tables, but he couldn't find him. Nathaniel woke from this dream, convinced Buddy was crying, and it wasn't until he reached the door of his cell that the realisation of where he was hit him again. He lay back down, and when he drifted off again he found himself back in the restaurant.

The table where he found Ida was set for two and covered in a bright white tablecloth; glasses and cutlery were laid out, ready for a meal. Nathaniel pulled out the only remaining chair and sat opposite her. It was dark all around them apart from the light of a storm lantern on the table and the little glowing orbs coming from the passing cars he could see through the large windows.

'Dad?' she said, looking up to meet his gaze.

'Yes, sweetheart?'

'Dad?'

'Yes, sweetheart.'

'Dad?'

'Yes, sweetheart?'

And so it went, like a film clip being repeated over and over again, only this was fluid, playing out before Nathaniel without any editing or cuts. Then she paused briefly to lift the glass from the table, and out of her mouth came a marble, then another and another.

'Talk to me, sweetheart. Come back to us. Tell us what happened,' Nathaniel heard himself saying to her.

She just smiled, looked contemplatively at him, then rolled the marbles over the table cloth towards him.

'Dad?'

'Yes?'

'Dad?'

'Yes?'

'Dad?'

There Nathaniel stayed, within that dream, happy to continue their stilted conversation. His daughter's beautiful face didn't alter at all – it glowed in the soft lighting, and she looked relaxed and happy caught in her linguistic loop. He was used to seeing her with a crumpled brow, stress she had started accumulating soon after she was born – violating the fresh features he remembered her having when she had been an innocent baby – from constantly worrying about her mother; a child who had swapped roles with her parent. All that had gone from her face now, and there was a solid peace, a grounding within this dark room with its empty tables and gentle atmosphere, people walking past the windows but no one coming in.

Nathaniel could have sat there forever, the mysterious atmospherics having a similar effect on him as they were clearly having on Ida. When he became aware of consciousness he tried to weigh himself down, so he could stay in the room of sleep with her. Nathaniel could feel he was waking up because he had begun to wonder why he hadn't seen her in such a long time. Why had he missed her? Where was she? Within the realms of sleep, it had all seemed quite normal, that his little girl was alive there. That's when Nathaniel woke up suddenly, a sharp clarity slapping him around the face.

CHAPTER THIRTY-SIX

Dan was quite different to all the other participants – even more so than Gerald, the man with no shoes.

Dan was one of the oldest volunteers and trickier than anyone I'd ever spoken to. He intrigued me, which was why I continued to search out his company. If I struck up a conversation with him he would snap at me like an aggravated dog, and he would return to his reading material, which was either a book or a broadsheet. Some minutes later he would ask me a question about some particular topic he'd been thinking about. So, quite quickly, I gathered we would be doing things on his terms – to a point, or so I thought until we arrived at the end of the game.

Dan had been a professor of quantum physics and now worked at a boarding school teaching maths. He'd retired from the university many years ago, but had continued his work, filling his time with the activity he loved the most – teaching. There was no wife nor children at home to occupy him.

This all made for some interesting conversations during our train journeys together. We argued and clashed over our views and opinions about the universe, like two ball bearings caught in a drum. The relationship we were forming shouldn't have worked at all, but it did. During the times we weren't locked in heated debate, we were polite to one another, in a very British manner. We talked about philosophy, touched on politics, and I probably shared more of my views with Dan than anyone else I met.

'What would you say about yourself if you were dead?' I asked him one day.

'I'd have to think about it.'

'When you have, write it down.'

'Why are you so interested?' Dan folded the broadsheet he was reading and placed it on the seat next to him.

'It's a good exercise for observing the life you have had from the outside. Maybe you could use it on your students.'

Dan shrugged, and the following week produced a one-page obituary. We were on a night-time train; he was only ever on that one or the early-morning one. The boarding school was situated in the north and he stayed there for his tutoring during the week, travelling home on a Friday night. It was during a Friday night, on the day he handed me his obituary, that we played the game.

It was quiet, the air tepid, still and cool. We were in a single carriage on our own and there was silence as I asked him if he wanted to shoot himself or be shot.

We'd discussed the Suicide Watcher, talked about me in the third person. Dan's feeling was that all my participants must have wanted to die on some level and had, in fact, killed themselves.

There was no question that Dan was going to win the game, that he'd be like Magda – brave and fearless until the very end. Not just because of his beliefs and candid approach to death, but because he had never allowed anyone to take control of his life.

The moment Dan put the gun to his head he died. I found out later he had an aortic aneurysm, a little ticking time bomb, prone to exploding under stress. What a waste of life.

CHAPTER THIRTY-SEVEN
THEN

Elise had risen from her drug-induced slumber, feeling no better for it. How anyone thought she would feel refreshed having a few hours' rest was beyond her. Asleep she might be, but the drugs just stopped her waking up from the nightmares she was swimming around in. All she was left with now was a strong urge to take more drugs.

Elise was struggling to recall what was real. Flashes of the past few days and how she'd ended up drugged and in bed were just that – brief sparks of memory she couldn't grasp. Ida was dead and her father and husband, the two people she needed the most, had been arrested. On top of all that, DC Chilvers had shown her a photograph of the man Elise believed was Steven Bridges, only to be told he was actually James Caddy. Nathaniel's friend, a man she'd once had a drunken fling with. Nathaniel had been working away and Steven had arrived at their apartment unannounced, as he always did, knowing there was always a bed and a meal on offer. Elise had seen no problem with him staying while Nathaniel wasn't there, but on the second night, having spent the day together, one thing had led to another after far too many drinks. Elise had never told Nathaniel, and Steven had agreed it was best kept a secret. They were all guilty of telling lies.

Elise had been staying in her bedroom, away from everyone and everything, finding comfort in the darkness. Friends and family had called round with flowers and food, wanting to show support or find out more information, but Sonny was staying with her, and he and DC Chilvers had managed to politely send them all away.

Ida's clothes were being kept for evidence, but Elise was given a bag containing her jewellery. When Elise realised one of the diamond studs they'd bought for Ida's fifteenth birthday was missing, she'd become hysterical.

'There's only one,' DC Chilvers had told her.

'One? Found on her, with her? Where?' Elise had felt her anxiety creep from high to extreme.

'There was only one in her ear. The other is missing.'

Elise had become fixated on the earrings, wondering if one had come loose and dropped out in the violent struggle she so desperately wanted to erase from her head. Or had Ida given someone one of her earrings – a stranger – another scenario that caused more anxiety.

'How are you doing?' Sonny got up from the kitchen table.

Elise just nodded, not wanting to answer anything about her well-being. There was no well-being, she was dead inside; the charcoal remnants of a raging fire. She went to the coffee maker and poured herself a cup.

'Where is everyone?' she asked.

'You've spoken to Nathaniel?'

'Yes, the custody sergeant allowed him to make a call last night. Where's Ray?'

'Ah. I was hoping DC Chilvers had spoken to you about Dad. He was rearrested and we're waiting to hear if he's going to be charged.'

'With what?'

'He's been questioned about trafficking; he's in a bit of hot water.'

'What sort of trafficking? About your adoption?'

'Not sure . . .' Sonny was being vague. 'Nick and Karen called and asked about having the boys for an extra couple of days – they thought it would give you a break.'

Elise sighed, fed up with people telling her what to do with her children.

'It might be a good idea to leave Miles and Buddy where they are,' he said. 'You need a rest.'

Elise knew he was right. The thought of having Buddy back filled her with dread. She knew something bad had happened, and although she couldn't quite recall what, it had led to Nick and Karen taking the boys back to theirs.

'I guess so. We've got a funeral to arrange.'

'Have they released Ida's body?'

'Tomorrow.' Elise sipped her coffee, watching him.

'Is she being buried?'

'Oh, yes.' It hung in the air between them; a possible exhumation if it was needed. Elise was well aware that if Ida was cremated, they could lose vital evidence.

'Elise, what an awful mess.' Sonny scratched his head, just on his hairline near his temple, something he always did when he was nervous. 'Can we talk for a minute?'

'Sure. What is it?' Elise sat on one of the chairs and tucked her feet behind the legs.

'I just wanted to check everything was okay? That we're all right?'

'Why wouldn't we be?' Elise's heart was thudding in her chest, but she remained calm.

'The other day, when Miles was being interviewed.' Sonny reached across the table and took Elise's hand. 'You got very upset when I told you about the allegation.'

Elise looked at him, puzzled by what he was talking about.

'When a client accused me of touching her in a police cell? The one who stabbed her sister?'

'Oh yes, I remember.' Elise sighed. 'I don't want to fight, Sonny. You're my brother and I believe what you told me. Dad would have checked you out anyway, you can be sure of that. I was upset and overreacted.'

'I wouldn't hurt any of you, I can promise you that.' Sonny's pull on Elise's hand was slightly firmer than she felt comfortable with.

'All I want is to find out who murdered my daughter.' Elise held Sonny's gaze.

They were interrupted by the doorbell, and Sonny got up to answer it. DC Chilvers came in, windswept and rain-soaked.

'Where have you been in this weather?' Elise got up to pour her some coffee.

'I've been to Magda King's. Nathaniel suggested I speak to her about the parcels.'

'Parcels?'

'He was worried about some items he thought Ida was having sent to Mrs King's house, but it seems to be a misunderstanding.'

'I don't know what you're talking about.'

'It's fine, honestly. If I thought there was anything to tell you, I would.' DC Chilvers unzipped her coat and hung it on one of the hooks in the hallway. 'I do need to speak to you about something. Can we have a few minutes, Sonny?'

'Sure. I've got some work to do anyway.'

When Sonny had gone, she pulled a chair out and sat down.

'I'm not sure how much you know at this point, but I've just had a call from the station.'

'I know my father has been arrested but I don't know what for.'

'I haven't had an update about your father, he's still being interviewed. Has anyone spoken to you about your husband?'

'I spoke to Nathaniel last night. I know what he's been charged with.'

'And do you understand he might not be granted bail?'

'Yes. I know that.' Elise was tired of people talking to her like she was an imbecile.

'Elise, you do know Nathaniel's been charged with downloading illegal images?'

'I know all that. I completely understand why you've felt it necessary to charge him, but you've got it all wrong. It would appear that James Caddy has been using the name Steven Bridges for years. Nathaniel had no idea who he really was, and neither did I until recently. We know him as Steven Bridges. When James Caddy was first mentioned, we didn't know anyone was talking about Steven. My father certainly didn't tell us he was a patient, and why would he? We'd have been none the wiser, Steven was using a different name.'

DC Chilvers nodded, waiting for Elise to continue.

'Tolek and Nathaniel came up with this big idea that they were going to net some high-profile paedophiles and expose them in a documentary. I told them it would backfire. As soon as they'd started it and people began contacting them, they decided it wasn't such a good idea. Alex, my husband is not a paedophile. Have you spoken to Tolek?'

'He's at the station now, being interviewed.'

Elise handed DC Chilvers a cup of coffee. 'What's really pissed me off is that you've charged Nathaniel, which means all this will be in the papers tomorrow and we'll have social services knocking on the door. Didn't you think about the consequences of this for us, with all the media camped outside?'

'Elise, downloading inappropriate material is illegal, regardless of the reasons behind it. This has to be dealt with like any other crime. We arrested him so we could protect you and your children. We are concerned about his connection to James Caddy. You can see how this looks. If he's innocent, he'll be released.'

'Mud sticks though, doesn't it?'

'Your husband needs to stay in custody until the CPS make a decision and we rule him out of any involvement with James Caddy.'

'Let me tell you something about Steven Bridges. I don't think he killed my daughter.'

'Steven Bridges doesn't exist.'

'Okay, James Caddy.'

'How can you be so sure?'

Elise's eyes were wide with anger. 'Because he doesn't have any reason to.'

'There isn't always a "reason", for want of a better word. James Caddy is a very dangerous individual.'

'It seems to me that you don't know what you're doing. One minute, Alistair's being questioned, then Sonny, then my father. You'll be accusing Nathaniel of killing her next.'

'We haven't charged anyone yet. This is normal in any investigation.'

Elise frowned. 'So, do you think the attack was sexually motivated?'

'There are no signs it was, but we're not ruling it out. It's more likely that Ida knew something that someone didn't want anyone else to find out. You know the photographs were taken by James Caddy, that they'd been talking online?'

'She wouldn't have done that without telling me.'

'All teenagers lie, Elise, even straight-A students. She probably didn't tell you because she knew you'd worry. The content of the messages is strange. It's not your run-of-the-mill grooming, there's no flirting or sexual references that we usually find when an adult is making contact.'

'Well, James Caddy didn't have anything to do with my daughter sexually.'

'Do you know why he lied to you all about his identity?'

'Is that a rhetorical question? Are you being sarcastic?' Elise was a bit wired from the tablets she'd taken and knew she sounded aggressive.

'It's just a regular question.' DC Chilvers sipped her coffee.

'Steven – I mean James Caddy, sorry – didn't want me to know he was seeing my father. He was embarrassed.'

'It sounds like you and Caddy were close?'

'He was a good friend until he and Nathaniel had a fight when he was staying over one evening.'

'Do you know why that was?'

'It's not what Nathaniel thinks. What other innocent explanation could there be for a man watching a young girl sleep?'

It was a few moments before the detective answered.

'A father watching his child?' DC Chilvers leant back in her seat. 'You and he were intimate?'

'Once. A long time ago, and Steven – James – convinced himself Ida was his. She's not, because I did a test.'

'Did you ever tell him that?'

'I never got the chance. He vanished the night Nathaniel threw him out.'

'You remember the conversation we had about his paranoid schizophrenia and how he attempted to kill his stepdaughter?'

'I'm telling you, he didn't do it.' Elise banged her hand on the table. 'He didn't do it because he wouldn't do that to someone he believed was his daughter.'

DC Chilvers didn't speak. Elise had stunned her into silence.

'Steven – James, whatever you want to call him – wouldn't hurt one of his own,' she continued. 'I know that for sure. I'll tell you who you need to have a closer look at.' Elise drained her coffee cup and lowered her voice. 'Sonny John Travers.'

'We have our eye on him. Why are you suspicious?'

The front doorbell rang, and Elise got up from the table, ignoring the question.

'Do you want me to get that?' DC Chilvers asked.

'I'm quite capable of answering the door, Detective. My daughter has been murdered, I haven't had my legs cut off.'

Elise was expecting to hear Nathaniel or her father on the intercom but it was someone totally unexpected.

'Elise, please let me in. It's your mother.'

CHAPTER THIRTY-EIGHT
NOW

It was the last day of Ray's trial and Elise was nowhere to be seen – she was missing, along with the Patons' son Louis. A police search had been set up and it was breaking news on two major news channels. Elise knew they'd be even more hated than they were before. No one would understand what had happened in the house with Mark Paton. Instead of going where the media speculated, which was her mother's place in Norway, Elise went straight to the house where she had lived with her mother a few miles away. It was where Ingrid had survived her fate and taken a new path, one that didn't involve her daughter. Elise had spent years believing her mother might have been a victim of the Suicide Watcher, and it had all been an excuse, a way of covering up what had really happened. Ingrid simply hadn't wanted Elise, and Ray couldn't accept that. Elise had never told her father about the many times Ingrid had told her she would be better off without her, that she was an awful mother, or the time just before she'd faked her suicide when she'd taken a shot at the bathroom mirror while she stared straight at Elise's reflection.

At least one day a week, Elise remembered, Ingrid would spend the morning washing, curling and styling her hair. She had beautiful, long blonde hair that hung down her back like an elongated bird's wing. It was heavy and thick, curled at the ends where her rollers had kinked it. Whilst her hair was setting, she would work on her make-up and nails, and Elise would sit and watch her, mesmerised.

Elise would always ask her mother where they were going, and she always replied with the same answer. A special place, just for me and you. Ingrid would bathe her, pay more attention to Elise's hair and lay a dress out on her bed. It was as though they were dressing each week for an occasion, but they always went to the same place.

There was another ritual before they left the house, and Elise would observe this routine as she followed Ingrid around. Her mother would run her hand along the kitchen table, the backs of the chairs, straighten the post she'd collected from the doormat and laid on the hall table, wipe the already sparkling surfaces for the fifth time. Then, upstairs, Elise would trundle behind her, awkward in her uncharacteristic clothing, and she would watch her mother straighten the bedclothes and the toilet roll, and make sure the shower curtain was symmetrical within its folds. Ingrid would linger, hover in each room much longer than when they went out for a walk or to the shops. Elise loved these days, they were such a treat for her – her mother was so present in her company, so focused on the two of them. But there was an underlying finality that Elise didn't identify until she was an adult. She now believed her mother was preparing to kill herself on these occasions, and it wasn't lost on Elise that she was probably part of these plans, but Ingrid always changed her mind.

Ingrid would hold Elise's hand tighter than normal as they would walk, and she'd tell her stories of when she was little, her life in Norway, somewhere Elise had never been.

They always went to the same place: a large hall that looked like a castle. They would pay to go in and make their way along the roped path, up the stone spiral staircase, the wind whistling down its cylindrical shape – even in the summer it was cold.

At the top, Ingrid and Elise would stand on the lead-lined roof and stare out across the landscape. If she was feeling brave, Elise would look over the turret wall on to the courtyard below, or run to the other side and stare down at the moat.

Not many people stayed up there for long; it was very high and usually quite windy. When there was no one up there and they were alone, her mother would lean forward, spreading her arms out like an eagle as she stared out across the vast landscape, her beautiful hair blowing in the breeze. She would hold Elise up in her arms, telling her to look straight ahead and not down.

For whatever reason, only known to herself, Ingrid decided it wasn't going to be the place they would die. Elise now knew that's what the ritual was about. They were in their Sunday best ready for their last journey once each week, and for some reason that last journey would be postponed, and they would always visit one of Ingrid's friends instead and return home, destined to repeat the ritual the following week, her mother a little more sombre than when they'd first set out.

Their old house was boarded up; Elise hadn't been there for many years and she guessed Ray had been silently dealing with its upkeep. It was her house, Ray had transferred the deeds, but Elise couldn't bring herself to sell it.

The sweep of the road made the houses look like a hand fan; they were duplicates, but the one they had lived in stood out from the rest, and not just because of its untidy and unkempt appearance.

Staring at the house, Elise began to wonder if the neighbours had been told the same story her father had spun her, or if he and Ingrid had just fled without saying a word.

Elise used to walk past on her way home from school, and sometimes she'd go in. Her desperate need to sit outside that bathroom door would drench her in a heavy grief, making her nauseous. Elise wanted to re-enact those last moments with Ingrid; she'd kid herself into thinking her mother would reappear and she'd hear her whispering through the bathroom door again.

Elise had found her old door key, which she had kept all these years, the hardness of it in her hand now reminding her of the days she used to return here, filled with a nervous excitement that Ingrid might be there, having momentarily blocked out the memory of her death.

Entering the house now, Elise found all the curtains partly drawn, casting shadows across the walls and floor, as though they were respecting the dead. Elise looked down at Louis, who had been very quiet for the entire walk there, thumb barely in his mouth.

'You okay, little man?'

Louis nodded but didn't speak. Elise wasn't surprised; she had no idea what he'd witnessed, on top of the horror that had occurred in her own home.

Elise squeezed her eyes shut when she reached the top of the stairs, breathing in the scent of the woman who for so many years had lived in her head – her voice, her skin, her hair, her laughter. Ingrid.

Louis temporarily removed his thumb and spoke. 'I don't like it here.'

'Neither do I. Let's go outside.' Elise reached for Louis and carried him downstairs.

The same sliding doors were still in situ in the lounge at the back of the house. The latch had always been faulty when Elise was a child, and if she pulled the handle hard enough the door would slide open. It was always handy when she'd forgotten her door key while Ingrid was at work.

Elise sat on the low brick wall that surrounded the patio and stared up at the windows. The bathroom still contained the opaque glass with a leafy pattern, the same one from when they lived there. The entire place was falling apart; she hadn't realised the state of the building. It reminded her of the old psychiatric hospital where Ingrid had occasionally worked, where she'd first met Ray. The hospital was an old, stately pile with turrets, surrounded by walled gardens. Elise had loved to spot it in the distance through the trees whenever her parents drove along the main road. The place had begun to crumble and there were no funds to maintain it. Eventually it was condemned, all the patients moved to other facilities, and it was bulldozed – a cricket pitch built in its place. Elise had cried that day, at the lost memories the building must have carried.

Sitting outside, the sound of the gunshot still cracked around the back of Elise's mind, ricocheting like a ball in a squash court. It was similar to the start of a panic attack, and however much she tried to stop it, the sound would still grip her by the arms and shake her violently. When Ida was first born, Nathaniel had suggested moving to the countryside for some peace and quiet but there had been too many random noises tearing through Elise's head. The peace was interrupted with a bullet-sprayed atmosphere, crow scarers banging in the distance, and they quickly moved back to the city. To the constant noise which muffled their own and allowed them the peace Elise required within its never-ending hum.

Louis slowly stood up from where he had been sitting on the patio wall and crouched down in the grass, where he'd spotted something shiny. He picked it up and handed it to Elise, a glimmer of a smile on his face. It was a marble; the largest one in the set she'd played with. Looking at the swirl of colour running through it, that had always fascinated her as a child, brought back all sorts of memories.

Elise remembered how Ingrid had talked to her through the bathroom door, her voice followed by the clunk of the marbles, bouncing down the stairs to the hallway below. Her mother told her it would be over soon and not to get upset. *Don't cry sweetheart*; her voice had been faint and alien to Elise. It felt like forever, but of course it wasn't. 'Nothing lasts forever' was something Ingrid often said. Elise wondered now, in light of the fact it had all been a lie, how two people could be so cruel.

Elise had been determined to be a good parent, so unlike her own, and she'd fought against her conditioning for years until, one day, it had drifted around her ankles like mist that eventually crept up over her body, up to her nostrils, her mouth, like a hand suffocating her, depriving her of oxygen. Elise grappled with it, this ghostly murderer threatening to kill her, until she and it settled in a gripping embrace where she was supposed to take her last breath. A stillness descended, as it does around prey and its predator, but instead of drowning, Elise's head pierced the surface and a rush of air filled her lungs. She was swimming again. From that point on, death was not her enemy, but a very dear friend.

Later that day, Elise took Louis to the police station and handed herself in. She knew it was the right thing to do. Seeing the old house, realising she was turning into her parents, had made her see she needed to start at the beginning and embark on the long process of changing her life.

CHAPTER THIRTY-NINE

We had a connection, my quixotic paramour and me. And when I say that, I don't mean in the transparent, weak sense that deniers understand.

When I wasn't in her presence, I could feel her. I only had to stand still for a few moments and missing her threatened to suffocate me, and I could feel her heart beating along with mine, hear her thoughts, feel her emotions. I didn't need to be with her physically to know her presence was there. I would hear her silky, gentle whisper – 'I miss you' – and know she was standing outside, as I was, hand to her chest, releasing the ache for me that I had for her.

Talking about everything has made me think of her more than I have for many years. It has unsettled me, filled my head with her presence, something I had worked hard to suppress but I am now questioning why. Why would I force away an emotion that I should have just accepted? We agreed to desire one another forever, whatever happened, because it's an essential part of life. It makes you feel alive. The deniers desire something and then immediately focus on how they are going to make it happen, and then all too quickly satiate that need. To yearn for something and not have it is a wonderful experience. The desire becomes stronger and almost sickeningly unbearable, and it fills your every thought. I would spend hours thinking of her, about her, a deliciously beautiful experience. Wanting her but not always being able to have her. But I knew, as happens with most of my lovers, as different as she was, that we would become too familiar with one another and the inevitable would occur; we would grow bored of each other. I used to try to convince myself it wouldn't be like that, as though I had a separate voice in my mind pushing me to fulfil my needs. A bloody denier had invaded my head, that's what it felt like. But I kept a hold of the mystery, languished in the desire when I couldn't be with her, torturing myself in the most exciting way by allowing time to lapse between us, and the joy in her face when she saw me was even more worth it.

It wasn't long after that that I met my next volunteer. Colin had lived with his mother all his life until she died recently. He'd never been married, and his father had left when he was a small boy. It was all so evident, and no surprise to me when he told me all of this. He talked freely, openly, as though he was nervous, and I discovered it was his first time on a long journey without the company of his mother, or anyone else for that matter.

It always amazed me how people, during a chat on the train, will give away so many facts about themselves. It never took me long to find out where they lived, and I would follow and watch them for a few days, sometimes weeks. I knew Colin was going to be on the train the same time the following week, so I made sure I was there to meet him. During that second encounter, he gave me his address and an invitation to visit for a cup of tea.

Colin was going to die, I knew that immediately. There was no way he was going to save himself – he just didn't have it in him, everything was an effort. Life was an effort for Colin. When I visited, and he presented me with a report about himself, which was to be his obituary, he said it had made him feel more positive about his life. That said, he still didn't work out the game. The only joy for me was the brief brush with Death that was always apparent.

Surprisingly, when I went to Colin's funeral, apart from his mother's friends of course, there was a woman there who had travelled from France to pay her respects. Sabine had been his penpal since they were teenagers at school. Even though she had never met him, they had been writing to one another three or four times a month. She painted a very different picture of Colin. In her mind, he was a very successful businessman who was married with two children. Talking to her at length I discovered he had created a monumental fantasy about himself, had lived a different life in Sabine's mind, through her eyes. It was sad and poignant that Colin had felt he couldn't achieve all these things in reality. Sabine had been his lifelong love via letter, making her promises he could never keep over the years. Now? Sabine was free. She was grieving but already making plans she'd kept on hold for so many years while she waited for Colin, a man who didn't exist.

CHAPTER FORTY
THEN

You can't go anywhere when you're in the media spotlight, and Elise knew this only too well, having experienced it several times throughout her life. Ray had caused a few controversial stirs with the social experiments he'd been involved with and because he'd been on a popular chat show. The press was never far behind, waiting for one of the country's best-known psychiatrists to make a mistake or cause another scandal, and Elise had got used to dodging them.

Walking at night was a way to release the pressures the days brought her; especially now, with everything that was going on, Elise regularly wandered the streets in the small hours. It was an activity Nathaniel didn't approve of – he thought it was dangerous – but he was asleep during the many times she left the apartment.

In the summer months, she liked to walk barefoot, to feel the smooth, cool concrete beneath her feet. Summer was her favourite time of year because it was so easy for her to walk straight out the door – there was no need to find boots and a coat. After learning that her father had been charged with several counts of murder, including her own daughter, she needed this walk more than ever – her head felt like it was going to crack open. Nathaniel was still in custody; another family liaison officer, Greg someone – she couldn't remember his name – had arrived at the house; and her mother, Ingrid, was insistent they meet and talk, after Elise had slammed the door in her face when she'd made an unexpected appearance. In Elise's opinion, she'd survived this long without her, so why did she need her now? And on top of that, she was so very, very angry at her parents for the lies they'd told. Elise had immediately alerted DC Chilvers to Ingrid's presence outside their apartment, and she'd been arrested and taken into custody for questioning about trafficking offences. Elise was going to explode, and she needed some freedom.

It was harder to walk freely now with journalists camped outside the door and family liaison officers who watched your every move. Elise hadn't clicked with DC Chilvers, and thought she looked like she'd just changed careers from army officer to police sergeant, and lived alone in a starchy, minimalistic terraced house. Elise had neither the energy nor the inclination to make her feel welcome. In fact, she'd tried ignoring her in the hopes she'd go away. So, without telling anyone, Elise crept out of the apartment, making her way out of the fire exit at the back and down to the communal garden, finding relief in the cold damp grass beneath her feet, and then began to make her way to the park.

'Where are you going? It's almost midnight.' DC Chilvers fell into step next to Elise, startling her.

'I need to walk, clear my head. Why don't you go home for the night?'

'Not tonight. I have to stay here.' DC Chilvers was dressed in some sort of sports gear, as if she were about to go for a run. 'Mind if I walk with you?'

'Whatever you like.' Elise pulled up her hood and began walking her usual route through the park. Ignoring her abrasive manner, DC Chilvers kept pace beside her, shivering as she zipped up her fleece.

'How come you have to stay at ours?' Elise focused on the concrete ahead of her.

'When things get a little fractious during an investigation, we always stay overnight, make sure everything's okay, especially now Ingrid has turned up. It's a very volatile situation. That's why Greg is there as well. You've all had a lot of news to take in over the last few days.'

'In other words, we're all being observed.'

'Partly, but we're here for your safety too and to offer support.'

Elise stopped walking. 'I don't need protecting from my own family.'

'Well, we're just taking precautions. It's our necks on the line if we don't.'

Elise shoved her hands into the pockets of her hoody and continued to walk. 'Whatever you think. All I want to focus on is giving my daughter a proper send-off, celebrating her life, so we can try to remember all the good parts.'

DC Chilvers reached across and squeezed Elise's arm – the first time the police officer had shown any emotion since the investigation started.

'Do you think Nathaniel will be charged?'

'Oh, he's been charged already, but it looks like he'll be released on bail. CPS will want to make an example of him, but it'll be a slap on the wrist and a fine. There's nothing to suggest there was anything sinister behind his actions, it was just a stupid idea. There's paedophile hunters everywhere right now; people wanting to take the law into their own hands.'

'Can we please try to keep this quiet? I really don't want to see this in the papers tomorrow.' Elise picked up her pace. 'It'll be enough seeing my parents all over the news.'

'We're trying our best.'

'You have concerns about Sonny, don't you?' Elise stopped in front of a bench and sat down, and DC Chilvers joined her.

'I wasn't going to tell you this just yet, in light of the day's news, but you may as well hear it now.'

'Go on?'

'During an investigation, we sometimes do a familial DNA sweep, to see if a close relative matches any samples we've found at a crime scene to a perpetrator's relative who happens to be on the national database. It's a long shot but has been known to work. We've solved a couple of historical cases this way.'

'I'm not sure I understand.'

'Okay, for example, we nicked a young woman for assault recently and we took a DNA sample, which is standard practice. The following year, the cold case team ran a familial DNA sweep in connection with the rape and murder of a young woman in the early eighties. Samples had been kept but DNA testing wasn't available in those days. This young girl's DNA showed up as a match against some DNA taken from the murder scene. Scientists were able to tell it was a close relative of the young woman – it had to be her father. They took swabs from him and it matched forensics from the crime scene.' DC Chilvers sighed. 'Sorry, I'm telling you all this and it has no bearing on what I'm about to say.'

Elise waited patiently for the officer to get to the point.

'The familial sweep that was taken from the DNA samples we took from you and your family showed up some interesting results. You and Sonny are not related. He's not related to your father, either.'

'That can't be right, surely? My father knows his adoptive parents. They were patients of his. He arranged for the adoption of Sonny.'

'I'm sorry, Elise. The couple your parents gave Sonny to aren't called Travers. Their name is Danes and they moved to France with your brother soon after he was born. His name is Christian, and he lives in the south of France with his wife and child.'

Elise thought about what she'd been told. Lies, all lies, and she'd believed every one of them. Sonny may as well be her father's son, given they were both so well-practised at deceiving people.

'Didn't you have any idea when Sonny first arrived?'

'Of course I was suspicious, but you have to understand, my father has always taken people in, looked after them, rehabilitated them. During my childhood, there were various people taking part in my father's social projects – most of them went along with it for free bed and board. Does he know about Sonny?'

'We're not sure. If he does, he's not letting on.'

'So who is Sonny John Travers? Another one of my father's warped deals, I suppose?'

'We're still trying to find that out.' Elise could see DC Chilvers was holding something back, keeping the rest of the story from her.

'Should I be worried? I mean, I've got to sleep in the same house tonight.'

'No. Greg and I are there. We don't think he's a danger to anyone and your children are staying with your father-in-law. It's fine, try not to worry.'

'What, because he's a barrister he couldn't possibly be a criminal?'

'Not at all, but we've checked him out and there's nothing showing up that causes us alarm. I think he just wanted to be accepted – recovering alcoholic, shunned by his family, and he knew your father would help him. I guess he gleaned information about your brother from your father and it was an opportunity to spin the story you were all related because he wanted to stay.'

Elise knew DC Chilvers had an idea who he really was but couldn't tell her because it hadn't been confirmed.

'Well, what a fucking day!' Elise threw her arms in the air and stood up, ready to continue her walk.

'I'm so sorry about your daughter.'

'Yep, everyone is.' Elise breathed in, pain tightening her chest.

'We lost our second child.' DC Chilvers stared at the plaque on the bench. 'We called her Zoe. She died just before I was due. It was a difficult pregnancy. And, being dead, the little sod wasn't able to help me.'

It was a bad joke and Elise didn't reply, just pushed her hands deeper into the pockets of her hoody, the single-person-living-alone profile dispersing. She was shocked by this relative stranger's candid comments.

'I'm sorry to hear that, but I don't want to compare war wounds.'

'Not at all. I'm not looking for anyone's sympathy. All I'm saying is, it's shit. Losing children is one of the worst things to go through.'

'Nobody gets a medal for it.' Elise started walking again. She knew what DC Chilvers was trying to do – she wanted her to talk about her personal life, see if she revealed anything incriminating about Ray. The bastards had probably sent her for this reason – the copper who appeared to have the most in common with them.

'We tried for another soon after and spent months feeling petrified about it, really scared she wouldn't survive. It turns out we were right to be worried – she has cerebral palsy . . .'

'Why are you telling me all this?' Elise paused again, hoping the woman would get the message, and preferably leave altogether.

'No reason. Just think we have some things in common.'

The two women walked in silence, striding through the cold night air until they reached a sectioned area of the park that was filled with flowerbeds. Elise led the way through the gate. The clang of the metal on the frame felt comforting; it was her favourite place to go and think.

'I'm sorry about your children . . . that was cruel of me.' Elise sat down on a familiar bench; the inscription on the plaque screwed to the back read: *In Memory of Louise Tate and her beloved dog, Dot.*

'Forget it.' DC Chilvers paused to read the inscription. 'That's got to be a small dog with a name like that, right?'

'No. Dot was a border collie. It was a nickname; he was actually called Billy.'

'You knew them?' The detective sat next to Elise and stretched her legs out.

'Kind of. We used to chat briefly whenever we crossed paths. I first met her at the support group. The one set up for victims of suicide?'

'Yes, I know about the support group. What was her story?'

'Louise's sister committed suicide . . . Well, Louise believed she was a victim of the Suicide Watcher, but as you know, not every case was proven.'

'What made her think that?' DC Chilvers sat forward and rested her elbows on her knees.

'I'm not really sure. I think it was the content of the letter she left. Louise said it didn't sound like her sister. They often wrote to one another, so I guess she would know.' Elise stood up. 'Let's walk, it's cold.'

'What happened to Louise – why is there a plaque?'

'She visited the park every day for years and fought to keep it in good order. All the pathways, play areas, plants and flowers are because of her. It was her favourite place. She and Dot were killed while they were on their way home one day – up on the main road.'

'Goodness. Was it a car?'

'No. Believe it or not, they were hit by a cyclist. It was awful. To live such a long life and end it in that way.'

'That's terrible.'

Elise looked across at DC Chilvers, realising that for the last ten minutes or so, she'd forgotten who the woman was and her determination not to like her. 'I'm sure you've seen lots of tragedy in your job.'

'It's different when it's not personally happening to you. I can go home at the end of a shift. I take it you go to the group because of what you thought happened to your mother?'

'Yes. I don't really go anymore, just as and when I can. Nathaniel goes quite a bit. His mother committed suicide around the same time as mine.' Elise stopped herself, realising how normal her mother's supposed death had become to her. She couldn't get used to the reality that it had all been a lie. 'I certainly won't be welcome there now my father's under suspicion.'

'You don't believe he had anything to do with the cases?' said DC Chilvers.

'I don't know anymore. I guess I'm past caring.'

'How can you say you don't care about all those people?'

'Why should I? They all wanted to die – ultimately, they were all going to kill themselves. How else would they be coerced?' Elise could see DC Chilvers was shocked by what she'd said. 'My mother was always trying to kill herself; it's only because my father took her away from me that things were better for her. Eventually, she'll probably go through with it. Don't you think if my father was going to kill her, he would have taken his opportunity back then, when he would have got away with it?'

'Okay, you have a point there.'

'I know a lot about it. I grew up with a suicidal parent and it makes you bitter. Don't ask me to have sympathy for those victims when my daughter has been murdered.' Elise turned and began walking back the other way. She had suddenly become extremely agitated; all the events of the past week were beginning to pile up on her.

'What are you hiding, Elise?'

Elise stopped walking. 'My father didn't murder my daughter, I know that for sure.'

CHAPTER FORTY-ONE
THEN

When Elise arrived back at the house, she discovered a voicemail message on her phone from Magda, asking her if she could call round. Elise made arrangements to go to Magda's instead, because Elise didn't want to discuss anything in front of the two police liaisons and it was late.

They gave one another a stiff embrace. Elise and Nathaniel had made it clear they didn't want to see Alistair for the time being, and even though Magda had respected their decision, she didn't necessarily like it. Alistair had written to them both, apologising for what he'd done, but the knowledge that Ida had accused him of rape was still hanging over them, however much he denied it.

Elise took her muddy trainers off and followed Magda into the kitchen. Sitting on the table was a large parcel addressed to Ida.

'That looks slightly too large for the doll's house.' Elise pulled it towards her, noting the London postmark. 'When did it arrive?'

'This morning. I didn't know whether to give it to you.'

Elise raised her eyebrows, unimpressed with Magda's secrecy. They'd been friends for a long time and it seemed that everyone around her was lying. She carefully opened the package while Magda poured them both a drink. Inside was a photo album with a thick cover. Elise turned it over, looking for a note from the sender, but there didn't appear to be anything. She opened it and flicked through the pages, frowning at the familiar faces she couldn't quite place.

The pictures were of a family from the seventies – a guess on Elise's part, by the looks of the clothes and wallpaper adorning the house, the tinted colour of the photos. There were various snaps of happy occasions: Christmas, New Year, birthdays and anniversaries, all captured on a Polaroid camera, the pages crowded with too many photos, causing the adhesive to loosen the cellophane covering.

Lifting the book up to her eyes, Elise made a closer inspection of the faces of the people in the photos. One of them stood out more than the others; she assumed it was the mother of the family. The woman's face was so familiar.

There was something beneath the smile, a glimmer of corrosion – it was there, and yet it wasn't, like a hologram. If Elise looked hard it wasn't visible, but if she moved the book away, it became obvious.

'Do you know whose album it is?' Magda set two glasses of red wine on the table.

'Not sure. I don't suppose you have any idea who sent it?'

'No, it came through the post – there's no return address.'

'I can see that. But Ida was having post delivered here. Did she ever say anything to you about someone other than a company that was sending her parcels? An individual?'

'I don't think so.'

Elise pulled out a chair and sat down, examining Magda's face, waiting for her to say something else. Then she turned her attention back to the photo album.

It was of a family Elise completely understood – how she imagined hers would have become, if her parents had stayed together. There would probably have been a sibling, maybe two, and so their family life would have trundled on, they would have built a history, like the family in the photos.

Like Elise's own mother, the woman in the photograph seemed to be a loner, the odd one out. One of the pages Elise turned to stood out more than the others and she immediately flipped it back to take another look.

'What do you see in that photograph?' Elise turned the book round so Magda could see.

The page contained just one photograph – the ghosts of other pictures were apparent by the light-brown square marks – unlike the other pages, which were cluttered with snaps, elbowing one another, desperate to be seen. But this one was solitary and stood alone, regally proud, embracing its oneness. Elise thought it was obvious that whoever sent the book had wanted Ida to look at this particular page.

'It's a picture of a family playing in the garden.' Magda frowned.

'Look again.'

At first glance, the photo showed two children playing swing ball in the garden with what was presumably the dad. They looked happy, laughing, contorting their bodies as they all tried to reach for the ball.

Magda peered at it again, and after a few moments Elise knew she'd spotted the same thing she had.

To the left could be seen what looked like the back of the house where this family lived. Faintly at first and then more prominently, as Elise's eyes had adjusted, she had seen the mother staring through the glass of the large French windows. Not laughing, not smiling, just staring past them; lost to somewhere else, her eyes vacant like derelict swimming pools, devoid of water.

'I wonder who took the photograph, and did they know she was there?' asked Magda.

Elise hadn't thought about who might have taken the photo. She was disturbed by the expression on the woman's face, a similar look she'd seen on Ingrid's when Elise was a child. It was the truest, most organic photo amongst them. The lady through the glass. Then it dawned on

Elise who it was. The photo album was of Nathaniel's family. The lady behind the glass was Anna, Nathaniel's mother.

Elise and Magda chatted for a while, the atmosphere easing, as they drank wine and talked about the photographs. Elise declined a second glass and stood up to leave. Grabbing the album, she made her way towards the hall and then stopped abruptly, gasping when she stood on something sharp in the shagpile rug. Lifting her foot up, she stared at her thermal sock, then plucked something from it.

'What is it?' Magda tried to look over her shoulder.

'Nothing, just a small stone stuck in my sock. I went for a walk in the park earlier.' Elise pretended to throw it out of the front door as she was leaving.

When Elise was quite a distance down the road, she stopped under a street lamp and looked at the object she'd found in her sock. It was Ida's diamond stud earring. She breathed in deeply, knowing if she tackled Alistair about it he'd just say she'd given it to him. It left her wondering if the boy had done something extremely clever by confessing and retracting his statement, a double bluff made to look like a desperate act of love. She needed to talk to Nathaniel about it.

CHAPTER FORTY-TWO

Magda was slightly startled to see me standing in the reception area of the school where she held her group meetings. We'd been in contact over the years, but I hadn't mentioned I was going to pay her a visit. After the initial shock, she gave me a beaming smile and we quickly left the stark building to find a pub where we could get a drink.

It was 1981 when I first met Magda; 1982 when her brother, Gordon, took his last breath. Magda had come to see me at my firm of solicitors about getting some kind of legal advice on behalf of her parents. Gordon lived with them and they were his carers – he had a severe personality disorder and, as they were growing older, they had no idea how long they would be able to continue caring for him. They wanted to sign the house over to Magda in case anything happened to them, and money was needed to pay for psychiatric care. Halfway through the process, Gordon had an unfortunate accident and died. I knew immediately it had something to do with Magda. There were a few details that didn't quite add up when she talked about his death – the story lacked conviction and she kept repeating it like she was justifying herself.

Magda came to see me shortly after his death. We had a friendship of sorts, a connection I suppose. I could see someone who had once been confident and successful underneath the nervous veneer that now faced me. I imagined she had been quite ruthless at one stage; she owned a very successful insurance company that she had built up by herself. I decided to give her a little advice.

'When you talk to anyone about Gordon's death, it's best not to say too much about it, especially as you claim not to have been there when it happened. Too many details and you'll slip up. No one is that good a liar, not even me.'

It was a while before Magda answered me; she was caught in the dilemma of admitting it or pretending to be mortally offended.

'Don't worry, Magda, your secret is well and truly safe with me. You obviously had your reasons and I have nothing to gain by telling anyone. I'm just giving you a bit of friendly advice.'

'Gordon tried to kill my mother. My parents would never have him placed in an institution and their wishes were that I should take over from them when they passed away.' Magda stared into her lap as she spoke, and I could see tears dropping from her face. 'I hated him. He's my older brother and I couldn't bear to be near him. I didn't want to spend the rest of my life looking after him.'

'I'm really sorry to hear that. You should have discussed it with me, I could have helped you.'

'We would never have been free of him. He told my parents he would kill them one night in their sleep. They were so scared of him, too frightened to take control of the situation. I mean, who makes these diagnoses anyway?'

'Are you saying you don't believe he was sick?'

'Mad or bad, someone once said to me. Sometimes I just thought Gordon was evil. He should have been in prison, but he never committed a crime – not one he was charged with, anyway – so no one would lock him up. He was sent to a psychiatric hospital when he was seventeen because he exposed himself to a young boy in the public toilets and he was displaying worrying behaviour. After three months of being there, he worked out how to get a glowing report from the psychiatrists assessing him. He was released, and my parents had been stuck with him ever since.'

Magda sobbed, not something I suspected she did very often, and I didn't believe it was born out of guilt, but rather because I think she was relieved her brother was dead. Tears poured from her – for years of frustration, for the lack of support they'd had in dealing with him.

'Do you know what Gordon used to do to me when I was a child? He used to make me touch him, do things to him.' I clenched my jaw and handed Magda a tissue. 'The thing I couldn't ever get used to was the assault within the assault. The perverted things he asked me to do were bad enough, but it was what he did afterwards that gave me nightmares. He would spit in my face. It made me wish he was dead. I should have been grateful he never touched me, but I wasn't; he made me feel so disgusting, I was repulsed by him.'

'When I said I could have helped you, I didn't mean from a legal point of view.'

Magda and I became friends after that. The only participant I hadn't met on the train, we shared a secret – one she didn't want revealed. Aside from her despair, Magda had been quite calculated about Gordon's death. Her happiness came from seeing her parents living their lives again. I liked that kind of spirit.

Many years had passed since I'd seen Magda, and even though she'd aged, there was a self-respect in her eyes that had been missing before.

'To what do I owe this pleasure?'

I laughed at this. 'A pleasure, is it?'

Magda smiled rather nervously, and I realised my visit had unsettled her. After all, the last time we'd seen each other, I'd offered her a handgun.

'Don't worry, it's nothing serious. I just wanted to tell you that whatever happens over the next few months, I won't be revealing anything about your past.'

'I don't understand. What's going on?' Magda glanced around, making sure no one was listening.

'Nothing. It's just time for me to tell the truth.'

CHAPTER FORTY-THREE
NOW

Elise emerged from the taxi feeling solid – whole – for the first time since she could remember. This was the first day of her life, the therapist had said, but to Elise, that had been the moment she walked into the rehabilitation centre. A few days before she'd left, Elise had sent her father a visiting order at the prison, and he'd returned it, agreeing she could come and see him. That was the first place she'd gone before coming here to his house.

Elise sighed, recalling the thin man with the sunken eyes she'd just sat opposite and tried to have a conversation with. It shocked her that someone could change so much in three months.

It was the first time she'd seen Ray since he'd been sentenced and found guilty of four counts of murder and six counts of human trafficking. He hadn't been charged with Ida's death. The only evidence had been blood spatter on his sweater, and a pathologist said the spray was from no more than an exhalation of breath as Ray lifted his granddaughter up from the floor, desperate to keep her alive. The media were still speculating about James Caddy, but there was no evidence to prove he'd even spoken to Ida that day, and the CPS had decided the case didn't hold enough weight to stand up in a court of law.

Ray had barely talked to Elise – only small talk and to tell her how proud he was of her sobriety. Every word he uttered carried such a heavy sadness that Elise thought her heart would break. It wasn't self-pity, it was acceptance of his fate, of what lay ahead and where he would end his days. To her astonishment, Ingrid had respected Elise's wishes to leave her alone. She just wasn't ready to talk to her mother and wasn't sure she ever would be. She was surprised Ray hadn't mentioned her during the visit.

Elise had decided when the visit was over that she would spend her time building an appeal for a retrial. Ray was unethical in his approach to things, but her father wasn't a murderer, that she would prove.

Chemicals lingered in the cold air as Elise walked into the hall of her father's Victorian villa. It felt so different now; the house echoed as though it had been emptied – but, of course, everything was where it always had been. It was devoid of Ray's presence, and that was why it felt so lonely.

Bracing herself, Elise clasped her fingers around the large crystal-shaped door knob which led to his office. She needed to go in there, feel what it was like, the remnants of an atmosphere. Elise turned the handle, and just as she began opening the door, she closed it again. She wasn't ready, couldn't face it just yet.

Instead, Elise made her way upstairs. She wanted to look in the rooms where they had all stayed during that terrible time that felt so long ago now. There were three large bedrooms apart from Ray's, and Elise was surprised to find all the beds neatly made and everything tidy apart from a thick layer of dust. After Scenes of Crime had finished, they'd arranged to have the place cleaned but she'd imagined they wouldn't bother, remembering all the police dramas she watched, where they ransacked houses, leaving them in a shambles.

Elise crept around, feeling like Goldilocks, like she shouldn't be there. It was an odd feeling; she had always felt so at home in the large old house. Something wasn't right, she could feel it.

Elise's phone began to vibrate in her pocket. It was Nathaniel calling.

'Where are you?'

'Just at Dad's checking on everything. I'll be home soon.'

'I said I'd pick you up from the prison; I've been sitting outside for ages. I was getting worried.'

'I'm fine. Just need a bit of time to myself and then I'll come home. Okay?'

'Elise. I actually called to tell you something. It's the day of the inquest.'

Elise had to think for a few seconds.

'The Patons?' Nathaniel sounded shocked she hadn't remembered.

'Oh, yes, yes, sorry. My head's all over the place today.'

'Sure. It was a few months ago. Well, it's as we expected. Murder, suicide.'

'Okay,' Elise said.

There was silence for a few moments.

'I'll let you go. Will you call me when you want picking up?'

'Yes. Give me twenty minutes, half an hour.'

'Are you sure you're all right there on your own?'

'Don't be silly. I'm just going to have a wander round and then I'll be ready.'

Elise hung up, not wanting to be suffocated, needing to hold on to everything she'd learnt over the past few months. She stared at the phone, thinking about the Patons, the sadness of it all. Poor little Louis, who had been adopted by a new family, and her own two sons.

Mark Paton had found the contract her father had drawn up for his wife Jane, where he'd offered to help her set up adoption for Louis when he was born. Mark had come to the conclusion that Ray had swapped

Louis for Buddy in aid of some weird social experiment, mainly based on information he'd read in the tabloids. The fact was, Jane had been so distraught about having a baby, a reminder of being raped, that she'd asked Ray to arrange everything and find a suitable set of parents for Louis. When the baby was born, she'd changed her mind, having bonded with him so strongly. Foolishly, Jane had filed the contract along with all their paperwork and forgotten about it. Elise couldn't help feeling partly to blame for their deaths. If it hadn't been for her neurosis, she wouldn't have had the crazy idea Buddy wasn't hers.

The obsession with the Patons had started when she'd seen Jane arrive at Ray's when she happened to be there one afternoon. Elise had peered at the newborn as she had every baby she saw, so convinced the one she rocked to sleep in his Moses basket wasn't hers, and had thought she was staring at her real son. The slight breeze of his baby smell as Jane walked past had convinced her that Louis belonged to her. But of course, he didn't.

Elise's phone began to ring just as she put it back in her jeans pocket. She tutted, thinking it was Nathaniel again, and then saw DC Chilvers's name on the screen.

'Hello,' Elise said quietly, not sure why she was keeping her voice low.

'Elise, where are you?'

'What's wrong?'

'We need to see you and Nathaniel. When will you both be at home?'

'I can be there in about an hour. Nathaniel is picking me up.'

'Where are you, Elise?'

'At a friend's. I'm leaving soon. Just having a coffee. Nathaniel should be at home now if you want to call round and see him. I can get a taxi, it's no problem.' Elise bit her lip. She had been told not to go to her father's alone – Ida's killer was still out there somewhere.

'We're sitting outside yours now, he's not here.'

'Tell me what's going on,' Elise said, wanting to know but not wanting to know.

'We need you to come home now, Elise. We've sent out a warrant for Sonny's arrest.'

'What for?' Elise could feel the tiny hairs on the back of her neck rising.

'We have new information about Ida's death. Sonny has a motive.'

Elise listened to what she had to say and ended the call, sitting down on the top of the staircase. It had been Sonny all along, and Elise had known that deep down – she suspected they all had. Sonny knew that too; he'd distanced himself from them all the last few months, moving nearer to his estranged wife and children, and the reason had seemed quite obvious when she'd been in rehab, though then she would find herself doubting it again. He had been a part of their family for so long – they trusted him, he was so familiar to them – that they couldn't see what was going on right in front of them. Elise would wake up thinking one thing and go to bed with an entirely different opinion.

Before Elise left, she went into Ray's bedroom and pulled back the quilt on the bed – delaying, not wanting to find out anything else, pausing time. Leaning forward, she pressed her face into his pillow, and her chest filled with so much pain she thought it would shock her heart into stopping. Elise ran her hand along the mattress as if she expected it to be warm. Lying down on the bed she turned on to her side and, pulling her knees up to her chest, released some of the emotion she had pent up. When she finally calmed, she swung her legs over the side of the bed, pulling herself up to a sitting position, her body heavy and sluggish. An old wallet of Ray's lay on his bedside table. Elise picked the wallet up and smelt the warm, earthy scent that always reminded her of her father. Opening it, she pulled out the pile of photographs he had tucked into the plastic picture holder. The first one was of Elise, and Ida when she was a baby. She let out a sob so loud she thought she was going to be sick. The rest of the photographs were of her, Nathaniel,

Ida, and a couple of Miles and Buddy. The last photo was the exception. It was a picture of two women she recognised. They were laughing, and it looked like it had been taken in a passport photo booth. One of them was Ingrid, and the other, she realised after a few moments, was Nathaniel's mother, Anna. She recognised her from the photo album, the one her mother had sent to Ida.

While Ida had been studying the family tree and sneaking into Ray's office, she'd discovered some secrets, one being that Ingrid was alive and living in Norway. Ida had talked Magda into agreeing she could have some post delivered there, although Elise hoped that Magda hadn't known who the mail was from. Her mother and her daughter had been writing to one another in secret for almost two years, and Elise had never known. It had made her feel desperately sad.

Elise looked at the photograph now and couldn't understand why Ray would keep a picture of Ingrid and Anna in his wallet, but then he had done a lot of strange things. Ingrid looked so happy in the photo; Elise had never seen her like that before, and guessed that was Ray's reason for keeping it.

A door closing downstairs and the sound of footsteps made Elise sit up. She hoped it was Nathaniel, that he hadn't been delayed talking to the police. She stayed where she was and held her breath as she dialled Nathaniel's phone, but he didn't answer. Elise then called DC Chilvers's phone, but she didn't answer either, so she whispered as quietly as she could, telling her where she was on her voicemail.

'You can come down, sweetheart, I know you're up there.' Elise heard Ingrid's voice – recognising her Norwegian accent immediately. She walked out of Ray's room and stopped on the landing. Her mother was standing at the bottom, a gun in each hand.

'Come with me, Elise.'

CHAPTER FORTY-FOUR

If you can be talked into killing yourself, how can it be murder? Ask yourself how precious your life is to you if you so easily give it away. It was a game, a simple puzzle I formulated. Magda was one of the few that worked it out.

There was a get-out. Isn't there always?

Think about why some people survive a fall from a high-rise or a car accident, and others don't. It's simple. They're making a choice. Some people resign themselves to there being only one pathway. The glass half full doesn't just apply to the small events, it is relevant in every area of our lives.

Imagine the police have arrived at your door to tell you a loved one has been in a car accident. Ask yourself if you are the kind of person who presumes they are dead or who assumes they've been taken to hospital.

I never told any of my participants they were going to die at that very moment. I just gave them two options: shoot yourself or be shot. One gun was loaded, the other was empty. If you were brave enough to opt to shoot yourself, I would pass you the empty gun. It's as simple as that, and yet it was rare that anyone worked it out.

I know one thing – there is a pattern within the folds of life, a hidden puzzle, but I haven't worked it out yet. It reminds me of the games in the newspaper supplement; they're commonly known as word searches. I have wastefully whiled away time on these frivolities by working out a strategy for solving them. There is a pattern that runs through these puzzles which makes them so simple to work out and saves time on searching for the words, and yet deniers will follow the trickier route, the one their ego dictates. Because, you see, we are told 'word search', and a robotic brain will do just that – search for the words. We try for the quickest time in which to find the words, but sadly, not in a strategic manner.

The reason why? There is this sickening desire to win, to be the best, to smugly know we are cleverer than anyone else. But at what, and who is it who sets these levels?

And yet people stumble through life without fulfilling their purpose, the calling which is so obviously put in front of us from birth.

Anything audible, aesthetic, oral or sensory passes by the deniers, unheard, unseen, untasted and without feeling. I've sat in a cab in the middle of London and watched empty humans passing one another in the street, existing but not present. Where are they? Lost somewhere in the past or the future, stuck in some pathetic memory or apathetic visualisation that rarely comes to fruition. The difference is, my desires serve me and me alone. I don't need to feed my ego. I am my ego, it is one and the same.

Should you be unfamiliar with my work, my participants are what society refer to as my victims. No one is a victim, it's an impossibility. A whimsical view from those who wish to heal others, to sympathise, empathise. The peeling away of these layers reveals a mass of rotting guilt.

A psychiatrist once asked me if I would like to possess these traits, if I had ever sat quietly and tried to imagine what they were like. I did not respond but I did give it some deep thought. Then I began to wonder if this counted in any way, the fact that I took the time to think about whether I wished for these traits. It's probably the closest I'll ever get to your superficial friends, empathy and sympathy. The question I began to ponder on was why he felt he needed me to explore this. What purpose did it have? For there is always a purpose, you can be sure of that. Even the so-called altruistic are squeezing their egos.

The conclusion I came to? That most people have a compulsion for us all to conform to what they want us to be. To fit in, to line up with the deniers, be someone they most clearly are not. Don't make a fuss, don't stand out from the crowd, eat your food, go to work, come home, and above all, shut up.

I've been questioned a lot about my ego, asked if I think I have an alter ego. Put another way, do I have multiple personalities? There are many facets to me and I am made up of many shards. I do not have to talk to or pretend to talk to someone else in order to satisfy desires or needs I am afraid to express. That, to me, is multiple personalities. The reality, for me, is that I am true to myself, at all times. To contort one's self involves the ego because you are displaying what you want others to see, what you believe to be the correct way to conduct your life.

Do I suffer from mental health issues? How can I, when I live the life I planned? There is no crack in my armour, I have no need to indulge in any frivolous activity – time is all too precious. Mental illness is sickness of the mind caused by the constant overwhelming battle one has with one's essence, beliefs and purpose.

When will you ever learn? There isn't time to wonder about things we can never understand; issues that are an extension of our surroundings. Live what's in your head, without thought or contemplation. There is a magnetism that leads us to the right way, the pushing and pulling of a life force.

CHAPTER FORTY-FIVE
NOW

As soon as Nathaniel saw the missed call from Elise on his phone, he knew there was something wrong. Every time he called her mobile it went straight to voicemail. Nathaniel drove round to Ray's, an acidic nausea scraping his throat. He just had the feeling this was it; there was a finality hanging in the air amidst his panic. Nathaniel pulled into the driveway praying Elise had decided to get a taxi home.

Running up the steps leading to Ray's front door, Nathaniel attempted to push the door open, but it was locked on the latch. His hand hovered over the bell as he pressed redial on his phone, and that's when he heard the striking sound of a gunshot splintering the bleak atmosphere. It was so loud, Nathaniel thought the sky was collapsing around him and he ducked briefly. The birds seemed to have been shocked into silence and the traffic sounded like it was passing in slow motion. This slow motion that had appeared around him suddenly accelerated as Nathaniel bashed at the door while he called 999. There was no way of getting around the back – the high gate was locked – so he ran along the front of the house to see if any of the windows were unlocked, trying to find a way in, then back up the steps to the front door. Sirens burst into the atmosphere like fireworks, and Nathaniel seemed to zone out. He didn't need to be told his wife was dead. And then he heard the click of the front door opening and there stood Elise, her face ashen, hair dishevelled. Clasped to her chest, her fingers splayed like a spider, was a handgun.

Elise's eyes stared right through Nathaniel; her mind appeared to be lost in another world as she lifted the gun to her head, pulling the trigger before he had a chance to stop her.

Later that night, after finally arriving back at the house, with the ridiculous idea he would sleep, Nathaniel got up from the sofa and went in search of the letters that he'd found in Ida's doll's house. Nathaniel hadn't shown them to Elise; he'd been so frightened of her reading them, scared the content might push her over the edge, throw her back into the addiction that had practically destroyed them all. Nathaniel opened one but decided to put it back in the envelope. He left them on the kitchen table, for Elise to read when she was ready. He had to let go, he was holding on to her too tightly. Nathaniel began to wonder if it was why she had always had a compulsion to end her life – because he was suffocating her.

There was an old boat moored in the river at the bottom of the garden when they'd bought the house, and Elise had made Nathaniel replace it, like for like, when it had practically sunk into the muddy silt of the riverbank. When they'd first moved in, they'd spent a few evenings on it, talking about their plans together, trying to weave a new life so that they would have something to live for, a reason to keep going for their remaining children.

Sitting out in that boat now, the bright light of the moon illuminating everything around him whenever the dark, silver-edged clouds crept past, Nathaniel wondered if he had died and was in some kind of limbo he couldn't escape. The one small hope he had, the one little spark that had kept him going, was that his sons might come home soon. There hadn't been a successful adoption for Buddy, and Miles was still with temporary foster parents.

As the clouds parted company again, Nathaniel looked up to see a figure standing on the riverbank beside him. He reached out and grasped Elise's hands, steadying her as she climbed on to the boat.

'How are you doing?'

'Okay . . . I think.'

The boat abruptly stopped swaying as they sat down on the wooden seats. It was a long time before either of them spoke again, but then the questions Nathaniel needed to ask her seemed to be spilling from his mouth.

'Did you know that gun was empty?' Nathaniel held her gaze.

It was a few moments before she answered. 'No . . . I'm sorry, I really am so sorry.' Elise reached forward and grasped his hand.

'Have you any idea what that was like for me, Elise?' The vision flashed before his eyes again, as he was sure it would do for years to come.

'I'm truly sorry. It was everything all at once and I just lost it for that moment . . .'

'I know . . .' Nathaniel couldn't stay angry with her; there was a huge part of him feeling a massive wave of compassion. 'I need to ask you something . . . did you kill Ingrid?'

'No. No I did not.' Elise stared into the water, avoiding Nathaniel's gaze. 'Maybe I wish I had.'

'When did you realise who she was? God, you must have been so scared, Elise.'

'Not really.' Elise let go of Nathaniel's hand and allowed her fingers to dance around in the water. 'I started to have an idea when DC Chilvers called and said they'd discovered some new information about Ida's death and were looking for Sonny. DC Chilvers had mentioned Benjamin Tilney to me on the phone, the little boy who had disappeared from the farm when his father was murdered . . .'

Nathaniel nodded, remembering he'd read the article and thought it was strange the body of the boy had never been found.

'DC Chilvers told me Ingrid had changed his name to Sonny after she'd taken him away the night she'd shot his father, John – her last suicide victim. She took the little boy back to Ray's house and told Ray what she'd done, begged him to help her. Ray knew of a couple desperate for a child, and he arranged an adoption of sorts for Sonny . . . or Ben. That's when they faked her suicide and Dad took Ingrid back to Norway. That's how much my father loved her.'

'It's just unbelievable,' Nathaniel said.

'I found a photograph of both our mothers in Ray's wallet and I started to piece a few things together, although I didn't know for sure. I just remembered odd things from when I was a child – she often travelled on the train but never said where she was going, I used to find the train tickets in the bin when I got home from school, and I knew she had a gun because she'd shut herself in the bathroom with it on more than one occasion. I could hear her talking but can't recall the content, apart from the odd sentence. I didn't really know the truth until she stood in front of me holding two revolvers.'

'What made her think Sonny did anything to Ida?'

'She worked it out when Ray visited her and told her what had happened when he'd found Ida. She wanted Sonny to play the game; she knew he'd fail and ask to be shot. Then she turned the gun on herself.' Nathaniel could see Elise's eyes glistening with tears.

'I'm so sorry, it's just awful.' Nathaniel reached out for her hand.

'Sonny was already dead when I got there. Ingrid made me go into Dad's office, and Sonny was just sitting there, behind his desk, gun lying on the floor.' Elise raised two fingers to the side of her head. 'Bang.'

'Don't do that, Elise.'

'All she said to me was he got what he deserved. Then that was it. Can you believe that's all my mother would say to me after all these years?'

'Try not to dwell on it. You're safe and that's all that matters.'

They sat silently for a while, taking it all in. Elise was biologically related to the person who had caused all this pain, to so many people, and they'd never known.

'There are some letters from Ingrid on the table. I found them in Ida's doll's house.'

'The ones Ingrid wrote to Ida?' Elise asked.

Nathaniel shifted uncomfortably in the boat, making it sway. 'No. They're from Ingrid, posted to Ray, although she hasn't addressed them to anyone in particular.'

'What's the content?'

It was a couple of moments before Nathaniel answered; he knew that Elise would work out the truth once she'd read them. 'They were about her victims. I think Ida probably found them in Ray's office, they were hidden in the roof of the doll's house.'

'Dad hasn't mentioned them. Why didn't you hand them in to the police?'

'You'll see why when you've read them. I think you'll understand it all better.' Nathaniel squeezed Elise's hand. 'Will Ray be released now?'

'DC Chilvers said he'll probably have to serve the rest of his sentence for trafficking, and then the courts will decide on a sentence for aiding and abetting. He certainly won't be serving the sentence he originally received.' Elise squeezed Nathaniel's hand, letting him know she was coming back to him, the way they used to be. 'You know, I always knew he hadn't hurt Ida. He would never do that. It was obvious it was Sonny, when you think about it.'

'It was too obvious, actually. And when you're that close to someone, you can't see it . . .' Nathaniel fell silent, his thoughts returning to the letters.

'He wanted to hurt Ray and Ingrid,' Elise said, 'and didn't believe the justice system would be punishment enough. Because Ida had been following the family tree, she'd worked out Sonny wasn't related to them and confronted him about it. My poor father.' She shook her head.

It wasn't the right time to point out that her father had lied to Elise for most of her life, and that Nathaniel was suspicious that Ray had known everything – that he'd had something to do with all the other victims. He was struggling to believe one person could coerce anyone into a game that ended in death.

'Ray really loved her.' Elise seemed to be talking to the sky.

'What makes you say that?'

'I just don't think he could let her go, but he couldn't be with her.'

Following her gaze upwards, Nathaniel couldn't help feeling a tug in his own stomach, her words ringing true with their own situation.

Sensing she didn't want to talk about it anymore, Nathaniel nodded, knowing she would tell him when she was ready. For now, he could only speculate what had happened in Ray's office earlier that day between Elise and Ingrid, or exactly what had happened to Ida on her last birthday, that 29th of February, the day that shouldn't exist. His head was spinning with all the events of that day, and he'd barely had time to think about any of it in detail. He was sure more revelations would come to light over the following months.

Before Elise went back to bed, she handed Nathaniel a letter. 'You should read this – it'll help you. Ingrid gave it to me before she died. I'm sorry about your mother.'

Nathaniel embraced her while she sobbed.

'You should have this too.' Elise pulled a small photograph from her back pocket. 'I found it in Ray's wallet.'

Once she had gone to bed, Nathaniel sat down to look at the photograph and read the letter she'd handed him. His mother and her lover, Ingrid – the only picture he'd ever seen of Anna looking genuinely happy.

The letter Elise had given him wasn't postmarked like the ones he'd found in the doll's house. Instead, *Elise* was written across the front of the envelope. Nathaniel took a deep breath and pulled the folded paper from its sleeve, and began to read.

Dear Elise,

Sometimes I wonder if I was born at the wrong time, as if my conception could have been prevented. I imagine my mother was waiting to jump off a moving train and kept missing the moment, and the result of this hesitation was catastrophe. She had an affair with a married man; that's how I know I was produced at the wrong time. My mother's sins became tangible in the form of a person. Me.

This misplacement has continued. It has to, you see, because once you are displaced, everyone else is out of kilter. And then I had this beautiful little girl with such a startling heritage I wondered often if I could shunt us all back into line by eradicating my physical self. Ray and I would often discuss my mental fracture. That's how the lines appeared on his handsome face; they are full of the perplexities inside my head. I know what's wrong with me, or maybe it's what's right with me. He's become too involved and that's not how it was supposed to be. I don't need someone to find a solution, I just need to understand myself in a better way.

Everything changed when you appeared, and it was then that I felt like two separate people. I've been apologising for my presence since I can remember, tentatively moving through life. And I say presence instead of existence because it's quieter, more of a whisper. A shush, a nervous cough, an uncomfortable clearing of the throat, that's what I represented as a child. Now I feel solid, louder, more alive, the constant need to apologise for my existence has lifted but then I had this fragile little person to care for, nurture, and I just didn't know how. My little Elise, a tiny stranger, a small misnomer.

This is where I am, where I know I am, and finally, in the place where I should be. Now. I could tell you this is the end, but it isn't, it's simply just the beginning. Perhaps it's a difficult concept for you to grasp, but you can, if you just look beyond my old frame, past the wilted skin, the strained eyes, grey hair. My soul will move on to a new life and I will start again, in a new guise, with the same intention. That's all any of us can hope to do, I think.

We met in the psychiatric hospital, your father and I — that's where it all began. He was a newly qualified psychiatrist, due to get married to a woman he met at university. I was the legal representative for some of the patients and their families. It wasn't supposed to happen — I know everyone says that — but it wasn't. Life is like that; we never learn to embrace the unexpected, always afraid to peer around that corner, in case what we see doesn't meet our expectations, living life tentatively on tiptoe.

The game had started well before we met, although there were no significant participants at that time, no victims as you like to call them — just potentials. You'd have thought we were complete opposites — his ideas were straight from a textbook — but he wasn't so very different to me once he loosened the restraints of his university indoctrination. Questions were asked, conversations started, and he shifted from being my travelling companion to a possible participant, to very quickly becoming my lover. Shortly after this I decided never to cross that line again, but of course 'never' is a ridiculous word. There is always a shift, a tilt in one's footing – position, if you like – within the confines of a relationship. And being a psychiatrist, it was within him to want to find a solution to what he saw as a problem. Therein lies the conflict, because there was no problem from my point of view. He helped me, there was no doubt about it, and it was something I needed, entirely due to the type of world we live in. My ideas were too advanced, beyond most people's comprehension. I'm not in any way suggesting my mind is or ever has been on any level of genius, but my notions for this period of time were too radical and he understood that. I was, had always been, out of time, out of sync, out of kilter with the rotation of the earth. Because, quite simply, I wasn't supposed to be here. My mother wasn't being cruel when she said that – she was absolutely right, one just doesn't realise in what capacity, the context in which she was saying it. Displaced, that's what I was. And once you accept you're dislocated from everyone else, life becomes a whole lot easier.

It was simpler for me to be dead and I did intend to kill myself that day, I felt so guilty about that little boy, but in the last few seconds before I fired the gun, my nerve was lost. Maybe it was because I wasn't ready; I had more to do in my life. Who knows. To anyone who knew me, I died that day in the bathroom and no one ever knew who I was. I wasn't prepared to alter, not for anyone, not even for my own flesh and blood. It's in you, the essence of who you are. What is the point of pretending to be someone you're not? It would surely be an insult to your existence. If it were the case for me, I may as well have been one of those people who were shot. Well, I would have, there's no doubt about it. A moment of weakness, grieving for my soulmate, my quixotic paramour, Anna. And I wanted to punish, to hurt myself. It warmed me to discover you married Anna's son, Nathaniel.

Dear Elise, you were always going to be better off with one fully functioning parent, and my absence offered you that. I shared something with you almost every day of your life. I was always there, in the background, you just couldn't see me. It is so important to me that you understand all this. I've never cared until now. I am aware this is all quite possibly too late.

I am signing off now as your mother, as Ingrid, fellow anonymous, a no one, some nemo, *the Suicide Watcher.*

CHAPTER FORTY-SIX
THEN

The rain began to sheet down as Ida stomped across the playing field, towards her grandfather's house, her coat pulled over her head to protect her hair. She thought Alistair had wanted to meet her to apologise, and now she was furious with him.

'Ida!' Alistair shouted after her. 'Come on, we can sort this out!'

'Leave me alone, Alistair!' Ida turned in his direction but carried on walking. 'Seriously, just leave me alone.'

Alistair stopped mid-stride, weighing up if he should follow her or return to the cricket pavilion. He chose the latter.

A few days before, they'd been giggling at YouTube videos in her bedroom, and now everything had changed. As Ida had told him, in half an hour he had destroyed their relationship. Their friendship had shifted into something else, and lying on the bed together after school, as they had done for years, meant something else entirely. Now he felt guilty, even though he wasn't sure he'd done anything wrong. Had he done anything wrong? They'd started kissing and it had quickly escalated into them both being naked. He hadn't heard her say no, didn't remember putting his hand over her mouth, and couldn't recall holding her wrists above her head. Why had she agreed to meet him after school today, if he'd done all those things to her? Alistair recalled the words she'd spat at him, after she'd quietly dressed herself in his bedroom and he'd offered to make her a cup of tea.

'You raped me.'

'No, I didn't,' he'd said, frowning at her, completely perplexed.

Ida had slammed the door on her way out, and Alistair had sat there staring out of the window at the early-night sky. It suddenly dawned on him, what she'd said, and he got into the shower and scrubbed himself clean.

Later that night, when his dad had gone to bed, he crept downstairs to talk to his mother about it. Magda's fingers had dug into his cheeks, her sharp nails pricking his skin.

'You must not tell another soul about this, do you understand? Not your mates, no one.'

'Oh fuck, what have I done?' Alistair began to cry.

'Don't you know the boundaries? No means no? Bloody hell, son, didn't we bring you up to understand all this?'

'Mum, I swear, I didn't hear her say stop, I promise. You know I'm not like that.' Alistair rested his head in his hands, tears dropping on to the floor. 'You know how much I love Ida. I would never hurt her.'

'Okay. Let's stop with the amateur dramatics. We need to think about what we're going to do. Did she say she was going to report you?'

'She isn't answering my texts . . .'

Magda grabbed Alistair. 'You haven't mentioned this in your messages?'

'No!' Alistair pulled his arm free. 'I've just asked her if she's okay with me and can we meet up.'

'Just carry on as normal. Listen to me, Alistair. She's not going to ruin your career. I'll go and talk to her, tell her she's making a big mistake. You haven't done anything wrong. I'll sort it.' Magda patted his knee.

Alistair glanced away from Magda, her last sentence said without conviction, because they both knew he had done something very wrong, and no amount of pushing it into the grey area was going to make it right. He'd had sex with Ida, she was underage, and she'd asked him to stop.

'I'll deal with it. Get some sleep.' Magda kissed his forehead.

Alistair had lain in bed later that night, unable to sleep. Most of what had happened now felt like visual white noise, it was all a blur. His mind fluttered back to what his mother had said. She was fiercely protective of his boxing career, and there wasn't anything or anyone who would get in the way of that. He curled up in a ball and clenched his stomach, wanting it all to go away. But as Magda had predicted, this wasn't going to go away, and he knew that.

CHAPTER FORTY-SEVEN
THEN

A mother's love, that's how Magda justified her actions – what she told herself when she got home from Ray's and stripped off her gym clothes and trainers. She shoved them into the washing machine and stood there in her bra and knickers, shivering from cold and shock. Visions of Ida collapsing on to the floor appeared violently in her mind; the sound of the heavy glass ashtray cracking the back of her skull, still so vivid.

It hadn't been her intention to kill her when she'd gone around there, but everything had turned white – a sharp, cold, icy white – before her eyes. Magda had tried to reason with Ida the day before, and that's when Ida had told her about the letters she'd found in Ray's office. Letters written by Ingrid, revealing incriminating facts about Magda and her brother. Ida had refused to hand them over; instead using them as blackmail against her and Alistair. And here she was again, pleading with Ida, having broken into Elise and Nathaniel's apartment earlier that day, trying to find the damn letters. Worried about being caught in the apartment, Magda had made her way to Ray's and found Ida there alone.

'Do you think I care about Alistair's boxing career?' the girl had said. 'He raped me, and if I choose to report it, that's up to me. If you try to stop me, I'll tell everyone who you really are and what you did to your brother.'

Magda opened her mouth, but nothing came out.

'And you'll never find those letters, they're somewhere safe.'

Those few words from Ida had done it. Magda had begged and pleaded, tried to reason with the teenager who she thought was far too grown-up for her age, too confident, too arrogant. A girl who Magda believed had influenced and brainwashed her son for far too long. And while Ida was searching for her mobile phone which she'd lost that day, Magda had hit her over the back of the head.

Magda switched the machine on to a hot wash and put her trainers in the shoe cupboard, relieved she'd had the forethought to take them off and put them in her gym bag when she was at Ray's. She didn't want anyone identifying a shoe print in the puddle of blood that had circled Ida's head like an expanding halo.

Time wasn't on her side, and she'd known Sonny or Ray could return at any minute. Just after Ida had collapsed on to the floor, Magda had heard a key in the front door and had quietly slipped out of the orangery, and she was making her way around the back when she heard Sonny shouting. She'd seen him chasing Alistair down the garden and out through the gate. She discovered later that Alistair had returned to the house to talk to Ida.

The less evidence, the better, and in that split second Magda made a decision to return to the orangery and remove Ida's body. Ray was with the girl, though. His face through the glass held an expression she would never forget, and she watched him for a few moments, rocking his granddaughter in his arms. She held her breath, waiting to see what he would do next, not daring to move in case he saw her. Deciding it was best to get out of there as quickly as possible, Magda waited for Ray to leave the room, so she could creep around the side of the house. Then she remembered she'd left her sports bag inside and could see it resting against the leg of the kitchen table, the bloody glass ashtray inside it. Her heart began to pound, filling her ears and making her dizzy. She had to get that bag. Ray had left the room, but she couldn't be sure where he was.

Magda had no idea how much time had passed; it felt like seconds but was probably quite a few minutes. There was still no sign of Sonny, and Ray had returned to the orangery, she could hear him talking to someone and they appeared to be giving him instructions. He'd called an ambulance. Magda realised Ida was still alive. Magda's heart seemed to slide up into the back of her throat and spread through her head.

Ray lifted the phone from the coffee table, turned the speakerphone off, and she heard him say he would go out the front and guide the ambulance in, and that's when she took her chance.

Magda retrieved the gym bag from by the kitchen table, and tried not to look around; she couldn't waste time seeing if anyone was coming. She put the bag over her shoulder and crept into the orangery. Crouching down, as she would if she was doing a dead lift in the gym, she deftly picked Ida up in her arms, swiftly manoeuvring her out of the door, somehow managing to push the door shut with her bottom.

When she stood on the path at the side of the house, she had an overwhelming feeling of horror, the shock of what she'd done and what she was about to do suddenly punching her in the gut. It was one thing killing someone in a rage, but finishing them off when your temper had calmed was another thing altogether. She had no idea where she was going to put Ida or how she would permanently silence her, and the security lights would illuminate her as they had Alistair. Panic embraced her. If it hadn't been for the sound of the gate clicking at the bottom of Ray's garden, she would have carried Ida to the cricket pavilion and dumped her in the basement, but it was too late now; she had to dump her and leave as quickly as she could.

Magda kept herself tight against the wall, and that's when she fell against the coal bunker. Having heard the back door slam and feeling assured that Sonny was back inside, she rested Ida on the top of the bunker and pulled her phone from her jacket pocket. Using the torch, she illuminated the large structure, trying to work out if it opened from the top. Once she'd established it had a lid, she lifted Ida off the bunker, heaving her over her shoulder. Her muscles were beginning to weaken, so with all the strength she had left, Magda lifted the lid and allowed Ida to flop into the bottom, flinching as she felt pain dart through her back. She carefully closed the bunker and tried to figure out how she was going to remove herself from the garden without being seen. There wasn't time to see if Ida was dead or think about her actions and if they were the right ones.

After a few seconds, Magda made a run for it through the shrubs, keeping her body against the wall as she tried to move quickly, whilst bent over, her heart beating like a jackrabbit's. The security lights hadn't been activated, so she managed to slip through the gate at the bottom of the garden, her dark gym clothing camouflaging her.

Once she had reached the corner of the park, she stopped briefly to calm herself. With shaking hands, she removed the trainers from her bag and put them on, feeling the weight of the ashtray she'd thrown in there after the attack. She had no idea what she was going to do with it. As she made her way home, she kept telling herself she'd just come directly from the gym.

Now, here she was, standing in her own home, having possibly killed a young girl, but if not, and she survived, she would tell everyone exactly what had happened. Magda gave herself a shake, carried the gym bag upstairs and got herself into the shower, taking the ashtray in there with her. She had to carry on as if it were a normal day. Alistair and her husband would be back soon, and the police would most definitely want to talk to them.

Magda turned the heat up in the shower, so it was almost unbearable, and allowed the water to pelt her skin. That was the second time she'd taken someone's life. The sounds of her brother, Gordon, tumbling down the cliff, and the thud of the ashtray on the back of Ida's head rang in her ears, making her squeeze her head with her hands, until she thought she'd crush her brains. She recalled the terrible, sickening guilt she'd felt after Gordon's death, which everyone mistook for grief. It had almost killed her, even though she had felt it was justified. But this was something else altogether. She'd killed a child, in a temper. There was no amount of mother's love that could convince her it was okay.

Thoughts of the ashtray brought Magda back to reality and she quickly scrubbed it with her fingers and then set about washing her hair and body while she racked her brains, trying to think of where to hide it. By the time she stepped out of the shower, she knew exactly where, and opted to place it in the lounge, like it was a familiar item in their home. Hiding the ashtray and risking it being found would immediately draw attention to it. Magda placed it on a table, deciding if Liam noticed and quizzed her about it, she'd say it was given to her or she'd found it at a flea market. She stepped back and observed the heavy glass object amongst their own things; it looked odd and awkward, but she didn't have time to worry about that now, then she ran back upstairs, pulling her towel off as she went.

Magda had just finished getting dressed when she heard Alistair's key in the door. She looked out of the window and he met her gaze. From the expression on his face, she couldn't help wondering if he knew what she'd done.

CHAPTER FORTY-EIGHT
NOW

Magda wasn't the only person to have worked out the Suicide Watcher's game. Nathaniel had researched it well enough over the years. And then he'd found the letters from Ingrid in Ida's doll's house and that gave Magda a motive. It was a theory and not a fact, but when he made his way to Magda's he didn't care about any of that. Somehow, Magda knew Ida had found those letters, and it was Magda who had broken into their apartment that day in search of them. It had to have been. She was the only one implicated in the letters. She'd killed his daughter, his little girl, and he wanted her to pay for it.

People rarely suspected women – he had learnt that being a journalist – and, granted, there weren't as many female killers as male, but there were enough. No one had spotted the motive, but Nathaniel had spent enough time with Magda to work it out. It was there in the words she spoke, you just had to look for it, or perhaps he noticed it, now he was equipped with new information. That's what Nathaniel thought, anyway. He'd interviewed people accused of crimes, and always knew if they were guilty or innocent.

Nathaniel acted as normal, ringing the bell and waiting for Magda to answer the door. He was nervous, filled with anger, but nervous all the same. Magda's reaction to his questions would determine her fate, because it was just a theory – she hadn't admitted anything to anyone, and Nathaniel had no proof, other than a motive and the earring Elise had found and shown him after her visit.

'This is a surprise, you normally text . . .' Magda stepped aside so he could enter the house.

'I was passing and fancied a coffee. Not disturbing you, am I?'

Magda looked at him. 'Is there something wrong?'

'No, no, not at all.' Nathaniel knew he was being weird, out of character. He needed to calm down and slow his heart, which was thundering in his ears. 'I've just been to the gym, ran too much probably.'

'Oh, did you see Alistair in there?'

'No. But then I didn't weight-train today. How's he doing?'

'Really well. Getting ready for this fight on Saturday. His coach says that if he wins this, he'll be heading for a professional career.'

'You must be really proud.' Nathaniel placed his rucksack on the floor, aware of the gun at the bottom of the bag making a soft thud. Magda didn't notice; she was busy making them coffee. She seemed nervous, and Nathaniel thought this was odd, considering she had no idea why he was there.

'I wanted to talk to you about something, actually.' Nathaniel pulled out a chair at the kitchen table and sat down.

'Oh yes?'

'I've been thinking about Ida's death . . .'

'Unsurprisingly.' Magda paused, catching Nathaniel's eye. He held her gaze for a moment – longer than was comfortable for either of them.

'I've been thinking about what happened that day and who would have a motive to kill my daughter.'

'Have the police closed the case?' Magda was still fiddling with the coffee machine.

Nathaniel decided to forget the questioning and get straight to the point. He had already decided what he was going to do – and no one, not even Elise, would know about it. That was the key to murder: bide your time and keep it to yourself.

'I know you killed Ida. I found the letters you were looking for when you broke into my apartment.'

Magda stopped what she was doing but didn't look at him. Nathaniel could see she was trying to decide whether to admit or deny. He carefully took some gloves from his pocket and placed them on his hands, keeping them concealed beneath the table.

'Come on, Magda. Tell me what happened.'

They stared at one another for a few moments.

'I don't know what you're talking about. Look, it was enough that you accused Alistair. Now me?' Magda's hand gently touched her chest. It was shaking, giving away her lies.

'I know, Magda. There's no point lying. The earring, the back injury, and let's not forget your motive of keeping your only child's name clear of any scandal – and, of course, your own.'

Magda stopped what she was doing and stared at Nathaniel. 'Firstly, I don't know anything about an earring. Secondly, what has a back injury got to do with it? And thirdly, I might have a motive, but I can assure you, it wasn't me.'

'When Elise visited you, she trod on a diamond stud earring in your hall. She knew straight away it belonged to Ida; she'd put them on, the morning of her birthday. It must have got caught in your clothing and dropped off when you got home. Error number one. Secondly, you'd hurt your back when I visited you after Ida was attacked – it's just an observation, an assumption, but I'm guessing you did it when you carried Ida out of Ray's house and dumped her in the coal bunker, like a piece of trash. And lastly, and most importantly, you had two motives, one being to protect Alistair and the other being that Ida had seen those incriminating letters.'

Magda took a deep breath, as if defeated.

'It was an accident. We got into a fight. I was defending myself. I honestly didn't mean to kill her.'

Nathaniel breathed in deeply, clenching his jaw, as he reached into his bag for the gun. Before Magda could run from the room, Nathaniel was on his feet and had grabbed her around the waist. She was strong, but she didn't have the strength he had. He dragged her back to the table and shoved her into the chair he'd been sitting in, and held the gun to her head.

'We're going to play a little game, Magda, and you're going to participate. Otherwise, I'll go straight to the police and tell them everything. It's a game I think you're familiar with. Only, the rules are slightly different to what you remember . . .'

ACKNOWLEDGMENTS

As always, a massive and heartfelt thank you to Paul and Susan Feldstein at The Feldstein Agency. I'm so lucky to have your fierce support and friendship. The entire team at Thomas and Mercer, particularly Jack Butler for championing me, and Dominic Myers, whose comment in *The Bookseller* made me beam. My editors, David Downing, Gemma Wain and Swati Gamble, I've loved working on this book with you all.

Endless appreciation to my husband, Christopher, particularly for his unwavering patience as I noisily interrupt his sleep to write at 2 a.m. Although, lately, I've noticed his smile has a whiff of hysteria about it.

A huge thank you to my parents, especially my mum, who is still wielding her red pen, ready for action. Please consider redundancy and go quietly. . .

If you're in my contacts list or on Facebook – thank you, I love you. A special thank you to the McMechans, Nicki Plaice, Michael Gibson, Fiona Murray, Arnie Cronin, Nikki Frater, Chris Whitaker, Alex Khan, Bev Langridge, Alison Stewart and Rick Cheal.

A nod to my cats, Sid, Nancy, Vivi and Barbara, for finding innovative ways of sabotaging my writing every day. Without you, I'd probably have finished another book by now.

Finally, I'd like to thank *myself* for regularly dragging *me* into the corner (so as not to embarrass *me* in front of Sybil or the cats), for a quiet but firm word in *my* ear.

ABOUT THE AUTHOR

Photo © 2014 Jamie Maxwell

When Gayle was five years old, she packed her little red suitcase and told her parents she was leaving Norfolk to find her fortune. Unable to reach the door handle, she decided to stay, set up an office under the stairs and started writing books. Gayle still lives in Norfolk with her husband and lots of cats. She is inspired by the beautiful countryside and coastline. Her novel *Too Close* was published in 2016. She has also self-published two novels, *Memory Scents* and *Shell House*, and a humour book about her cat, entitled *Wilfred, Fanny and Floyd*.

Printed in Great Britain
by Amazon